Dragon Queens

Kathleen de Plume

This novel is entirely a work of fiction. The names, characters and incidents portrayed in it are the work of the author's imagination. Any resemblance to actual persons, living or dead, events or localities is entirely coincidental.

Art by StarsColdNight

www.bookcoversrealm.com

For all the women out there, both young and young at heart, who dreamed of facing the dragon to rescue the princess. May you all have your own happily ever after.

Contents

Kathleen de Plume

Dragon Queens

Kathleen de Plume

Chapter One – The Bounty Hunter

She shoved the man forward. His hands bound, he stumbled to his knees beside the Keeper.

"Which one is this, Gwen?"

"John Little. Breaking the King's Peace, public drunkenness, and poaching. Twelve shillings."

"Twelve? Are you sure? That list doesn't sound worth more than four or five."

Gwen shrugged. "I don't go out hunting for less than ten. I'm sure it's in your notices if you want to check."

James held his hands up placatingly. "I believe you. Maybe there's more to this little twerp than meets the eye."

He rummaged through his saddlebags. Keeper of the King's Peace sounded a grand title, and at twenty-four years old he was proud to hold it, but in truth his position was more like that of a petty constable from one of the groves. Still, he kept track of bounties and paid them out, and Gwendoline Carter was efficient enough to make him look good.

"Here you go." He tossed her a small purse.

She caught it and counted quickly. "Any news?" she asked curtly. She didn't care much for him, and it showed.

"Two new bounties." He passed her the notices. Unlike a lot of bounty hunters, she could read them for herself. "And I hear a rumour that Princess Ava has gone missing."

That brought her head up sharply. "The princess? Are you sure?"

"No. It's just a rumour, for now. But if it's true it'd be worth a mite more than what you're picking up on these outings – King Harald loves his daughter more than life."

"Hah! If she's wandered into the dragon's lair, the rate is half the kingdom. He knows that, same as anyone."

He barked a laugh, as if the thought hadn't even occurred to him until then. "If she's been taken by the dragon, even you might not be able to bring her out alive."

She sobered at his words, passing the purse gently from hand to hand as she thought. Prophecy always gets garbled when it becomes legend, but there's no denying a dragon would be a deadly foe. James held Little's collar and waited.

"Missing person," she said at last. "I might stay in town for a couple of nights. If the princess is missing, it might not be the dragon. Might be easy work and good pay. Worth a few nights at the inn, at least, to find out."

"Good luck," said James, pulling Little to his feet and walking him off toward the cells. Gwen watched him for a second before turning to go.

Gwen strode into The Bull and Goose, feeling optimistic. She scanned the tavern for outlanders – preferably well-to-do ones.

Spotting a well-dressed young man by the bar, she let her long dark hair out of its plait, relaxed her stride into more of a saunter, and made her approach. She asked barkeep for a wine.

She didn't have long to wait.

"What's a nice lass like you doing in a place like this?"

So. Zero points for imagination, then. Hopefully it just meant he wouldn't embellish what he knew of affairs at the Capital.

Taking a small sip of her wine, she gave a friendly smile. "Hoping for news of the world. Have you been on the road long?"

"I was at the King's court not two days past." She broadened her smile at him encouragingly, and he preened a little under her attention. "I know the latest news of alliances, marriages, rebellions and wars. What news would you hear?"

"Any news of the royal family? Last I heard the princess was still not betrothed, and she must be nearing twenty-five by now." Better he think it his own idea to tell her the princess was missing. *If* the princess was missing.

"Ah! Of course you would not have heard. In truth, the betrothal papers have not been formally signed, but our dear sweet Princess Ava is to be married to Reginald, the first Lord Forquitte. Only an Earl, of course, but he commands lands as large as any Duke in the Realm – larger than many foreign Princes – and he has personally led men to victory on the battlefields against odds lesser commanders deemed insurmountable. What he lacks in rank he makes up for in reputation. A veritable giant among men." At this he glanced up at her, as if noticing her height for the first time. "I think he may even stand taller than you yourself."

Okay, then. Maybe she didn't so much run away as elope – rumour had it that she was unmarried only because her father indulged her desire to choose her own spouse. This Reginald sounded suitably impressive; perhaps she didn't want to wait the traditional three months?

"Were you around court long enough to see the princess? Did she seem delighted by the match?"

He frowned slightly. Evidently it hadn't occurred to him before to wonder what she thought of her betrothed. Highborn ladies usually married for alliance, after all, not for love. In many ways it was better to be born common as muck.

"I only saw her once after the rumours began of her betrothal. She did not look well and took to her bedchambers shortly thereafter. I hadn't seen her in three days when I left court." He brightened suddenly. "But she must be thrilled. She must. Perhaps her excitement and joy upset her stomach."

Gwen hummed neutrally and took a small sip of her wine. She waited for the well-dressed young man to say something more.

"I did hear some stirrings, now that I think of it." He looked troubled at his own words. "Apparently some of the palace servants did not believe she was so well pleased by her betrothal." He frowned a little deeper, before his face cleared. "But what would servants know? The last day I was there, word was that the servants thought our beloved princess had run away! The very idea." He laughed, and she smiled with him.

"I have no doubt you are right," she said.

Getting free of him without making a scene was easier than she had feared. The lad was almost sweet, really, if you didn't mind the vanity of wealthy young men.

She walked up the stairs to her room with her head full of thoughts and plans. Putting the two rumours together, it seemed most likely that the princess was sulking and hiding somewhere in the palace. It was also possible she had eloped, or had run away to avoid betrothal. At least she could dismiss Jack's worry about dragons.

If it was the first, no official news would ever be heard. A sulking princess might worry the serving staff who can't find her for meals or dressing, but it would not be news the Realm needed to hear.

If it was the second, there would be carefully curated news of a low-key royal wedding, with only the most honoured guests invited. Within a month every courtier who passed through town would claim to have been there.

The third was the interesting one. Not very likely, but if Princess Ava was on the run to avoid this Lord Forquitte, then the decision to put a bounty on her safe return would have been made by now. An official herald would be here with the proclamation within three days.

She had more than enough money for three nights. And her horse could use some rest.

As it turned out, it only took two.

"Hear ye, hear ye, hear ye! By order of His Grace, King Harald von Tryptshire, Lord of the Marshes, Emperor of the Realm

13

Without Night, High King of the Eastern Isles, and Champion of the Faith, heed my words!

"Her Royal Highness, the Princess Ava, beloved Daughter and only Heir of our precious Monarch, has vanished! The King calls upon all able-bodied men of honour to ride to her rescue!

"The person who returns our Princess to her Royal Father unharmed shall be rewarded with whatsoever they may carry from the treasury using nothing but the strength of their own two arms."

The lass making the proclamation had a strong voice, for all she looked around fifteen years old. An audience of perhaps thirty people, mostly men, had gathered to hear. Now she was nailing a proclamation to the notice board in the town square.

"As much gold as you can carry in your arms." The speaker was Derrick, a bounty hunter like Gwen, but well past his prime. These days he spent a lot of his time in the tavern, buying the company of travelling women with tales from his glory years. "That's more'n any of us'll see in a lifetime, but isn't the traditional fee for returning a princess half the kingdom?"

"Hah! And her hand in marriage." This was the Keeper. James had obviously been thinking about this for the past two days. His very posture proclaimed that he saw himself as far more handsome than his face could prove.

"I'm fairly certain *that* tradition only applies if you defeat the dragon to do it." Gwen was surprised to find herself speaking up. "Besides, isn't the Dragon Prize linked to the sort of prophecy you don't want to be on the wrong side of?"

James sneered at her. He probably thought it was a handsome sneer. He may even have been trying to flirt.

"Who's to say what I might face on my daring rescue? Everyone knows the dragon stirs when royalty rides unguarded. The King will believe me when I tell him of our harrowing ordeal." His sneer became a smirk. "Do prophetic warnings apply to the sort of epic tale of heroism that leaves no dragon corpse behind?" Gwen decided she didn't just dislike James. She loathed him.

At the mention of draconic stirrings, several of the men at the edges of the crowd peeled off.

Gwen stayed a while longer to hear what the others thought, but it soon proved to be more bravado about how they would spend their prize. No one had any more idea where the princess had gone than she did.

Chapter Two – Venturing Forth

Two days later she stepped into The King's Head, a few streets out from the intricately carved stone walls of the Royal Palace. She scanned the patrons quickly, until she saw the bright blue silks of Lady Deidre.

"You?" Lady Deidre questioned quietly as Gwen approached. "I was under the impression you'd be more... martial." She looked Gwen up and down briefly. "Muscular enough, I suppose. You'll do."

"You thought I was a man?"

"I was told I'd be meeting the best bounty hunter west of the Capital," Deidre shrugged. "Should have figured you'd be a woman. A man wouldn't bother talking to the princess' lady-in-waiting."

"If anyone can give me insight into why Princess Ava left, and where she might have gone, it's you."

The pause was only a few seconds. But it seemed longer.

"I don't know anything definite."

"But if you knew nothing at all, you wouldn't have wasted your time coming to see me." Gwen swiftly sat down across from her, leaning across the table. "Anything you can tell me, Lady Deidre. Anything at all."

Deidre sighed. "I'll give you what I know. It isn't much, though. And most of it is speculative."

"I'd take your speculation over any man's truths. To begin, how was she feeling in the days before she left?"

Deidre smiled at the compliment, then stiffened at the question. "Grim. She had been despondent, but right before she disappeared she seemed grimly determined."

"This was around a week ago, yes?"

"A week ago yesterday she vanished, yes."

"Do you know what made her despondent?" It seemed clear to Gwen that a decision to leave would explain the grim determination.

"Yes. She had been given an ultimatum by her Lord Father a month or so back. She had turned twenty-five, and he bade her choose someone to marry else have someone chosen for her. Well, she did make more effort in meeting eligible nobles in the weeks that followed, both here and from abroad, but the King was meeting nobles, too, and had found someone he deemed suitable."

Nobles. The lack of gender caught Gwen's ear. She'd heard that the aristocracy did things differently – and more often – but didn't realise a royal heir might have that freedom.

"Speaking of her Lord Father. It seems he sent for bounty hunters when she had been missing – what, a day? Two? Is that normal? Stories are unreliable as far from the Capital as I live, but I'm led to believe the King has thousands of trained armsmen at his disposal, along with…" She trailed off, trying to find words that wouldn't make her sound like a country oaf. "More arcane solutions?"

"Arcane?" Deidre looked puzzled for a moment. "Oh, you mean the seers? They talk a big game, and the official reason they're never called in for matters like this is that their remit is far too lofty to be bothered for something so small as one Royal Princess. But if you ask me, they weren't asked because the King knew damn well it would take them six months of argument to decide that the winds of prophecy blew her away for a reason, and it would be foolhardy in the extreme to use their mystic knowledge to anger the Gods." Her snort wasn't particularly ladylike.

"And the army? Why send for bounty hunters like me when you have sworn soldiers you could send instead?"

There was a very careful pause. "You noticed a few days delay between the princess going missing and sending the news throughout the Realm. Well, I'm not privy to his inner council, but I spotted several familiar faces prowling the city during that time. I think that before word was sent to the countryside, the city itself was thoroughly searched by every man the King trusted with the task. When that failed…" She gestured, but Gwen didn't follow. "You have to understand, armies are expensive. The King raises troops when he needs them – lords' men form units of pike from the manors and farms; common free folk form units of archers from the townships and villages like your own – but when he doesn't there are only a few hundred men and women employed as full-time soldiers. On the other hand, there are two or three full time professional bounty hunters – such as yourself – in each flyspeck village in the Realm, and a large enough bounty will draw two dozen more, even if all they do is keep watch on the local taverns."

Gwen gave her most winning smile. "So what you're telling me is that magic is bunk, and there's nothing suspicious about the timeline of the King's actions – am I correct?"

Deidre smiled back. "I wouldn't say *bunk*, exactly – and I certainly wouldn't say it in a seer's earshot. But I would definitely be willing to say that 'magic', as you put it, wouldn't be the most useful in situations such as this, no."

"I think that makes sense – let's get back to the princess' nuptials. She has to marry a man while she is young enough to carry lots of babies?" She should really be asking about the Earl, but she had a suspicion to confirm first.

"It's less about the babies – though her mother, our dear Queen Constance, would surely love to have grandchildren running around. She has cousins with children who could secure the succession if she were to die without issue. But she needs to marry, and to do it soon enough for the King and Queen to train her spouse up in how to be consort and help rule the kingdom. They aren't getting any younger, you know."

That didn't really answer her question, though it did tell her that the answer might not be important. "Are you married, Lady Deidre?" Now, why had she asked that?

"Yes, to Lord Mountfeather. He's a good man."

Gwen nodded. She didn't really have a follow up question for that. Oh, that's right – nobles. "Was there a certain minimum rank the princess had to look for, when selecting her consort?"

Deidre hesitated. "Not really. By law, the prince or princess may marry whomever they choose. Though if she's turned down a Duke to marry a cobbler's boy she'd better *really* love him, or the Duke might start a rebellion for the insult. In practice, she would never try looking outside the hereditary lordships. Occasionally a particularly impressive knight might catch the eye of a princess, but the Ogres haven't stirred in decades, so the opportunity for heroics isn't what it once was."

This was fascinating to Gwen, but it wasn't really giving her the answers she needed right now. Might as well ask a question she thought she knew the answer to. "And who did the King deem suitable?"

Deidre grimaced. "Reginald Lord Forquitte."

"Now, *there's* a face. I hadn't heard of the man five days ago – what has the Earl of Lubrey done to make the princess run rather than wed him?"

"I don't know. Not for sure. Lady Eveline – Princess Ava's younger lady-in-waiting – never confided in me. And as far as I know he has never done anything directly to the princess. But the man is cold, cunning, ruthless, and wants to be King. I'm not sure I trust him to be content merely being consort."

"He can't, though, can he?" Gwen was confused. "If the Queen dies before her consort, her heir is her child, or her sibling, or her cousin. Not her husband. Or have I heard incorrectly?"

"You've heard correctly. Though laws can be changed. It might be that he can't change them enough to be King, but if he can then he will."

"Doesn't this worry the King as well?"

"No." Deidre looked frustrated, now. "The King thinks the Earl's ambition is for his son to be King, and to rule equally with his wife as consort. That level of ambition doesn't worry him. In fact, he thinks it will be good for the Realm; after all, Lord Reginald's lands have become more fertile and thus more lucrative in the years since he took over their management."

Gwen nodded slowly, digesting all of this. "Okay, so she's running away from a marriage she doesn't want. And she's been gone eight days. What did she take with her when she left?"

"Riding boots, a couple of cloaks and other clothes. The kitchens were missing some food, but not enough for more than a few days; she'd have run out by now. I don't know how much money she had, several guineas at least. She didn't take any jewellery." Deidre frowned in concentration, evidently trying hard to think of anything that might help. "Oh! Her mare, Beauty. She's quite striking – a beautiful solid chestnut brown, except for a pure white diamond on her forehead, one white hoof, and a pattern on one flank. Um. A bit like a heart pierced by a lightning bolt?"

While Deidre had been talking, Gwen had been pulling paper from her belt bag, along with a charcoal pencil. "Which hoof? Which flank? Can you draw the pattern for me?"

"Umm, front foot. It's the opposite to the flank – I think it's right hoof and left flank, but it's not my horse so I could be mistaken. I'm no artist, but I'll do my best to draw it for you."

"Thank you. I really do appreciate it. Lastly," she pulled out some maps, "where do you think Princess Ava would go?"

A rueful smile as Deidre finished her rough sketch. "That's what I thought you'd ask to begin with. I don't know. I can tell you she's got a poor stomach for sailing, so I doubt she's taken a boat. I can tell you where her mother's family is from." Here, she pointed to an area of the map several days south of the Capital. "And I can tell you where her best friend, Lady Eveline, will have gone," she pointed to a town not too far from where Gwen had come from, to the west. "But if I were a betting woman, I'd put my money on her heading east."

"Why east?"

"Closest foreign border. She's always wanted to see the land where silk comes from, and to hear foreign languages used by people who see the world differently to her. She's never travelled outside the Realm, you see. She has dreams. Why wouldn't she try to live them, if she's leaving her home anyway?"

And if she went where her family or friends live, people might try to return her to her father's house, too.

"Descriptions of the princess that make it out to us have her as short, slender, blonde and beautiful. I assume all royals are described as beautiful, but how small is she? Are there any paintings that are fairly accurate, so I know who I'm looking for? I doubt she's announcing her presence when she rides into town."

"She *is* beautiful. Her hair is very long; it almost reaches her waist – though when she travels she usually keeps it in a plait like yours, so the end would hang just below her shoulders. She uses soot to dull the golden shine when she doesn't want to be recognised. As for how small she is – if you stand I can show you where she would reach on you?"

Gwen stood, and Deidre indicated perhaps the top of her shoulder. Small, yes, but not the shortest woman in the world. Deidre herself was only very slightly taller.

"You could wait for Audience Day to see the throne room with the royal portraits, but I have a woodcut that isn't too bad. You might be able to recognise her from this." Deidre handed her a folded piece of paper. It seemed to Gwen that Deidre really wanted her to succeed. She appreciated that.

"I guess I ride east. Is there any particular city she spoke of often? Somewhere she might be headed?" If not, she was just going to ride east and hope to learn more as she went.

"Not really. Izantium is the closest centre of the Silk trade, though. I hope you catch up to her before she gets there."

"Me too."

Three days hard riding down the road. Four tavern owners who were fairly sure they'd seen a small blonde woman with a long plait a week earlier. One who was absolutely *definite* about the horse.

But, more troublingly, there were also rumours about other things. Grass fires. Missing sheep. Cattle stampedes.

A superstitious woman might think of dragons.

Everyone knew an unguarded royal was catnip to a dragon. Gwen had been hoping that what everyone knew was wrong. Still, if we're in realms of legend, here, at least she knew that dragons didn't kill and eat princesses. They capture them as trophies; much like the legendary hoard of gold and jewels that no one had ever seen.

Perhaps that was just a metaphor.

The next tavern on her journey was The Barbed Tail. This marked the edge of the lands where dragons had been sighted in living memory.

Possibly just one dragon.

Hopefully just one dragon.

One dragon is terrifying enough.

She pushed her hood back off her head as she walked in. Her cloak covered her boiled leather breastplate. She knew she was nervous when she was wearing it on the King's Highway, but never mind that right now. It was time for more news.

"Wine, please." She took her gloves off at the bar and found some pennies in her purse.

The innkeeper put her drink in front of her, and asked "Anything else?"

"News, if you have it." For once she didn't lead with the woodcut of the princess. Her gut told her that the dragon would be news on its own.

"My, my," she said. "You've heard that there have been dragon sightings already, have you? Word travels quick – first sighting was the day afore yesterday."

"Actual sightings? No, news hasn't travelled that fast. So far, I've only heard reports of fires and missing livestock. I can add two and two, though."

This got her an approving nod. "So can we, missy, but them bloody Kingsguards can't. They still think we're making it all up. Think it's a coincidence that a lass who looks a smidge like the princess comes in here, two days later the Heralds announce her missing, and two days later again there's a dragon flying by? I don't."

"This lass who looks like the princess. Was she riding a horse?"

"Aye, that she was. A fine mare, beautiful brown with a white diamond on the forehead. Coat looked like it would glow like burnished bronze if it weren't so dusty from travel."

"Any local bounty hunters go chasing after her?"

"No, miss. No bounty hunters around here. All our menfolk are sensible enough not to pull the tail of the dragon."

"And your womenfolk?"

"More sensible'n the men!"

They laughed together. Gwen was seriously doubting her own common sense by now, but she felt committed. Bloody Deidre. Without her, she might have decided her own skin was worth more than the princess' royal hide.

Oh well.

"What can you tell me of local geography? My maps are from the Capital, and they get sparser the further out you go."

"Show me what you've got; I'll tell you if you're missing anything important."

Gwen pulled out her map of the area and smoothed it over the bar. They poured over it together, adding annotations of missing landmarks. Most importantly, at least to Gwen, was the missing castle ruins in an otherwise very empty section of the countryside, maybe two days ride away.

"I'm not surprised the Capital's cartographers have forgotten that exists."

"You're not?"

"Local legend has it that castle was built near a thousand years ago. When dragons were common, but the King knew how to fight them. They put that castle right in the middle of the Hatching Grounds, to make sure humanity always had the upper hand over the dragons."

"If the castle kept the dragons under control, why is it now a ruin?"

"Well, the castle did its job, see, and after a few generations of peace no one really thought it was a good idea to keep sending men and food and supplies to this castle that didn't seem to be doing anything. So, they stopped."

"Ah. Cursed by their own success, then?"

"Well, that and the land around it seems to hold an actual curse. You can't farm it, you see. Not for miles. Crops won't grow, and livestock run away."

"Or are eaten by the dragon?" Gwen guessed.

"Possibly, possibly. Most outlanders think we're being superstitious when we suggest things like that."

"Outlanders? We're still in the Realm, aren't we?"

"Oh, aye. We pay our taxes to the King, and his Kingsguard see to safety on the highway. But it's different here. Almost all travellers are people looking to cross the border east, or those who have already crossed. Mostly merchants. We don't get many folks from the rest of the Realm. Sometimes it feels like we're a land to ourselves out here."

Fascinating. Half a week's hard riding from the Capital and you feel like you're in another country.

"I think I'm going to need a good meal, a better bed, and as many days travel rations as you can spare."

"You're going after the princess, then? You're brave."

"Or foolish."

"Or that, aye."

She probably had too much food. Optimistically, she needed enough to get the princess back as far as the inn. Pessimistically, it might slow her horse down too much and the dragon might get her. Best not to think too hard about that.

She'd seen it last night. There had been a beating of wings, like thunder in the dark of night, and when she looked to where the sound had come from, there had been the flame. Her mouth had gone dry with terror. Now, she waited to see it fly again.

Her horse was tied up in the thickest part of the forest, half a mile or so behind her. He was well trained, but she hoped the dragon was looking for prey in the open. Tales tended to speak of missing cows, goats, and sheep, but she had no doubt a horse would be a meal if the dragon was hungry.

Still, as much as she loved her horse, if it was her horse or her, she knew which way she'd choose.

Why was she even out here? Because she'd promised some noblewoman who she'd probably never meet again? Stupid.

It was a pity her mother's collection of books contained so little on myth, legend, and prophecy. She'd never had her little brother's knack for working out which parts of a tall tale should be believed, and which were pure embellishment.

She thought she'd heard something following her earlier. Now that *was* stupid. A dragon would be flying overhead, not slinking through the forest behind her. Her imagination was playing tricks. Like when you see faces in trees, or shapes in clouds.

She crept to the edge of the trees. There was a quarter mile of open grassland between the last tree and the dilapidated castle. There was no way she could cross it unseen when the dragon was inside. And the castle was larger than she'd expected.

You could fit a whole village in the open courtyard, visible through a hole in the wall. Only one tower was still whole enough to keep the weather out, but all four had parts intact. If the princess wasn't in that first tower, it might take hours to find her. And she didn't have hours.

She was still studying the castle ahead when she heard the wings. It was just taking off from the ground, and at this close range the sound was almost deafening. Her heart thundered in her chest as she watched the dragon fly off, nearly overhead. Her faltering fingers fumbled the hourglass at her belt twice as she turned it over. Sitting down to wait, she told herself her caution was prudence, not cowardice. Princess Ava was in no more danger tonight than on any of the last four nights, wherever she was held. And Gwen needed to know how much time she had.

The dragon was out of earshot in just over a minute. There would be enough warning to make a mad dash for the tree line, then, if it were just her searching the ruins. But not enough time if the princess was with her. Especially not if they were still in the tower. Damn. Her hands steady once more, she settled down to sharpen her sword. It had been a while since she'd had to use it. Not that it would be much use against a dragon. How *had* the old knights beaten them?

No. She wasn't trying to beat it. She didn't want to get caught up in whatever part of the legends might actually be true. Her life was complicated enough. Sneaking in and out without being seen was the plan. A good plan.

A plan that involved her surviving this foolhardy rescue.

Bloody Deidre. Bloody noblewomen and their bloody expectations.

The sands ran out, and she turned the glass. Maybe she'd have enough time. Tomorrow.

She oiled the leather of her breastplate. It was thick enough to stop an arrow, and a stab would need to be hitting one of the joins to do more than push her around. A heavy crossbow would make her life difficult. Or, you know, any of them could take her in the throat. Or the legs. Armour doesn't do much against fire anyway.

Better to get in and out without fighting. She was here for the bounty, not the glory.

The hourglass had nearly emptied a second time when she heard wings in the distance. She flattened herself on the ground under some bushes, holding her breath as she watched the skies. A minute later, the dragon beat past overhead, and returned to the castle. It circled the intact tower once, before settling in the courtyard.

A similar length of time to last night, then.

After a few minutes, Gwen eased her way back from the tree line. She stole away to her horse as quietly as possible and made camp without a fire.

She was back at the tree line the next night. The knowledge that she was going to act had her on edge. Twice now she had jumped at a rustle in the leaves behind her. No one was there, of course. Probably the wind. Maybe a fox. Not a dragon.

She was getting cold while she waited. Her cloak had a hood, but with no fire overnight the damp seemed to have seeped into everything. Brambles dug into her side as she shifted position. She eased her sword in its scabbard as a nervous habit.

There. The clap of great wings, followed by the sight of the dragon rising over the crumbling walls. Her heart hammered hard enough to feel in her chest, her stomach, her ears. Surely she should be used to this sound by now? She lay very still until it was gone. Not quite the same direction as last night. Could she trust it would still be close to two hours? She didn't have a whole lot of choice.

As soon as it was out of earshot, she ran. Scabbard held still in one hand, cloak held closed in the other, she dashed across the open fields. Letting both go might be faster, but tripping wouldn't be fun, and she didn't need full speed right now. She just needed to be fast enough. At least she'd left her bow at home – it would be no use against a dragon and would just slow her down.

She slowed as she approached the walls. The old moat had long reverted into a mere grassy hollow, barely visible unless you expected it. There was no point trying to find the drawbridge – this crumbling section of wall was good enough. She clambered up.

Turning to her left, she followed the dilapidated corridor toward the miraculously untouched tower. The dragon had circled it last night – she had to believe the princess was in there.

She reached the door at the top of the stairs. Locked. Not entirely unexpected – though a thousand years of rust had her hopeful that her dagger could be used to pry something loose. If not, well, there would be something in the rubble she could use as a crowbar. She wasn't going to ruin her sword.

Nothing around the lock. Rust, yes, but the iron underneath was thick and strong. The hinges stretched across the entire door face, and the bolts holding them into the door were huge. She traced her fingers over them, refusing to let frustration overwhelm her.

Her fingertips traced the ornate hinges right to the edge of the door, and she stopped, barely breathing. The pins! They weren't even rusted solid – this door could open. And the pins could be forced out.

She pulled a pritchel out of her belt bag. No idea why she'd taken it with her – she wasn't going to be forging horseshoes on the road – but it was about the right size to push the pins out of the hinges. With them gone, the door fell towards her. She flinched, but it stopped falling when the lock caught it. She eased it open as far as it would go and stepped inside.

"Brave Sir Knight" came a melodious voice from deeper in the room. A beautiful young woman, somewhat below average height with a long golden plait, stepped out of the shadows. Her blue riding dress was travel stained, yet she carried herself with such grace and elegance that Gwen couldn't look away. "May I see the face of my rescuer?"

Chapter Three – The Princess

Gwen hesitated briefly. Her face was hidden by the hood of her cloak, her breastplate betrayed nothing of the shape underneath it, and her height was above that of most men. Combined with her broad shoulders, it was no surprise the princess assumed her to be male. Best to fix the misunderstanding right away.

She stood up straight and lowered her hood. "Princess Ava, I am here to take you home."

The princess gave a small gasp. Her eyes widened. The small "Oh" she gave sounded disappointed.

What had Gwen expected? The princess probably had a romantic ideal of being swept away by a handsome and dashing prince. A knight, at the very least. She certainly didn't want to be returned to her father's court, and the betrothal she had already run away from once. Gwen was counting on her wanting to flee the dragon more than Lord Forquitte. Persuading her to come all the way home was a problem for after they'd escaped.

"Are you coming, your Highness?"

"I – yes. Yes, of course." The princess gave her an appraising look, seeming to quickly recover from her shock, and stepped over to Gwen's side.

Together, they edged under the unhinged door. Ava put her hand in Gwen's, and Gwen couldn't help noticing how small and vulnerable she was. She hoped this would make the princess easy to get home. She had a bounty to collect, after all.

"The climb down the rubble is going to be a bit rough. While your boots are solidly built, I don't think your dress was made for scrambling. Follow me closely and try to let me know if you're going to fall into me." Gwen released her hand. The night air felt cool on her palm.

"Of course," Ava replied in a meek voice. "How long do you think we have? Before the dragon returns, I mean."

Gwen checked her hourglass. The first turn was almost complete. "Maybe an hour. Can't be certain, of course. We need to be careful." Gwen looked at Ava's fearful expression. "Do you know how it tracked you? I know it didn't abduct you at random."

"No. I know the legends – and they're very specific about *unguarded* royalty. My only hope is that whatever method it used won't be effective with you guarding me."

Gwen snorted. She couldn't see how her presence could possibly help. Then again, she had no idea how the dragon had sniffed Ava out in the first place, so maybe she wasn't in the best place to be judging.

"Do you know what happened to your horse?"

Ava's face morphed from fear to sadness. "No, but I doubt she survived. I hope she did; if so, she could be anywhere by now."

"You don't know if she survived?" By now they were scrambling slowly down the rubble ramp. "Surely you would have seen if the dragon killed her while taking you?"

"I – no, I didn't. I don't know. I remember big wings, and flame, and Beauty running for our lives to take me away." She picked her way carefully down a few more blocks. "And then there was blackness. But I don't seem to have any injuries. I think the dragon has some kind of magic. I woke up in that tower."

Gwen nodded slowly as she took this in. It sounded farfetched, but so did dragons. She watched Ava deftly descend a few more steps, before tackling the next part herself. So far, the princess had been surer of her footing than Gwen had expected.

"What's your name, anyway?"

Gwen couldn't stop the look of surprise that crossed her features. "Gwen. Gwendoline Carter, your Highness." She gave a tiny bow, careful of her footing.

"Are you surprised that I care to know? What must you think of pampered nobles, Gwendoline?"

"Please, your Highness, call me Gwen. And no, I just forgot that I hadn't said my name yet. I know yours already, you see." Gwen blushed slightly, feeling foolish.

"Then call me Ava. We have many days ahead of us. If we are lucky."

"As you wish, Ava."

"How much longer, do you think?" Ava asked when they reached the bottom of the rubble.

"Not sure. Maybe half an hour? Perhaps a little longer. Perhaps a little less."

Ava nodded. "What's the plan?"

"We get to the trees over there," Gwen pointed and began walking. "Then my horse and supplies are about half a mile or so deeper into the forest. We camp for tonight, without a fire, and set off at daybreak. It's probably two more days to the first inn; maybe three if we take it slow and rest the horse."

"How are your supplies?" Ava asked as she followed. "Do you have three days of food for two people? What about bedrolls and blankets? It's cold tonight."

"Food, yes. We won't starve, Princess. Bedding is another story. We might need to huddle together next to the horse for warmth. It won't be luxury, but we'll survive."

Ava looked up at her. Gwen couldn't quite read her expression.

"What's in all of this for you, Gwen? Why risk a dragon to rescue me?"

Gwen was surprised at the question. "Gold, of course. Your father promised the one who returns you safely as much as they can carry out of the treasury. I figure I can carry enough to live handsomely for at least a couple of years, even if I'm not allowed a bag to fill."

Ava looked shocked. "Just money? No promise of land and titles? You'd risk dying to a dragon just for an armload of coins?"

"Hey, it might not seem a lot to you, but to me it's enough to buy safety for a couple of years. And I can send some home to my ma, too – she's been raising my little brother on her own since our da died. Besides, when I came looking for you I didn't know there would be a dragon."

"But you didn't turn back when you found out there was."

She didn't have an immediate answer to that.

They were almost at the tree line. A young man stepped out, one hand on the hilt of his sword, the other raised in the universal gesture of 'halt'. Gwen recognised him immediately. James.

"Stop right there, Gwen. I'll be taking the princess from here."

"Lay off it, James. I got her out of her prison; I take her home and claim the bounty. You know that's how it works."

"Not today. I have six men with bows hidden in the trees. Hand her over, or you'll look like a pincushion."

Gwen actually laughed at that. "No, you don't. You don't have the money to hire men to follow you, and you don't have the charisma for them to do it without pay up front. There are no archers in the trees. Now push off."

James scowled angrily. His hand tightened on his sword hilt, and the first few inches of blade came free of its scabbard. "Hand her over, Gwen. I intend to claim the Dragon Prize."

At this, Ava spoke up. "Half the kingdom and my hand in marriage? No. You won't get that, so go."

His scowl deepened, and he fully drew his sword. Seeing this, Gwen drew hers as well, but spoke calmly. "You really don't want to do this, James. You can't claim the Dragon Prize without consent of the rescued, and she's said she won't. The best you can claim is the same handful of coins I'm after, and I'd hope that's not worth killing a friend over. Even if you think you can win."

"Oh, we're friends now, are we? Does that mean you're going to share your haul?" He sneered as he spoke. It wasn't handsome at all.

Gwen sighed. "No, James. If you'd asked before I got to the tower I probably would have agreed. But you've drawn your sword now." A thought struck her. "Is my horse still where I left it?"

"I haven't touched your rotten horse. I've got my own." He still had his sword raised.

"Well, then. Why don't you go get it, and ride home? There are still bounties coming in, and if it's personal glory you're after I'm sure there are some that you could do in your sleep. Put your sword down, and go home."

"I could win, you know. You don't want to kill me. And you're not enough bigger and stronger to win when you handicap yourself."

Gwen deliberately set her features as hard as stone. "James. You can't win. You're right that I don't want to kill you. I want you to go home. But if you attack me, I will *not* handicap myself. You will die. Now. *Go.*" That last word had all the strength of command she could draw upon.

She saw his sword waver. He was reconsidering. She was careful not to show relief on her face while he made up his mind. Finally, he sheathed his sword. Without another word, he turned and stalked away.

Gwen listened carefully. The sound of hoofbeats began far too soon for it to be her horse. She relaxed the tension from her shoulders and led Ava into the trees.

Gwen's horse had just come into view when she heard the wings. They sounded too close for her comfort – or for Ava's. The tiny princess grabbed her arm and bore her to the ground, whispering with intense fear and purpose.

"Gwen! Am I unguarded?"

"What?" Gwen's whisper was more bewildered than anything else.

"Are. You. Guarding. Me?"

"Yes! Of course I am!"

"Then cover me and say the oath."

Ava had fallen into a sitting position with her back to a tree. She picked up the edge of Gwen's cloak and hid under it like she was a small child playing games. The wings beat again, and it almost sounded like the dragon was circling overhead.

"I don't know the oath, but I swear to protect you." Gwen shifted closer, so that she was practically on top of her. She spread her cloak to better cover the smaller woman.

"Repeat after me: My blood spilled for hers. My life given for hers. I protect the heir."

Gwen repeated it. She was confused, but Ava sounded so certain. They huddled together in silence after that. Gwen could feel her own heart thudding in her chest. She could also feel Ava's.

The dragon circled overhead one more time before flying off into the night. Gwen didn't think it was heading back to the castle, but she couldn't be sure. She could feel the princess shaking with relief under her; it was only then that she realised she was trembling too.

They sat together in silence for several minutes before either of them spoke.

"How –" Gwen began, her voice unnaturally high. She cleared her throat and tried again. "How did you know that would work?"

"I didn't. But every version of the legend includes the word 'unguarded', and that's the oath the Heir's Bodyguard gives ceremonially each time we leave the Capital. I've never seen a dragon while out with my bodyguard, so I hoped."

Gwen nodded slowly. "Am I a member of your bodyguard, now?"

"No. Well, maybe. Honorary for the interim. And only if you meant it."

They sat in silence a little longer. Then Ava spoke again. "Of course, if you *didn't* mean it, I suspect we'd both be dragon fodder by now."

Gwen considered this a moment. "Thanks," she said, simply.

Ava looked surprised. Gwen wondered if she'd expected her to be angry about the quick thinking that saved both their lives. "You're... welcome?" Maybe she just thought Gwen would be embarrassed because she pointed out the fact that she'd meant it.

Maybe it should be embarrassing. Gwen was feeling too relieved to care.

They ate cold bread and cheese out of the saddlebags that evening. Gwen laid her bedroll beside her horse and spread out her blankets and her cloak. She laid her sword and dagger aside and removed her armour.

"Well, Princess, it's not much but between the three of us we ought to be warm enough at least."

"Thank you. For everything."

Gwen raised her eyebrows a smidgeon, but only said "You're welcome, your Highness."

They shifted a little to get warm. Gwen could feel the small body next to hers, shuffling so her back was completely against the horse's flank and her right-side flush against Gwen's. Ava didn't seem to have any qualms about sharing heat. Though Gwen didn't fool herself into believing she could read the princess at all.

"I'm glad it was you, you know."

"Hmm? Princess?"

"Who rescued me. I'm glad it was you, not him."

"Who, James? The boy's a fool."

"Boy? He wouldn't be much younger than you, would he?"

"I think I was five or six when he was born. It might have been a year or so after the heralds came to proclaim your birth. Sure, he's grown tall, but he's still a fool in boyish ways. Still thinks he can slay the dragon and marry the princess – and doesn't yet realise that princesses are allowed to say no, even to dragon slayers."

"I gathered that much." Ava sighed. "If he *did* kill the dragon my father wouldn't be able to avoid giving half his land holdings. The seers disagree about a lot of things, but one thing they all agree on is that refusing to pay a prophesised debt is a bad idea. I don't honestly think it's possible, though. The best you can do is a daring rescue, and make the beast quieten down for a while." She shifted slightly, and Gwen thought maybe she turned to look up at her in the dark. "Like you did. As I said, I'm glad it was you."

"We don't yet know if the beast is quiet. It just seems to have lost interest in *you*."

"Well, I'll take it."

"As will I."

There was a time of silence. It felt companiable, and Gwen was just starting to relax into sleep when Ava asked, "How did you find me, anyway?"

"Hmm? Oh, I went to the Capital and asked Lady Deidre some questions."

"I never told her where I was going. What did she say?"

"That you were displeased with your betrothal. That you had plenty of money but not much food. That you were most likely not going to friends or family, but rather to see the world. She thought you'd gone east. Turns out she was right."

"Displeased with my betrothal. That's one way of putting it."

"Are you going to run away again? Once we're out of the dragon's lands, I mean. Are you going to try to escape me? Your circumstances haven't changed."

"Are you asking if you need to tie me up to bring me home? No. Running away did not go well. I'm going to have to find another solution." She paused, and Gwen could feel the muscles in her arm tense against her thigh. "Besides, for the next few days you're my protector, so we need to see that you get paid."

"I do like being paid, your Highness." She decided to take a stab in the dark. "If the Earl has done something that might get a bounty on his head, well, I'm a pretty decent bounty hunter. I specialise in bringing people in alive, but it wouldn't be the first time I had to bring a corpse in for justice."

Ava flinched, her hand jerking to land partially on Gwen's leg. "I'm not going to ask what Deidre told you. She doesn't have proof. Neither do I. And Reginald Lord Forquitte is powerful enough that proof would need to be incontrovertible." Her voice had become bitter at the end. She shook herself, squeezed Gwen's thigh, then removed her hand. "Thank you, though. I wish that were a remedy we could use."

Gwen's leg burned where Ava had squeezed her. How can such a small person produce so much heat? And why wasn't it cooling down after the touch departed? Best not to think too hard about that.

Sleep was a long time coming.

She woke to the slight tickle of a hand under her shirt, just above her belt. Somehow during the night they'd gone from sitting with their backs to the horse, to lying on the bedroll, Gwen underneath. Ava's weight was warm and almost comforting. Gwen didn't really want to move, but now that she was awake the call of nature was becoming irresistible.

She slipped out as quietly as possible and found a private section of the forest with good leafy bushes.

When she returned, Ava was brushing her horse.

"Are you rested? We've got a long ride today." Gwen buckled her breastplate back on before apportioning more dried rations for them both.

"Yes, thank you," came the quiet voice from behind her horse. "Do you think we'll make it to a proper bed tonight?"

"Not tonight. Possibly tomorrow. We'll need to rest the horse, though. That means getting off to walk some of the time."

"I do know how to care for horses, you know."

"Of course. But I wasn't sure you'd ever had to think about weight considerations." She looked at Ava, who was slight of build, and raised an eyebrow. "Have you ever had to ride double without pack animals before?"

"No. But Beauty always tired more easily when I had full saddle bags. Your horse is bigger, but he's still flesh. He'll tire."

Gwen nodded. She was glad Ava wasn't completely cut off from the considerations of the real world.

They ate quickly and set off, each lost in her own thoughts. For Gwen's part, she was worried about the dragon returning, wondering if James was going to leave them alone for good, and trying not to think about the closeness she and Ava had shared last night.

"Do you want to talk about it?"

Gwen had run out of ways to distract herself quietly. She figured while they were walking the horse was as good a time as any to see if she could get her companion to open up.

"Just trying to find another plan to not marry the Earl."

"Well, we can talk about your plans, if you like. Or you can tell me how you see the problem and we can try to come up with something together."

Ava sighed. "Reginald is a bully. He's closer to my father's age than mine; he has bastards up and down the Realm, and I have grave suspicions that not all of the mothers were willing." Her eyes flashed with fury. "No, it's worse than that – I have reason to believe he shuns willing women for unwilling. He enjoys the *sport*." She spat the last word with ferocity.

"Ah. So, you're not angry that he had dalliances before betrothal – you think your marriage bed will be an unpleasant place. Or is it more the moral outrage of knowing what he has done to others, regardless of whether he does the same to you?"

"Both. And I wouldn't have an issue with a nobleman sowing his wild oats. The Gods know, all of them do it. An honourable lord treats his lovers well and provides for any fruit of the unions. Many a common woman has been set up for life, her son named Fitz and no need to marry if she does not choose it. I know how the world works. I'm not a child."

"Is it just his sexual proclivities that anger you?"

"Is that not enough?" Now her glare was turned on Gwen, who held her free hand up placatingly without interrupting. "No, it's not *just* his sexual proclivities, as you call them. My father is impressed by his prowess on the battlefield, and with the rise in his wealth over the fifteen years he has been in control of his Earldom. But he delights in torture – he has ridden away from enemies who were mortally wounded, when it would have cost him nothing to end their suffering. Worse, I have heard from a man who served in his army that he has added cuts to a dying man that did nothing but increase pain without hastening the end."

Gwen grimaced. She had had need to end a man's suffering once. It was an unpleasant duty, but far less so than dragging the man to die in town of festering wounds.

"Also, his wealth. He takes more from his tenants and serfs than any other noble, gives less in return, and is harsh with runaways. Even with his reputation for cruel punishments, more serfs attempt to flee the lands of Lubrey than those of any other lord in the Realm. He requires them to work harder, on more dangerous land, and he gives them less in return. His is not a

44

model of leadership I want for this country, even without any fears of his personal sadism."

"Lady Deidre thought you were worried that he would try to have himself named your heir and then eliminate you."

Ava snorted. It was a charmingly unladylike sound. "Lady Deidre is a wonderful woman and a dear friend, but she has very little understanding of law, and even less imagination once she has decided she knows what is right. No, I'm not at all worried about being killed for the throne. The most plausible way for him to try that would be to wait for me to have a child and then make himself regent after I'm gone. But the man is shrewd enough to see some holes in that plan. For one, my father is quite likely to live at least another fifteen years, and it is not unlikely that he lives twenty or more. Our child could come of age while his or her grandfather still reigns. For another, if he somehow managed to get both my father and I out of the picture at once, it is highly unlikely that he could do that without some suspicion ending on him. He would be the target of assassination attempts from my cousins, and if he protected himself well enough, well, a babe is more difficult to defend. No, he wouldn't see killing me as his path to more power. And why would he even bother when he could terrorise me and rule in my name anyway?"

"I can see you've thought this through."

"Of course I have. There are enough real problems without jumping at shadows."

"You say you have no fear of your father dying in the next decade or two. Why is he in such a rush to have you married off, then? I'd been given to understand it was so that he could train your consort, but that doesn't sit right with what you're telling me. Is there some symbolic significance about your age?" This question had been bothering at Gwen for a while.

"I think I mentioned the seers yesterday?" Ava waited for her nod before continuing. "As the heir I am not permitted to receive instruction in Prophecy and the Scrolls, but I've heard my father discussing our current epoch with his advisors. If I understood them correctly we are in an age of flux – where small changes can drastically alter the course of history." She paused for a few seconds, looking uncharacteristically unsure of herself.

Gwen waited, before prodding gently. "And? Is your age when you take your vows one of these small changes?"

"I don't know." Ava frowned, looking frustrated. "I don't think the seers know, either. But several of the precursors to the – well, to the Dragon Prize, I guess – are in place, so people are worried."

"Should I have let James try his luck after all?" Gwen's attempt at humour fell flat.

"That could have been a disaster. If the wrong person fights the dragon, or if they lose, or if events aren't in exactly the right position before they try..." She trailed off and shrugged, looking helpless.

Gwen nodded. "Well, are we ready to think about ways to circumvent this betrothal? Or is there more?"

"If you have a brilliant plan – one that doesn't involve you murdering an Earl or sending a boy off to fight a dragon – I'm all ears."

"Nothing yet. Though I heard your father truly wants you to marry for love – have you told him of your misgivings?"

"Oh, no, I completely forgot to think of that!" This glare made the earlier one look tame. "Of course I have. My father believes that I would have exactly as many issues with whoever he chose for me, and that I am just making up excuses. He thinks the rumours of mistreated common women are overblown, and that all serfs complain of their masters. He sees me as a child, running from my responsibility."

"Why does he think you'd object to whoever he chose? Have you objected to others before?"

"No. But I have objected to being forced to choose. The seers don't even know what they fear. If I were born male this would never have become an issue – my father would have trusted my instincts and trained me to lead." Ava looked frustrated. Gwen couldn't blame her.

"Is he at all concerned about your future children? Lady Deidre thought not, but I can see she doesn't know the whole story."

Ava paused and thought. When she spoke, her "No," was drawn out, and Gwen could hear the "But" forming in the air between them.

"But?"

"If I am going to have children, he wants the man I have them with to look a certain way."

"That seems odd. Doesn't he trust you to find a handsome man yourself?"

"No. I haven't responded to pretty boys he has paraded in front of me in the past. Besides, he mostly wants his grandchildren to be dark haired, blue eyed and tall. Broad shouldered. Like the warriors of old." Her voice took a grand, theatrical cast, and she waved her hand regally for emphasis.

Gwen schooled herself not to preen. She wasn't noble, and she wasn't male. This wasn't about her.

"Were you deliberately not responding? Or did you just not find them interesting?"

"It's hard to find someone interesting when all you can see is the transparent motives behind them being there. It would be like appreciating the beauty of a single rose, when all around it were garishly painted signs saying exactly what the sender hopes you will do with your gratitude. It's exhausting."

"It sounds it. It also sounds like you never had the opportunity to meet anyone suitable without the pressure from your father to choose your consort. Do you think he would relent on the Earl if you chose someone else?"

Ava's brow furrowed. It looked less like she hadn't thought of the question, and more like she had, but still wasn't sure of the answer.

"I honestly don't know. The betrothal papers haven't been signed – I'm old enough that he can't sign them on my behalf – but the talks had reached a gentlemen's agreement. The news was out. Rejecting the Earl now would have political consequences – possibly as grave as rebellion, if the other lords didn't like my reason well enough."

"And mistreatment of women and serfs wouldn't be considered a good enough reason?"

"Is this some form of a jest? No. Nobles would want loftier reasons."

"I thought the canonical Noble Ideals were Justice, Liberty and Brotherhood. Wouldn't mistreatment of common folks strike against the heart of those?"

"You're not joking, are you?" It was more a statement than a question. "I must assume you've learned to read but have never conversed with other learned scholars – am I correct?" She didn't sound unkind.

"My mother taught me my letters. There are some books at home. Not a palace library, but more than you could count with one hand. I was fortunate."

"Yes." Ava's voice was soft. Almost tender. "You were. I wish we had more people in the Capital who had read without hearing the definitions our current crop of noblemen put on those words. You see, they feel that Justice is the lords bending knee to the power of the King, and the peasantry bending knee to the power of the lords – accepting Justice as meted out by one's superior. Liberty is the freedom of landed gentry to do whatsoever they will with their own property – including the people bound to those lands. And Brotherhood is understood to mean the Chivalric code – and is only between men who have been trained in arms, and who can afford a horse and armour and a squire to help them ready for battle. Some would go so far as to say that the ideal of Brotherhood *requires* they take the Earl's side against any woman who names him beast."

"What I'm hearing is that Justice and Equality are out. What other lofty ideals could you appeal to?"

"Honour, duty and love. Unfortunately, honour and duty both declare I should wed him. If I'd made a secret promise to another before my father made his promise to the Earl that could satisfy honour, but not now. Duty for a son might be the duty to fight in wars before choosing a consort, or the duty to care for bastard children before fathering legitimate heirs, but as a daughter my duty is to wed."

"And love? Would unending love for another be sufficient reason to break your unofficial betrothal?"

"While it is unofficial, yes. Once the paper is signed, no. But there is no one I love with such fire."

"You have friends who know you don't want to wed Lord Forquitte. Would one of them be willing to claim their friendship is actually love and marry you instead?"

A startled look passed across Ava's face so quickly Gwen wasn't sure she'd seen it. Not knowing its origin, she quickly dismissed it.

A rueful expression remained. "Deidre probably would have. But she's married, and even if she were willing to brave the scandal to save me, the whole world knows her dedication to her husband."

Gwen blinked, temporarily lost for words.

"Will, the stable hand, is only a few years younger than me," Ava continued, "and he is absolutely devoted. If I crooked my finger he would declare his love and fight for me, I know he would."

"Sounds like a plan?"

Ava grimaced. "It could have been a plan six months ago, when he reached majority. As it is, everyone knows that I am fond of him, but I haven't shown any romantic interest before now. His love for me on its own would be enough if he outranked Forquitte – but he doesn't. He's a common boy with no education and no prospects. Choosing him over an Earl would be a grave insult unless there was a level of Fairytale Romance that can't believably spring up overnight between people who are already friends."

Gwen was puzzled. "Some of the best marriages I know of started as friendships. Why must passion burn so fast?"

"Because we're not talking about a basis for a good marriage. We're talking about a story for the Nobility to hear. A story so that they accept my refusal of an Earl my father has chosen for me with no insult. We're talking politics, Gwen. Not love. Not really."

"Oh." Gwen felt a little sad at that. "Do you think you would have chosen this boy if you were free to?"

"Probably not." Ava shrugged. "Affection without passion is better than passion without affection. But I would prefer both – or else no marriage at all."

Gwen could relate to that.

Chapter Four – A Proposition

They'd spent their riding leg in silence, each woman with her own thoughts. After eating a quiet lunch they set off again, walking beside the horse. Gwen was relieved not to have Ava's slender form sitting in front of her anymore. She'd been practically in her lap, and all Gwen could think of was how Ava had said she'd considered asking Deidre to marry her.

Marriages of convenience happen. But where Gwen came from, even a marriage of convenience was intended to be able to produce offspring.

"Your father's dead, isn't he?"

Ava clearly didn't believe breaking a long silence required more small talk.

"Yes; he died shortly after my brother was born. I was sixteen."

"And you're not married?"

"No."

"Is that why the money is so important to you? So you can look after your mother and brother?"

"Yes. It will buy me some time away from bounties, but also my brother is getting old enough to be apprenticed. If I want him to have choice in where he goes, I need enough money to pay guild fees. Otherwise, he can only choose to go where his labour is payment enough."

"You said your mother taught you your letters. Can you brother also read?"

"Yes, though he has never been as interested as I am. He hasn't read all ma's books, and his lettering is crude, but he can read and write." Gwen smiled, thinking of her brother. "Nick's never been interested in books, but he can pick up languages faster than you'd believe, just from listening to people speak."

"Are there a lot of foreigners in your village?"

Gwen felt her lips twitch in mirth. "Not hardly. But we're close enough to the Capital that traders come through occasionally. He's picked up Varouvian, Tenerian, and even a few words of Nidywhonyniaith just from listening to caravan guards – and I don't even know how he manages to pronounce that last one."

Ava nodded thoughtfully. She appeared to be making her mind up.

"You know, the brother of the heir's consort would be accepted as apprentice into any guild in the Capital – including some that are extremely choosy about their membership."

Was Ava offering what it sounded like? Gwen was extremely careful of her tone. "I imagine he would."

"I've been thinking of what you said this morning," the princess said, her voice nervous and her words a little rushed. "You're right – the best plan to get out of marrying Forquitte is by being head over heels in love with someone else. And who could possibly question a princess falling in love with the valiant knight who rescued her from the dragon?"

Gwen blinked a few times. Her brain did not want to process this as fast as she needed it to. "I'm not a knight, your Highness."

"I know. So we'll have to appear even more in love than if you had rank. But it's a believable story – and your brother would have opportunities he couldn't dream of otherwise. Will you do it?"

"Let me get this absolutely straight. Are you asking me to marry you?"

"Yes. And to pretend to be so absurdly in love with me that songs will tell of us through all the ages." Her hands made grandiose gestures through the air, as if conducting a symphony.

"Will I get murdered by an Earl if I say yes?"

"No. If he were feeling vindictive, he would aim at the one who insulted him. But he is far more likely to try to stir rebellion than to attempt assassination – which is why we need to be utterly believable. Do you think you *can* act besotted with me?" It looked like a thought struck her suddenly. "Please tell me you don't have a long history of publicly lusting for men. One or two we can probably get around, but if it's a new man every month with no women between I might need a new plan."

Gwen coughed. "No history of publicly lusting for men. The only man who ever thought I lusted for him was that buffoon we encountered last night. But he thinks all women want him, and I corrected him swiftly."

"And the other question?"

"Can I act besotted with you? I don't know. I don't know the normal way to act around princesses, nor what Courtiers expect from a woman in love. I'd never been to the Capital until you went missing."

"Well, you sounded sincere enough when you said the Oath, so we have something to work with. We have a few days to practice before we get home. What do you say? Will you marry me?"

Who could reject a proposal like that? "It would be an honour, your Highness. Yes."

Gwen found it very hard to concentrate while they were riding. The thought that she had agreed to marry this beautiful young woman had her mind completely jumbled. They'd met yesterday! She was a commoner. And she had no idea how Ava felt about marrying her, except that it was preferable to marrying the Earl of Lubrey.

It sounded like cutting her own arm off was preferable to marrying the Earl of Lubrey.

They made camp less than halfway to The Barbed Tail. There hadn't been any sign of the dragon today, but they made their fire small and hid it as well as they could in a hollow. The dragon would have to be practically overhead to see it. She took off her armour and tried to relax.

Gwen felt a lot better for a warm meal inside her – even if it was just warmed up travellers' rations. It looked like Ava felt the same. They loosened up a little and told each other stories from their childhoods. It was easy to warm up to the princess. Probably too easy – though Gwen told herself it was necessary to feel some fondness if she was going to pretend to feel more.

After food was in their bellies, conversation turned to their plans.

"What's our story going to be? Are we going to arrive at the castle betrothed to each other? Or do I need to ask your father for your hand? Or what?"

Ava burst into giggles at this. "We aren't betrothed, silly. That's a ceremony in its own right that we'll get to when we get home. We're just going to get married, that's all."

"Well, forgive me for not knowing all the correct words, your Highness," her tone was playful, teasing the princess. "I'm just a poor country lass, never had no need to know such grand words as those."

"Oh, you!" Ava jumped at her and tickled her sides mercilessly. Gwen fell to the ground laughing, batting Ava's hands away ineffectually. When they came to rest, Ava was on top of Gwen, still filled with mirth. "All right, all right, I'll try to be serious." Her smile was still wide. "What exactly did the bounty notice say about your reward?"

"Are you thinking of having me claim the Dragon Prize?"

"No. You didn't slay the dragon, and if you claim me as a prize through such a broad interpretation of tradition the Earl may well convince some of the other lords that they should all ride in to rescue me. But what did the notice actually say?"

"It said the one who brought you safely back to your father could have whatever they can carry from the Royal Treasury using nothing but their own arms."

Ava grinned. "That sounds like the kind of thing my father would write. Do you think you could pick me up and carry me?"

Gwen chuckled as she worked this out. "Such theatrics! Yes, of course I can. Want me to show you?"

"Better to be sure," laughed Ava, standing up.

Gwen got up beside her and swept her off her feet, one arm under her shoulders and the other under her knees. She smiled and carried the princess around the campfire twice before setting her back down. "Satisfied?"

"Very." Ava did indeed look satisfied with herself. "It might not come to that – if we're acting like there has never been a love so great as ours, it might draw my father's attention well before you get around to claiming your prize. But it would definitely make an impression."

"Is there anything I need to do to show love? Or not do?"

"Well, we should be unable to take our eyes off each other for more than a moment. That's easy out here where there's no one else to distract you, but keep doing it in town, too."

Gwen tried not to blush. She hadn't realised she'd been staring so much. "Anything else?"

"Affectionate touching. We've got the playful touches working well, but we need to be able to just reach out and touch each other as if we're not even thinking about it. You need to touch me like it's the only thing keeping you from floating away." She giggled. "You know – romantic idiocy, but in touch form."

"Okay, longing looks and affectionate touches. Got it. If that's all, I think I can handle it."

"Well..." Ava's mirth subsided, and she looked a little uncomfortable. "We probably need to be caught in slightly compromising positions a time or two to really convince all onlookers that we're just too in love to pay any heed to my father's plans."

"Compromising? How compromising are we talking about, here?"

"Kissing ought to be enough, as long as it looks like we didn't mean to get caught. And like we might have gone further if we weren't. Do you think you can do that? Kiss me, I mean?"

Gwen couldn't speak. She could hardly breathe. All of a sudden her mind was flooded with images of kissing Princess Ava, of the feel of her body in her arms, of her lips so soft, of her... *snap out of it! It's just for show.*

"Gwen? Have you ever kissed a woman before?"

She finally found her voice. "No," she said, quietly.

"Oh. Well, if it makes you feel any better, neither have I."

Gwen wasn't sure that did make her feel any better. After all, was it worse to feel these flashes of desire for a woman who liked women too? Or one who only liked men that way?

"It's alright," said Ava, soothingly. "We can practice, and it won't be so bad." At Gwen's terrified expression she added, "But maybe not tonight."

Gwen nodded mutely.

Despite the cold, they were careful to sleep slightly apart that night.

She woke with the princess sprawled on top of her again. The fire had burned down overnight, and the warmth of the body in her arms was welcome. She lay there for a time, awake but content.

Then she remembered their conversation from last night. She thought about kissing the princess, about "practice" coming up in the next few days. Heat started gathering low in her belly, twisting into an ache that spread deeper within her. The more she tried not to think about kissing her, the more she thought, and the worse the ache got.

She eased her way out, attended to nature, and remade the fire. By the time it was strong and warm she'd managed to get her body mostly under control again. She was just heating breakfast when Ava joined her, looking like she'd freshened her face in the nearby stream.

"Sorry. I seem to be a bit of a cuddler."

Gwen gave a lopsided smile. "You could say that. It's okay – I've got to get comfortable with touching you somehow, right?"

"True." Ava reached out and squeezed Gwen's forearm briefly, smiling. "Try to touch me a little more today. And I'll do the same. If we can look natural with each other, that's half the job done."

Gwen reached out hesitantly and put two fingers on Ava's wrist. She grimaced at how unnatural the gesture felt. And even more at how much it made her heart race. "I definitely need practice at this. How long do we need to keep up the façade?"

Ava thought for a moment, frowning pensively. "Depends on what you mean. Ideally this arrangement isn't too onerous on either of us, and we just stay in a marriage of convenience permanently. Or are you still looking for true love?"

Gwen huffed a quiet laugh. "I gave up on love years ago. I'm okay with the marriage being permanent. What I was asking was, how long do we have to pretend to be smitten with each other?"

"Ah. Well, most marriages drop to gentler affections over time, and often very little of that is in public. We must be outrageous in our display before we wed, and then we have to look blissfully happy for a while after. Maybe a year? Certainly, until the Earl moves on in his life. Long enough for the songs to be written and for little girls to wish they had what we do." Ava flashed a cheeky smile at that. "I have it on the best authority that most of the grand romances of history were played up for the public. It's just good politics."

Gwen laughed in frank disbelief. "Have you always been so cynical, your Highness?"

"Enough with the Highness. You're in love, remember? It's Ava, or cute pet names I'd never let anyone else use." She paused, then grinned rakishly. "And yes, I'm cynical about history. It's written by the victors, after all."

"Alright, then, snookums." Gwen tapped Ava gently on the nose, grinning like a fool. "Your wish is, as ever, my command."

"Are we going to make it to a real inn tonight?" Ava asked, as the sun was dropping toward the horizon.

"Not unless we keep going well past eventide. I think it might be for the best if we have another night out here, anyway."

"Really? Because I for one could use a bath."

Gwen laughed. "Me too, sweetie." The endearments were getting easier, but still sounded a little forced. "And The Barbed Tail has an excellent bath house attached. But the innkeeper recognised you on your way through, so I'd like to have a plan before we get there."

"Oh? She never said anything while I was there."

"No – this one's my fault, your Highness. I was being nosey, and she told me that a young woman who looked a bit like the princess had come through a few days earlier, right before the heralds came and announced your disappearance."

"We have to work on that 'Highness' thing. You still drop into it when you're feeling anxious. Or guilty." Ava gave her a wry smile. "Sounds like it's as likely she guessed from the proclamations as from your questioning, anyway. I guess this will be our first road test?"

Gwen smiled. "What, you're thinking of trying to scandalise everyone and get the news out ahead of us?"

"Well, I wasn't actually thinking anything too scandalous, but now that you mention it..." She tapped her finger on her chin in overly theatrical thought.

"What *were* you thinking, then?"

"Oh, just seeing if we could act enough like a couple in public that we get offered rooms with a joining door – easy access, you see." Her grin was wicked, and Gwen felt her stomach muscles tighten involuntarily at the suggestion.

"Ah." Gwen felt for her unfortunately light belt pouch. "Do you still have any of the money you came with? I only have a few shillings left; we might not be able to afford separate rooms in any case."

"No; my purse was with all my other things." Ava looked sad for a moment, probably thinking of her horse. Her wicked smirk came back quickly. "Scandalise everyone it is, then."

They made camp a little early that evening. After all, they were planning to spend the next night at The Barbed Tail, and it would look odd if they arrived there before mid-afternoon. They made good use of the daylight to refill their waterskins and wash as much of their faces and limbs as they could reach. Actual baths and fresh clothing would need to wait until tomorrow.

"Are you ready to practice some more... intimate affection?" Ava asked quietly. It almost sounded like she was nervous about this, too. Gwen wondered if she was worried kissing would be unpleasant, or if she was just worried Gwen would mess it up.

If it were the first, too much practice would be cruel. But if it were the second, too much practice might not be enough. Gwen would have to watch her very carefully.

"Alright. What did you have in mind?" She was proud of how even her voice sounded.

"Standing, to start with." Ava sounded determined. Gwen was really starting to worry that this was going to be a hardship for the small princess. "Most of our public appearances together will be while we're standing up."

"As you wish." Gwen stood in front of Ava, and gently placed her hands on her waist. It felt unnatural. It felt terrifying.

It felt blissful.

Ava smiled encouragingly up at her, her hands snaking up to Gwen's shoulders. They stood like that for a few seconds, as Gwen felt her heart pound so hard there was no way Ava couldn't feel it. She hoped the princess just assumed it was nerves. If Ava could feel how aroused... She stopped that thought right there. No. It *was* just nerves. Just nerves.

"If you stand with your feet a little further apart, you won't need to bend down as far." Gwen obediently widened her stance and slouched her shoulders just a little. Now if they were both to tilt their heads just right...

Softness. Such a featherlight touch, and the softest, most beautiful thing she had ever felt. Gwen felt a soft moan leave her as Ava's lips moved under hers, pressing infinitesimally harder. Her lips parted without her conscious volition, just the barest gap, not trying to intensify the kiss, just taking pure pleasure in what she was offered.

Ava's hands had moved from her shoulders to behind her neck and head, holding her in place. She felt the tiniest flick of tongue on her lower lip, and moaned again, pulling Ava's body more firmly against her own. She could feel a damp heat spreading between her thighs, but her mind was too full of sensation to care. Her lips parted a little wider, and her tongue met Ava's on the next tiny flick.

Ava pulled back suddenly, flushed. Reality came crashing back, and Gwen dropped her hands as if burned. Both women stood staring at each other, neither knowing what to say.

Gwen broke eye contact first. *Oh Gods, there's no way she missed how turned on I am.* Would she end up with an appointment with the headsman, rather than the priest? Gwen's reddened cheeks now held as much fear as arousal.

"Wow," Ava said, and then cleared her throat a little roughly. "Are you sure you've never kissed a woman before, Gwen?"

Gwen stammered "No! I mean, yes. No, I haven't kissed a woman before. Yes, I'm sure. Sorry. I'm sorry, your Highness. I won't –"

"Relax. I'm not angry." And, wonder of wonders, she didn't sound it. "Far from it. If you kiss me like that where we can be interrupted… well, whoever catches us will certainly believe our charade."

Gwen started to breathe more easily. She was still a little frightened, but she had it under control. Mostly. Ava didn't seem to know she wasn't acting.

Thank the Gods.

They were a little subdued while eating their dinner. Ava insisted on practicing affectionate touches, so Gwen had been careful to touch her arms frequently and her face on occasion. She made sure not to touch her waist – the memory of the kiss they'd just shared was far too strong for that.

Ava reached out to touch her, pausing with her hand on her shoulder. "We should practice from a seated position, too," she said quietly, her fingertips moving again slowly and lightly up to Gwen's exposed neck. Gwen's eyes closed involuntarily, though she controlled her slight gasp well enough to be inaudible.

"As you wish," she said when her eyes opened again. Gwen managed a steady voice, trying not to let the princess know just how much she was affecting her. "How would you like to begin?"

"I'd love to," grinned Ava, deliberately misinterpreting her. "No, seriously, just stay seated where you are. I'll take the lead." Gwen nodded, and Ava climbed somewhat inelegantly into her lap. At first, she sat side-saddle, twisting to put her arms around Gwen's neck. This felt slightly awkward, and it seemed Ava felt it too. She shifted to face her, one knee passing through between them, so she was straddling Gwen's lap. She sat herself back down, her thighs firmly positioned around Gwen's waist.

She made the mistake of looking down. The princess was in dark blue riding skirts, so there was no bare leg, but she could see

64

where their bodies joined, and... *Oh hells*. The rush of liquid warmth to her centre felt like it could give her away on its own, but her stomach also clenched right where her muscles pressed between Ava's thighs. She hoped the princess just thought she was bracing to steady her.

Ava leaned forward, her hips tilting against Gwen's stomach. She slid her hands up Gwen's arms, the little squeezes as she traced the muscles under her fingers surprising the taller woman. Her hands paused briefly on either side of Gwen's neck, before her fingers linked together behind her head.

Her eyes closed just before their lips met. Gwen felt her own eyes drift shut in response. The kiss began with more heat than the last one, though still exquisitely tender. Ava's lips were the softest thing she'd ever felt. She could lose herself in the feeling... and was in danger of doing so.

Ava's lips parted, and her tongue very gently probed the line of Gwen's mouth. She gave her entrance; she could as soon have resisted the pull of gravity as that gentle request. When she felt their tongues meet with the lightest of possible strokes, she felt an inferno in her lower belly, and her stomach began a rhythmic clench and unclench.

Ava deepened the kiss further, and her hips began to move seemingly of their own accord, her centre rubbing up and down Gwen's stomach, shifting her shirt out of position a little more with each undulation. Gwen could feel heat, so much heat through Ava's divided skirts onto her bare skin. Her moan sounded loud in her own ears.

The princess broke the kiss with a gasp, and sat motionless in her lap, their foreheads pressed together as they each caught their breath. When they had themselves under control again, Ava stood up a little shakily and took a position a few steps back from her, smiling as if proud of herself. "Well. Was I convincing?"

Too convincing. While they'd been joined, Gwen hadn't remembered that this was all a ruse. It had felt real, and she'd let herself get carried away. She'd have to be more careful in future.

She schooled her features to an impressed smile. "Yes, your Highness. Very."

They had a fire again that night and did not cuddle together as they fell asleep. Gwen was glad of the space. Her mind was racing. Who would have thought the princess could kiss like that? And why hadn't she guessed how much she'd enjoy it?

Her dreams were a chaotic mess, full of Ava moaning in her ear and rubbing her naked body all over Gwen's. She felt like she was on fire. She couldn't make out details, but she couldn't get enough of what was just beyond sight. Just as her dream woman stiffened, arching her back in ecstasy, she felt a very real thigh slide down between her own. She woke with a gasp, her own pleasure pulsing out from her core. She felt the aftershocks spasm through her body, causing tremors in the smaller woman asleep on top of her.

Asleep. Gods. Gwen was suddenly very aware of her body and that of her princess. She *hoped* Ava was still asleep. That her thigh moving at exactly the wrong time was just her shifting in her sleep, like she had the previous two nights. That she hadn't suddenly woken up to her rescuer convulsing underneath her like some twisted creep.

Gwen was disgusted with herself. She'd said she would keep herself more under control, but as soon as her dreaming self took over, there she was, taking perverse pleasure in the woman she had come to save. The woman who wanted her to pretend to be in love, but not to actually fall for her. Whatever would Ava think of her?

She didn't sneak out this time. It was still night, and besides, if she woke Ava by leaving their blankets now, the princess might piece together the meaning of her earlier movement. Best to stay very still and hope for sleep.

Chapter Five – Scandalous

"Mmm, I can't wait for a bath this evening," the princess declared, lifting herself off Gwen's chest and yawning.

Gwen was surprised to discover she had actually slept well. The fear and self-loathing had faded quickly, replaced by a lethargy that pulled her back under and let her sleep soundly. And while this was the first time Ava had woken while still cuddled up to her, it didn't seem to make her unhappy. In fact, she looked positively radiant.

"Sleep well, Princess?"

"Pet names, Gwenny dear," Ava teased. "And yes, I slept very well indeed."

"Have you decided which it's going to be this afternoon, Pookie? Subtle or scandal?"

"I thought we'd already agreed on scandal, hadn't we, Honeycakes?"

They were both struggling not to laugh, and at this point they gave up.

"Maybe we should actually agree on pet names so we can use them with a straight face," Gwen suggested.

"Maybe. I quite like hearing new ones, though, darling." She made the word sound like it had at least five 'a's. "Scandal in the bath house?"

"How do we scandalise a bath house?"

Ava's grin was positively wicked. "You'll see."

"You know, a lot of couples actually use 'princess' as a pet name."

Ava looked at her in confusion for a second, before laughing. "Sure. And if I wasn't one, it would work. But since I am, people are going to hear it as a title, not an endearment. Choose something else."

"How about 'precious'?"

"Precious could work. But you're going to mess up and say Princess instead, aren't you?"

"Probably. Sweetheart?"

"Sure, darling," Ava smiled. "We should really have spent more time practicing these, shouldn't we?"

Gwen hoped she didn't notice her blush at the word 'practice'. "We're here, my sweet."

"So we are, my love." Ava's dimples flashed as she grinned. They gave her an air of impish mischief. "I really hope that when I say that people think I'm laughing out of affection and not at absurdity."

She handed the horse's reins to a stable boy and entered the inn.

As they went inside, Ava pressed close to her side. She draped her arm across the smaller woman's shoulders and smiled at the innkeeper. Ava's arm snaked around her waist, holding her even closer.

"Well now," said the innkeeper. "Here be two faces I didn't think I'd be seeing again. Welcome, and what can I get for you?"

"A room, and use of your bath house, if you please." Gwen's smile only broadened.

"Just the one room?" The innkeeper raised her eyebrow at the pair of them.

"One room is all I can afford, my good woman." Her tone was rueful now. "But if you could launder our clothes while we bathe, we would greatly appreciate that."

"As you say, then. I'll show you to your room."

"Here we go, your Highness, my Lady. Drop your bags and we'll go downstairs to the bath." The innkeeper waited outside the door as they went in to leave their bags and cloaks.

The room was small, and the bed a simple straw mattress. Compared with what they had been sleeping on previously, it looked heavenly. Gwen noticed it was small enough that the two of them would be touching the whole night. Not that it made any difference – she was already realising that the princess was always going to end up on top of her regardless.

They followed the innkeeper downstairs. Gwen idly wondered if she should have asked the woman her name – and then realised that she was just avoiding thinking of what was about to happen.

"Do you have towels and soaps?" Ava asked.

"Aye, that we do, your Highness," the stout woman replied. "And our bath is large enough to submerge your whole body at once – even when you're sharing two to the tub."

Two to the tub. *Oh Gods*. She was about to be naked in a bath with Ava. Her breathing picked up pace until she deliberately slowed it down.

They entered the room. It was filled with steam, and a serving girl was just pouring a bucket of steaming water into the largest bath Gwen had ever seen. It was round, like half a barrel, but close to her own height across. There were steps leading up the side, the edge of which was just about the height of her waist. The surface of the water was covered in bubbles.

Ava dipped her hand into the suds as the serving girl waited. "The heat is good. Thank you. We shall let you know if we need more hot water by and by."

"Leave your clothes on the stool by the door. I'll be back in a bit to collect them, and we'll have them returned to you shortly." The innkeeper indicated a stool, and the pair of them bustled off to other tasks within the inn.

As soon as they'd gone, Ava began undoing her plait with a relieved sigh. Gwen followed suit, running her fingers through her dark wavy hair. It had been weeks since she last washed it, and it felt a little greasy, but it had been worse a time or two before.

"At least neither of us are wearing dresses we need help getting out of," Ava smiled a little cheekily. "Though that would have let us put on a bit of a show and get the scandal started."

Gwen blushed, her fingers tripping as she undid the laces of her shirt. "And how exactly do you plan to scandalise the locals, Ava?"

Ava had her shirt off and was pushing down her riding skirts. Gwen tried hard not to stare but couldn't help noticing her small round breasts with nipples pointing just higher than the horizon. She looked away before she could think too hard about that perfectly flat stomach and the flare of her... *Damn it, Gwen, you're trying* not *to think about her that way!*

"Well, the good innkeeper will be down in a few minutes to collect our clothes. I don't think we should be doing too much when she does – it risks looking crude, or worse, staged."

"But it *is* staged."

"Right, hence why we must be careful not to look it. So, when she comes down the first time, we ought to just look nice and cosy and close. Scrubbing each other's back and washing each other's hair, you know?" Ava glanced down and added "We'll need to do something about that when we get back to the Capital."

About what? Gwen looked down at her own nude form, following the princess' line of sight to her unruly thatch of hair. She glanced over to where Ava was now also perfectly naked, and saw that her golden curls were far shorter, and appeared to be growing in a very neat patch. "What? Why?" She looked away quickly, careful not to stare.

"It might not be necessary. Maybe no one will ever see you in a state of undress. But I don't want anyone having reason to leave certain speculation off the table, so we're going to groom you."

Gwen was bewildered but decided to drop it. She could ask later.

"After you?" She extended her hand. Ava took it and climbed gracefully into the tub. Gwen checked that the soap and washcloths were within reach and followed with somewhat less elegance. At least she didn't trip as she clambered in.

She felt a lot less nervous once she was in the water, the suds covering her to her armpits as she sat on the submerged shelf. Ava was divinely beautiful, covered so that only the very top of her shoulders peeked out from the water. "Would you like me to scrub your back, my sweet?"

"Hmmm… yes, but hair first, I think. My love." Ava smiled. The endearments were coming more easily to both of them, but they still sounded strange.

The feel of Ava's hand on her bare shoulder, a rough cloth scrubbing over her back, was blissfully relaxing to Gwen after so long on the road. She heard the door open, but didn't turn, knowing the innkeeper could see exactly what Ava wanted her to see.

"You two ladies just relax while I go get these clean. Shan't be more than an hour." The door closed again, and both women giggled like they were children caught stealing sweetcakes.

"Alright," Ava said, gathering her damp hair around the front of her left shoulder. "My turn." She turned so her back was to Gwen, handing her the cloth as she did so.

Gwen gazed at the perfectly smooth back and shoulders in front of her. Ava was leaning with her elbows on the edge of the bath, so her entire back was visible down to her hips. The very beginning of curved buttock was at the edge of the bubbles, and Gwen willed herself not to fixate on how beautiful the princess was.

"There's no one watching – you don't have to stare." Ava sounded amused.

Gwen blushed. "Right. Sorry." She stood close behind the princess, and placed her left hand on Ava's hip, holding her steady as her right hand began soaping up that glorious back. She was careful not to touch the princess any more than strictly necessary. Even just this much contact was setting her body on fire. She didn't want to know what could happen with more.

"Ohhh yes, that feels amazing," the princess groaned with deep contentment. "Do you think I can put somewhere in our wedding vows that you promise to scrub my back every day? Because this is heavenly."

Her fingers tightened on Ava's hip in response to the sensual groan. Her thigh bumped up against the princess' smaller one as she moved to scrub further up her back. She took too long to answer, but finally managed to get some words out. "Your wish is my command, of course."

Really? That's the best you could come up with? Pathetic. Still, at least she'd managed to respond, and not just with an aroused moan. This whole bath was doing disastrous things to her libido.

Several seconds passed in silence, save for the appreciative murmurs from the princess. A minute stretched to two, then three. Gwen could feel the tension building within her and sought to relieve it a little. "Don't you have attendants to scrub your back for you in the palace?"

"Hmm? Oh. Yes, I suppose so. I've asked my chambermaid to scrub my back before, but she's rough and quick, getting me clean like I'm a child. Not like…" Ava paused, looking for the right word. Gwen winced, worrying that she was being too obvious in her admiration, but unable to stop the slow movements of her hand on Ava's back. "Not like you." Well, that was a neutral way to end the sentence. She relaxed very slightly and continued scrubbing her upper back and shoulders in silence.

"Thank you," Ava said eventually, and gave a slightly forced laugh. "I think my back is clean, now." She slipped below the water again before turning around. Her smile looked a little forced.

Gwen hoped she hadn't done anything to displease her. She smiled back, but she knew her smile was somewhat weak as well. "You're welcome. Any time."

Ava glanced away, blushing slightly. "We should really make sure we're keeping up the touches. I think we'll hear if anyone approaches the door, but it's easier to put on a show if we're already sitting close and touching each other." The words were rushed. Possibly she was nervous, though of what Gwen couldn't guess.

"Of course, my sweet." She put a little cheek in her smile and scooted across on the submerged bench until their thighs touched. She reached her hand across her body to touch the smaller woman's arm.

Ava's smile in return looked relieved. *I wonder why?* This whole situation was awkward and slightly scary, but also thrilling. Ava's hand came around, touching her upper arm hesitantly, then moving more confidently to caress her over her collarbone. Gwen tried hard to keep her breathing even. She could do nothing about her heart, which was threatening to beat its way out of her chest.

They sat like that in silence for a time, their bodies joined from one hip down the length of their thighs. Their upper bodies were twisted to face each other, their hands roaming. These weren't tiny touches to give the illusion of seeking comfort in each other's presence; these were continuous caresses, albeit relatively chaste ones. Their hands moved over each other's arms and shoulders, up to stroke a neck, a cheek, down to trail a finger over ribs and waist.

They were careful to avoid touching each other more intimately, but this much was enough to have Gwen's senses reeling. She could feel her inner thighs becoming slick even through the water. If Ava's hand ever strayed down that far...

There was the sound of footsteps approaching. Ava moved suddenly, straddling her thighs, and leaning forward to whisper urgently in her ear. "Hold me, and moan like this is the best thing you've ever felt in your life."

Suddenly they were kissing, the princess' tongue seeking entrance more roughly than she had done before. Gwen was happy to give it to her, deepening the kiss and moaning in pleasure as their breasts slipped against each other in the soapy water. Ava had one hand on her shoulder, and the other was between them. She could feel a fist between their lower stomachs, moving around their belly buttons as Ava's arm made pumping motions that would be visible from the doorway.

Understanding dawned, and Gwen stopped trying to control her moans. Her hands explored Ava's back, and each time their nipples crossed paths the bolt of pleasure drew even deeper groans from her throat. She arched her back as the door opened, closing her eyes as Ava's mouth dropped to her throat. If this didn't stop soon she was going to find out whether she could pass a real orgasm off as merely incredibly good acting.

"By all the Gods! I'm so sorry, your Highness. Here are your clean clothes. We won't bother you again." The words had tumbled out as fast as lightning, but the final sentence was still spoken from part way down the hall, as the innkeeper dropped their things and rushed off.

Ava stopped pumping immediately and stifled a giggle against Gwen's neck. Gwen gave one last, loud, moan for effect, then stopped and giggled along with her. The tension was broken, but she was still very much aware of the gorgeous nude woman in her arms. Her clit was throbbing, but at least it didn't feel like she was in imminent danger of embarrassing herself.

"Well." Their giggling had subsided, and the princess sounded extremely pleased with herself. "If my Lord Father hasn't heard rumours before we get home to him, I'll eat my hat."

They lay next to each other that evening, wearing only their undergarments and a shirt each. Compared to the bath it was positively demure, but it still felt intimate.

"These rumours that are racing ahead of us," Gwen began.

"Yes?"

"The King is going to believe that I've deflowered his daughter."

"That's the idea, yes."

"How much trouble am I going to be in, here? I mean, I know he'll be happy that I rescued you, and I hope the rumours that reach him contain some dragon in them too, but I've known a few fathers in my day and none of them would be happy with a person they never met having their way with their daughter. Even less so if it's a woman."

"Why? At least with a woman there's no chance of pregnancy."

Gwen gaped at her. That was what she was focussed on right now?

"You're seriously worried, aren't you?"

"Well, yes. I don't want to be beheaded."

Ava gave a slight smile at that. "You won't be. Unless you refuse to go through with the wedding, of course. Father might have very firm opinions about a rogue who takes his daughter's virginity without marrying her. But I actually think he'll be relieved to hear I've finally shown interest in taking a consort, even if he has to unruffle some feathers to make it happen."

"And your mother?"

Ava hesitated. "She'll be disappointed you can't get me pregnant," she admitted. "The deflowering won't worry her. She says everyone pretends to be pure on their wedding day, but only fools actually are. No one wants to be saddled with a dud now, do they?" She grinned.

Maybe everything she'd heard about nobles was true. This was surreal. "You honestly think there won't be consequences to the whole world thinking we're…" she searched for a way to put it delicately. "Making love?"

"Of course there will be consequences. You'll have to marry me. That's the whole point." Ava looked at her like she was being a bit stupid. "I can't very well be known to have made love to a person I did not go on to marry. My father will need to make it happen. I'm not embarrassing both of us for no reason, you know."

"No, I know. I just didn't appreciate how different sexual mores could be at court, I think."

Ava grinned a little impishly. "I don't think it's that different, really. You mentioned knowing fathers – what would one of those fathers do, do you think, if he found out his daughter had been rolling in the hay with some village boy?"

"Drag him out in the fields with a hunting crossbow?"

"Possibly. But what if consequences had already happened? What if she was pregnant? Would that change anything?"

Realisation dawned. "He'd make the boy marry her and take responsibility for the baby."

"Right. Especially if the two of them looked to be madly in love, correct? He might be annoyed at the pair of them, but he'll hope the boy makes his girl happy, and he'll make him be responsible."

Gwen nodded. This did seem to make sense. She just couldn't imagine a girl from home pulling a stunt like this. Then again, she couldn't imagine a girl from home needing to. No one got forced into marriages they didn't want – well, not like Ava was, anyway. She wasn't stupid enough to think all marriages were for love. But no one had to marry someone they actively despised.

"Will the whole dragon situation make things better or worse?" She hoped the rumours flying ahead of them contained dragon. It was an explanation for why Ava might have fallen for her. It also just made her look pretty heroic, which was always nice.

Ava shrugged. "I suspect it will make him worried that whatever the seers have scared him with is actually coming to pass. With any luck, it will have him champing at the bit to marry me off without too many questions."

Gwen snorted and looked away. "Four days to the Capital from here. Three more inns. Are we going to be seeding rumours the whole way home?"

"A display like today shouldn't be necessary again. If the rumours are travelling ahead of us – and we were caught early enough in the afternoon that they should be – then just being seen kissing in the dining room or similar should be enough to reinforce them. Certainly, when combined with sharing a room." Ava grinned, showing her dimples. "At the next inn, don't justify the single room – just ask for it."

"Alright. And if the rumours haven't preceded us?"

"Well, if they haven't, we might need to retire to bed early and be *extremely* loud."

Gwen blushed a deep red. She hid this by turning to snuff out the candles beside the bed. "I guess we have a plan, then."

"That we do. Goodnight, Gwenny dear."

"Goodnight, snookums."

"You're a very convincing actress, you know," Ava spoke suddenly as they were riding together along the highway.

Gwen tensed at that, then forced her posture to relax, making her voice as nonchalant as she could manage. "What makes you say that, sweetheart?" She was relieved she hadn't dropped a 'Highness' in there. Ava had already told her she did that when she was nervous.

"Last night. In the bath," Ava giggled. "When the innkeeper walked in on us? I would never have known you were faking it if I didn't know my hand was nowhere near you." She blushed suddenly, apparently realising what that sounded like. "Not that I actually know, of course. What a woman sounds like, I mean. When she's with another woman."

Gwen was glad Ava was feeling flustered about her own inexperience because all Gwen could think of while she was stammering was how her nipples had felt, how her body had felt, how her mouth had felt. She wondered if the princess thought the only sexual act was one of penetration. Did she not feel their breasts together? Maybe she wasn't sensitive there. She'd heard that not all women were – usually she pitied those who were not, but right now she almost envied them. But to not even think of kisses as able to cause such moans? The princess must find women so completely devoid of attraction that she could only imagine a woman reacting to things that would work if she did them to herself. Gwen was relieved, but also felt guilty for finding such pleasure in her touch when she clearly did not return the sentiment. She tried to reassure herself that even if Ava would be repulsed by her attraction, it was at least useful for the moment in making their ruse believable.

"Oh no, please tell me you're not upset," Ava looked stricken.

"Upset, Princess? No, of course not."

"Only, you were so quiet, and now you're calling me Princess. I've offended you, haven't I? Talking about what a woman might sound like with another woman?"

"No, no, Ava, of course not." Gwen tried to sound reassuring, but she was terrified that she'd be caught lusting for the princess. "I'm not offended at all."

"It's hard for you, though, isn't it? Having to pretend you're in love with me? Having to pretend you lust after me? I was just trying to compliment you for being so good at it, but I know it must be difficult." Ava took a deep breath as Gwen stayed quiet, and then continued. "Up until just now I'd hoped it at least wasn't utterly repellent to you; but it is, isn't it?"

Gwen was completely torn. How did she respond to this? She wanted to reassure the princess, but she didn't want to make her feel used or dirty. She opted for a very careful tone. "It's not repellent, your Highness. You're a beautiful woman, a princess, and anyone would be proud to have you on their arm, telling the whole Realm that you love them."

"There's that 'Highness' again. I need you to act like you're in love in front of everyone else, and I'd like you to practice showing affection out here, so we don't mess it up, but you don't have to lie to protect my feelings."

"I'm not, Ava. And I'm only not telling the whole truth in as much as I don't know the whole truth myself. I don't know how I feel about being able to convince strangers that your touch does... *that*... to me. Does it bother you? If I look like I'm enjoying myself too much, will it disgust you? Because that's what's been worrying *me*."

Ava's laugh sounded relieved. "No, Gwen, I promise not to be disgusted if you look like you're enjoying yourself. I want you to look that way. Gods, I *need* you to look that way. And I know it's not real, so you don't have to worry. I know how good you are at pretending this."

Gwen relaxed a little. "Still planning on scandalising innocent innkeepers all the way to the Capital?"

"Never met an innocent one yet, but yes. Them and all the tavern patrons if we can manage it," Ava sounded positively mischievous. Back to her normal self.

The sun was going down by the time they could see the village in the distance. There was an inn there, which was all that mattered to Gwen.

Ava had been making plans. "I know we already talked about being more definite about only needing one room. But I've also been thinking. Rumours racing ahead of me having my wicked way with you," here Ava grinned in a truly devilish manner, "are all well and good, but we need some of *you* having your way with *me*, too."

"And how do you suggest we do that, snookums?" Gwen put a teasing note in her voice to cover her nervousness.

"I stayed here on my way out. There's a dark little corridor that leads from the taproom to the outhouse. It's poorly lit and would look like you'd get privacy there if you didn't know better, but people need the privy all night long."

"So, we order a meal, and then, what? While we're waiting for service, I drag you into a dark corridor and have my way with you? Is that the idea?"

"More or less. We'll choose a table nearby. I'll leave the details up to you."

"What if I do something you don't like? If I go too far and you react badly it'll ruin the illusion. And if I don't go far enough and it looks like I'm afraid to touch you it could also ruin everything."

"I trust you. But err on the side of going too far – I won't react badly in the moment, and believe me that I'll say something later if I want you to change what you're doing."

Gwen was deeply uncomfortable with this. But all she said was, "As you wish."

The horse was stabled, their bags were up in their room (and by the lack of surprise on the innkeeper's face when they said they only needed one it seemed stories had indeed travelled ahead of them), and they'd just ordered a meal in the taproom. Gwen knew what she was about to do, and she was nervous. And also excited.

"Are you ready, sweetie pie?" she murmured, taking Ava's hand.

"I'm all yours, darling," came the princess' breathy reply.

She led her into the dark corridor, past a set of stacked crates that provided some barrier to prying eyes, and pushed her gently but firmly up against the wall. "Are you sure you're up for this?"

"Stop questioning yourself and take me." Ava was on her tiptoes, her mouth beside Gwen's ear. "Better too much than too little, yes?"

She finished her sentence with a brief nip to the earlobe. Gwen gasped, feeling her nipples tighten in her shirt. She reached down, taking one thigh in each hand, and hoisted Ava up onto her hips. The princess took the hint immediately, wrapping her legs tight around her waist. Leaning in to pin her against the wall once more took some of the weight off Gwen's arms, but honestly, she didn't need it. Ava's weight was light and stable, her body melded perfectly to hers.

Gwen's mouth took Ava's firmly, her tongue demanding entrance. Ava surrendered, their kiss deepening as if in desperation. Both women moaned, the sound swallowed between them. Ava's hips started rocking, her legs tightening and loosening to give her motion. It seemed Ava meant what she'd said – she intended to look like she was being taken roughly, and like she was enjoying every second of it.

Her hands were still on Ava's buttocks. She didn't need much support, but her fingers started kneading the beautiful roundness of their own accord. The princess moaned with each firm stroke of her thumbs. Gods she was beautiful. Gwen angled her body a little, so instead of leaning front-on into her princess she had the bone of her hip placed firmly against the smaller woman's centre.

She leaned her weight forward further and began rocking in a slow but insistent rhythm.

Ava broke the kiss, gasping. "Oh, my fucking Gods," she groaned out. Gwen stilled instantly, thrilled by the vulgarity on the princess' tongue, but terrified she really had gone too far with this. "Don't you fucking *dare* stop!" Ava's head went back against the wall, and her hips never stopped moving.

Gwen leaned in, taking up her rhythm again. That outburst almost certainly got some attention. She fixed her lips to the neck that was being so beautifully offered to her, pressing her tongue to where she could feel Ava's pulse hammering. Did such a thundering heartbeat mean the princess was feeling triumphant that her plan was working? Or was she so angry she could barely contain herself? Gwen desperately hoped it was the former.

She sucked at Ava's neck, gently at first but growing more insistent as her moans encouraged her. She shifted one hand from a perfect hip and ran it up a leg, under Ava's flowing divided skirts. She passed the knee, stroking up the inner thigh toward her core.

Wet. Oh Gods, Princess Ava is so fucking wet. Does this turn her on for real? Gwen was too terrified to leap to any conclusions but knowing Ava had soaked through her undergarments made her at least a little less self-conscious about the state of her own. She clenched and unclenched her fist in time to the thrust of her hips, moving her hand along Ava's upper thigh as she had done last night in the bath. Her lips fixed more firmly on her throat, her teeth scraping as she sucked relentlessly.

She thought she saw some heads silhouetted at the taproom end of the corridor, but by now she couldn't even care. She might not be inside her, but her hand was pumping, her hip providing resistance, and the princess was rubbing herself against her like she was planning on reaching climax whether she touched her or not. She bit down and the faintest metallic tang of blood met her tongue.

"Gods! *Yes!*" The scream was divine. Ava was convulsing in her arms, gripping her shoulders hard enough to bruise. Her hips were jumping up and down erratically like they had a life of their own. Ava let out a series of quieter moans, sounding hoarse and exhausted. She let go of Gwen's shoulders, and gently held her face. Her eyes looked deeply troubled for a second before she laid the gentlest of kisses on Gwen's lips. Her stomach was still quivering, shockwaves passing through her body at longer and longer intervals.

Gwen could feel wetness dripping down her thighs. Her clit throbbed almost painfully. The slightest pressure would make her climax every bit as hard as Ava had just done – and hers wouldn't be faked. Best be careful not to brush against anything, then.

She heard some wolf whistles from the taproom. She raised an eyebrow at Ava, waiting for her lead.

Ava straightened her clothes, put her hair back in order as much as possible, and did the same for Gwen. She gave a shaky smile. "Success. Now, we go back out there to eat our dinner. Remember: we're deeply in love, unable to keep our hands off each other, and mortified that we just got caught. Got it?"

"Got it."

They'd both managed to look happy but sheepish when they returned. Most of the looks they got were indulgently amused – people who either remembered being newly in love or hoped to be one day. They ate quickly and returned to their room.

As soon as they were out of the public eye, Ava found something to be very interested in on the other side of the room and avoided Gwen's gaze. Gwen didn't know what the matter was. Well, she *knew*, but hadn't the princess promised to tell her if she overstepped? And she'd said not to stop. And it had worked! Everyone had thought that was real. She'd even seen some patrons slip out after they returned, presumably to spread the latest gossip far and wide.

The silence stretched on as Gwen readied herself for bed. She decided she needed to spread her bedroll and leave the bed to Ava – after all, she'd clearly violated the princess' trust. Not to mention her body. No wonder she was avoiding her – she wasn't going to force her to lie beside her after what she'd done. Still, she did wish the princess had said something. And she needed to clear the air. She spread her blankets out between the bed and the door, took a deep breath, squared her shoulders, and faced the smaller woman.

"I'm really truly sorry, your Highness. I got carried away and should never have touched you like that. I know you're stuck with this marriage now, and I won't mess that up for you, but you don't have to worry about me doing anything like that again." Ava's head snapped around to look at her, and her stare was frosty. "I don't expect you to forgive me. But I *am* sorry."

"You? What on earth do *you* have to be sorry about? I was such a pig that you're spreading blankets to get away from me! I'm the one who should be apologising, here." Ava had tears in her eyes. Maybe 'frosty' hadn't been the right word for the stare. Maybe 'distraught' was closer to the truth.

"Princess? I was trying to give you space! I took advantage of you, and as soon as nobody could see you couldn't bear to even look at me! Of course I spread my blankets."

"I reacted too much. You wanted to stop but I ordered you not to. You agreed to a marriage of convenience, and you agreed to faking true love to get me out of a bind. You never agreed to be my whore." Her voice was bitter, full of disgust.

The silence stretched out. Gwen wasn't sure she understood. "Is that how you see me? As a whore?"

"No!" The vehemence in Ava's voice matched the fire in her eyes. "No, you're not! And that makes me a..." Whatever word she was thinking of, she couldn't say it. "That makes me as bad as Forquitte."

Comprehension dawned. "Never!" Gwen's forcefulness matched that of the princess. "You could *never* be as awful as him. You are *not* as awful as him." Ava clearly felt she'd pushed Gwen into something she didn't want. Gwen wasn't sure she was willing to tell Ava exactly how wrong she was – she didn't want Ava flipping from feeling like an abuser to feeling like she'd been abused – but she needed to make her understand that Gwen was a willing participant.

"And now my father will have your head if you don't marry me. You don't have freedom, here. And I made you take me anyway."

"I don't have freedom to refuse the marriage now, no. But I didn't feel forced into *tonight*. Gods, if anything, that was what put the headsman's axe into play." Gwen wasn't reassuring her well enough. She took two steps over and enfolded the princess in her arms. Ava tensed for a moment, then melted against her, sobbing into her shirt. Gwen stroked her back gently, being as comforting as she knew how. She felt guilty, and confused, but hopefully it would all be alright.

Eventually, Ava's tears subsided, and she raised her head hesitantly. "So... you don't hate me, then?"

"I could never hate you, Ava." Gwen was shocked to realise that was the simple truth. "How about you? Do you hate me?"

"Never. I couldn't have asked for a better friend through all this. Thank you." Her hands gripped tightly to Gwen's shirt.

"Can I put my bedroll away and take you to bed, then? After all of this, I'd quite like to just hold you for a while."

Ava smiled shyly. "I'd like that."

She woke in the middle of the night from a dream where she and Ava were doing what they'd done tonight, but without any pretence. It took her several seconds to process what was fantasy and what was reality, and she froze in horror when she realised where her hand was.

They'd gone to sleep spooning, Gwen behind, legs tangled together, one arm under Ava's neck and the other over her hip. Not exactly how platonic friends would sleep, but nothing too outlandish. Well, the arm that had been resting on her hip as they drifted off was now up under her shirt, holding one breast, and until just now, rolling a very stiff nipple between her thumb and first two fingers.

Ava made a sleepy murmur of protest at the cessation of movement. She arched her breast into Gwen's hand further, simultaneously pushing her shapely backside firmly into her lap. Gwen considered her options at lightning-fast speed. She could either remove her hand, risking Ava waking but possibly being able to deny anything untoward took place. Risky – you tended to remember the thing that woke you up, even if it wouldn't have stayed in memory had you slept through. Or she could go back to her gentle fondling, and hope Ava went back into deeper sleep again. And *then* remove her hand.

Her fingers resumed their caresses, and Ava made a sleepily satisfied noise. Her hips started rubbing up and down in Gwen's lap, reminding her that she had been incredibly turned on for days now with no opportunity to give herself any real relief. Her clit began to throb perfectly in time with Ava's hips. If she angled her own hips upward just a fraction...

Gwen, what are you doing? She's definitely *going to wake up if she feels you explode all over her perfect royal behind!* She couldn't stop herself, though. Her fingers increased their tempo, hearing Ava's breathing getting faster and shallower, with some soft whimpers thrown in. She couldn't resist flexing one thigh slightly, giving the rocking princess something to rub herself on. Fresh wetness met her bare thigh, and she couldn't fully stifle her groan. She was so close – she didn't know how she was going to stop herself climaxing, but there was nothing she could do about that now.

Ava's whimpers became an almost constant whine. *She must be having some amazing dreams right now.* Her back arched as her whole body stiffened in Gwen's arms. She ground her centre down hard on Gwen's thigh, pumping a flood of slick wetness out with each downward thrust. Gwen pushed her own core into Ava's hips, and let her orgasm overtake her. She felt her body shuddering hard against Ava's and was helpless to stop it. Many long seconds later, the tremors stopped, and she stuttered to a halt, panting.

Gwen carefully reduced her touches until she was still. She even more carefully withdrew her thigh and returned her wandering hand to the safety of the princess' hip.

Ava gave a very contented "Mmm" in her sleep and relaxed completely in her arms. Gwen was astounded, but so relieved that she quickly followed her into slumber. Never in her life had she had such a blissfully restful sleep.

When she next woke up, the sun was streaming in through the window. Ava was sprawled across her chest, as had become her custom, and was just beginning to stir.

"Good morning, sleepyhead," she said with a smile. "Did you sleep well?"

"I did, actually." Ava gave an impish smile. "I can't ever seem to remember my dreams, but I think I had some nice ones last night." The smile deepened, and she looked away briefly. "How about you? Do you ever remember your dreams?"

"Sometimes, though the details seem to fade pretty quickly."

"Do you sleepwalk at all?"

Now, why had the princess asked her that? "I don't think so. I know *you* do."

"Oh? Where have I walked to?"

"Right across my chest. Every night so far," Gwen laughed. "I'm assuming you don't wake in the middle of the night and decide to sprawl on top of me like that?"

Ava blushed. "Oh, that. No, I'm a cuddler, and I make myself comfortable when I sleep. I don't think I get up and walk, though. At least, no one's ever told me I do."

Gwen laughed again. "Have you had much opportunity to cuddle? Or, indeed, anyone to tell you that you'd walked?"

"Hey, you know no one's shared my bed like *that*." Ava gave a playful glare, but Gwen knew she wasn't really upset. "But I had sleepovers when I was a child, and I've shared with cousins while travelling the Realm. I usually end up pressed into their side by morning. Not generally on top of them – but you're a fair bit bigger than anyone I've shared a bed with before."

"And the sleepwalking?"

"Well, there are guards outside the room, so if I wander, I know I don't wander far."

Gwen was shocked. "What, every night?"

"Yes?" Ava looked confused.

"Is the door soundproof at least?"

"No? If I need them, they need to be able to hear me."

"So, your previous chastity really is well and truly documented, then."

Ava's confusion vanished, and she blushed. "Well, I *am* a Royal Princess. It's kind of expected."

Gwen had so many questions. "Will you at least be given some privacy on your wedding night?"

"Oh Gods." Ava's eyes went wide. "No. It might not just be the guards, either."

"What?" Gwen hoped this didn't mean what she thought it meant.

"Umm… it isn't exactly tradition, but let's just say it's *common* for several of the newly married royal's family members to sneak up and check that the night is going the way it's meant to." Her blush was so red it was threatening to singe her eyebrows. "The closer the royal is to the throne the more likely, too."

"Ah." Gwen felt her own cheeks start to burn, too.

"Since I'm the heir, it's almost certain." Ava was staring out the window, now, looking mortified. "Having just snubbed an Earl to marry you, there might be other nobles coming to check us out, too."

"Ah." Gwen was usually more eloquent than this, but words had just failed her. She stared out the window next to Ava, who took a deep breath and turned to face her.

"I'm really sorry about this. I should have thought of it beforehand and warned you before you said yes." She winced a little. "It won't be as bad as last night, though. We'll need to be louder, and it'll go on for longer, but at least you won't have to touch me."

"The guards will stop busybodies interrupting, at least?"

"Yeah."

"Is this where we thank the Gods for small mercies?"

"Something like that."

They both returned to staring out the window, lost in thought.

The shadows were getting long when the town appeared. There was an inn there. Gwen checked her purse quickly – it was a lot lighter than when she'd started this venture. Should still have enough for two more nights. And after that, well, hopefully money wouldn't be a problem anymore.

"Are you ready for a slightly different display?" Ava asked quietly.

Gwen nodded. "Any specific instructions, or do I just follow your lead?"

"Just be as sweet and loving as possible. We're not going to be caught with our hands up each other's clothes this time; we're just going to have a lot of soft looks and softer kisses."

Gwen nodded, and they rode the rest of the way to the inn in silence.

After handing over the horse, Ava stopped her right outside the inn's door. She smiled up with the most loving look Gwen had ever seen in her eyes, touched her ever so gently on the cheek, and let her lips part softly. Gwen took the hint. Caressing her cheek with one hand, she bent her head down and kissed Ava with the softest of touches, lip to lip.

She hated that her body reacted so strongly to even this light a touch. She didn't deepen the kiss, and neither did Ava. They stood there, kissing gently, tenderly, reverently, showing nothing but the purest love for each other. And it was fake. And Gwen's traitorous body loved every second of it.

Several townsfolk walked or rode by while they shared their romantic moment. Some stopped to stare, but most barely glanced at them. When they finally parted, Ava was looking very believably breathless, her eyes bright with the love she was projecting. For Gwen's part, her breathlessness was very genuine, and she had no idea what was in her eyes at all.

The following evening, they were approaching their last inn before they reached the Capital. Rumours had been flying ahead of them, and they were finally starting to fly back.

It seems the Earl had heard of their displays and was not amused.

There had been no word as to how the King felt. Gwen had an itch right at the nape of her neck.

Where the headsman's axe would come down if this didn't go to plan.

It had better go to plan.

Chapter Six – Returning Home

"Wine, please." They had left their bags in their room and were at the bar. "And news from the Capital, if you have any?"

The innkeeper gave a short laugh as he fetched their wines. "All the news I've been hearing concerns the two of you. Sure you don't already know?"

"Well, I have some idea what news might have gone *to* the Capital," Gwen coughed delicately, and gave Ava her very best lovesick look. "But we were hoping to find out how…" she paused, searching for the correct word, and gave up. "How certain news may have been received, shall we say."

Ava smiled and sipped her wine, content to let her take the lead in the conversation.

"Well, the King is relieved you've been found safe and sound, your Highness," the innkeeper nodded to Ava. "The fellow he promised your hand to, though?" Here, the innkeeper shook his head and gave a guffaw. "I don't think he's happy about any of it, no." More laughter. "No, I daresay he isn't."

"He's unhappy Princess Ava has been found safe and well?" Gwen tried to sound surprised and a little disappointed. As if she didn't understand the implications. She didn't succeed.

"Not that, my Lady, as I'm sure you're well aware." He still had mirth in his eyes, but gave her a level look, darling her to deny the rumours he had already heard. Of course, she did not. He turned his attention back to Ava. "Anyhow, word is he's expecting you tomorrow, and plans to ride out to meet you. Him and Lord What's-his-face. Full regalia to bring the Royal Princess home."

"Is Mother planning to ride out, too?" Ava sounded a little nervous. They were her first words this evening.

"Not a clue, your Highness. Does she usually, when they make a pageant of it?"

"Sometimes," the princess said, quietly.

"I want you to wear your breastplate tomorrow."

They were in their room, and Ava had been thinking very hard about the following morning. This was where they found out if all their plans would come to fruition. She was clearly nervous, and Gwen ached to comfort her – but she also didn't want to step out of line.

"Wouldn't that make your father think I came to fight?"

"No. You're bringing me home; he's not going to see you as an enemy. But he might see you as a peasant if you're just in your shirtsleeves. I know the breastplate is leather and not steel, but you keep it oiled and it looks of better quality than the rest of your clothes. Wearing well-maintained armour, he'll see you as the equivalent of a knight. I hope."

"Someone it might be okay for you to fall in love with and marry?" Gwen guessed.

"Something like that." She paused, weighing her next words. "And also because it's far too possible that Forquitte will challenge you to a duel."

"Wait, what?" Gwen was shocked. "Ava, I asked you days ago if you thought the Earl would try to kill me, and you said no!"

"I said he wouldn't try to assassinate you. And he won't. But I've been thinking, and you're near enough as big as he is, so he will likely think he can challenge you to a duel for my hand without losing any honour. And I can't see any way to make it dishonourable for him to challenge you without making it just as dishonourable for you to marry me, so I'm stuck. The best I can come up with is making you look like you'd win." She drew a deep breath and continued. "If he thinks he might lose he'll hide behind the fig leaf of it not being Lordly to duel a woman. But if he thinks he will win easily, you being a woman won't faze him in the slightest."

"Alright, I'm looking my best and I'm ready to fight. What else?"

"I'd rather you didn't fight. You got out of fighting before; I hope you can again. But yes, be ready."

"You don't think it would be better if he died in an honourable duel that no one saw as a murder? I thought you hated him enough to want him dead."

"I do. And I can see you have faith in your fighting abilities. But he is one of the best, both in tourneys and in war, which are far more like duelling than the bounties you are familiar with." Ava looked troubled. "If I were certain you'd win, I'd urge you to ride him down. But I can't bear the thought of you losing." She didn't say it was because then she'd have to marry him. She didn't need to.

"I'm putting more value on my own skin than his. Got it. Is there anything else? I get the feeling there are things you're not telling me."

"Nothing specific." Ava still looked discomfited. "I'm just worried about how we're going to tread the fine line of appearing besotted with each other without committing any gross improprieties."

"Ah. I take it you'd prefer I didn't just push you up against a tree with your whole court watching?" She waggled her eyebrows suggestively.

Ava glared at her. "Gwen! Please don't joke about this. If tomorrow goes wrong, I could wind up married to that monster, and your head could end up over a gate."

Gwen sobered right up. "We don't want that."

"No. No, we don't."

"So, what do you suggest?"

They talked long into the night.

Around mid-morning they saw the colourful banners and shining armour of the welcoming party ahead of them.

"Looks like mother decided to join us after all," said Ava, pointing to the three largest pennants raised over the main group. "Remember how we planned this."

Gwen nodded, pushed her hood back and threw her cloak as far over her shoulders as she could. Her plait was thick and shone in the morning sunlight, and the hilt of her sword gleamed brightly at her side. Brushing and polishing had taken hours, but the effect was what they had hoped for. Her cloak flapped in the breeze.

As they approached, the main party stopped, and a smaller group came forward to greet them. She saw the King at the front of the group with the Queen, and a large dark-haired man she had to assume was the Earl. Alongside them rode six guardsmen. From what Ava had told her, they would be two from each of their personal bodyguards.

"Well met!" Came the booming voice of King Harald. "And to whom do I owe my thanks for the return of my wayward daughter?" His smile took the sting out of his words, and he alighted from his horse.

"Well met, your Majesty," Gwen called back with rather more confidence than she felt. "Gwendoline Carter, of Farrowdown, if it pleases you." She swung her leg over the back of the horse, letting herself down with all the grace she possessed. She immediately turned to help Princess Ava dismount.

Ava had swung her leg over, so she was sitting side-saddle. Gwen put her hands on her waist, and the princess leaned over with her hands on Gwen's shoulders. They paused for the merest second or two, gazing into each other's eyes with as much love as they were able to show, before Gwen set her down lightly beside her. So far, so good.

"Good morning, Father," Ava said once she had turned to face him. Gwen had no idea how she managed to put spots of colour into her cheeks like that. "Mother."

"My beautiful child," came the voice of Queen Constance for the first time. "We are so glad to have you home."

"You have our gratitude, Gwendoline Carter of Farrowdown," said the King. "We will see to your reward when we return. For now, will you accept our hospitality?"

"I would be most honoured, your Majesty," Gwen said with as formal a bow as she could muster. They had practiced last night, but she had been taught as a child that women curtsey and it still felt strange. Ava stood to her right, close enough to feel her breath on her neck.

"Then come, let us take our midday meal in the pavilion yonder."

Lord Reginald had still not said a word. They walked toward the tent.

The pavilion was huge. There were chairs. Upholstered chairs. And rugs. A grand mahogany table. Gwen looked around, almost surprised there wasn't a fireplace. It was an absurd amount of luxury to have been picked up and transported to a luncheon several miles from the Capital.

She had held Ava's hand for the walk. Again, planned subtle intimacy. The princess had known the broad strokes of how this would go, and Gwen was glad for the preparation. The King had made small talk with her about her parents, her brother, where she grew up, and her life as a bounty hunter. She wondered if this was his way of setting her at ease. If so, it wasn't working.

And here they all were, sitting around an enormous table, dining on cold meats and pastries. Gwen had been allowed to sit beside Ava, for which she was glad. She would not have enjoyed sitting near Lord Reginald Forquitte.

"And now, my dear, we must turn to more practical matters," the King smiled at his daughter. "I'm sure you are aware of certain gossip that has reached us ahead of you. With that in mind, we must insist that you and Gwendoline be accompanied by a chaperone if you spend any time together while she is staying with us at the castle." He held up a hand, forestalling her protests. "We must of course extend our hospitality to her during the celebrations of your return, in gratitude for her heroic rescue. She may not have done battle, but a dragon is not something to be crossed lightly, and we recognise that."

Gwen was shocked. She was grateful that news of the dragon had preceded them. While she was still trying to figure out how everything else had gone so completely against their careful plans, Ava spoke up.

"Father, if you are aware of 'certain gossip', as you put it, then you know we need to do more than extend our hospitality. And if you already knew I was being held prisoner by a dragon, then you know why 'certain gossip' is entirely factually correct!" Her eyes were ablaze, darling her father to skirt the issues any further.

"Ava, my darling daughter, you know I made certain alliances concerning you. What would you have me do? Break my word out of gratitude to a sellsword?" Gwen felt her anger rise at that. She knew that there wasn't a lot of distance between a bounty hunter and a mercenary in the eyes of most, but the differences were important to her.

The Earl of Lubrey spoke for the first time. "Your Majesties, your Highness, I do not see any need to concern ourselves unduly with the prattling of idle commoners." He ran his gaze over Gwen, appraising her and then clearly dismissing her as unworthy of his concern. "I understand that emotions can run high after one's life has hung in the balance. It is the reason for battle lust. I will not hold any indiscretions my future wife may have made against her during our marriage." His eyes were now on Ava, and he made no effort to disguise his desire to own her.

Gwen's anger was no longer on her own behalf. The arrogant tone, the casual dismissal of their love, the disregard of Ava's wishes – it was enraging. It was almost enough to make her forget for the moment that this love of theirs was fictional.

He stood from his chair and addressed the King and Queen. "Your wisdom is unparalleled, and of course you must hold grand feasts, honouring the return of our lovely Princess Ava, and the bravery of her rescuer. And then, once the fêting has run its course – a week, say – the mercenary should be showered in gold and silver, given a patch of land to call her own on the far edges of the Realm, and firmly instructed to never set foot in the Capital again." At this he turned his eyes to Gwen. They were hard and cold. "Do we understand one another?"

Gwen placed her hands on the table, deliberately keeping her breathing calm and even. When Ava placed her hand atop Gwen's, the calmness she was pretending became closer to reality. They hadn't planned for this, but she knew what to do. "Why do you call her your future wife, my Lord?" She remained seated, her voice steady and assured. "As far as I am aware, there has been no betrothal. Have you even asked her if she consents to be your wife?"

"Now, now," the King began. "The papers aren't signed, but he and I have come to an agreement. He is not being presumptuous. Ava is to sign her betrothal papers tonight."

Ava stood at this, still holding Gwen's hand. "I will sign betrothal papers tonight if it please you, Father. But not to Lord Reginald." She took a deep breath, squeezed Gwen's hand once before letting it go, and took the two steps necessary to stand before the King. "Father, six nights ago I asked Gwendoline to be my wife. She did me the great honour of saying yes. We're in love, Father, and I want to marry her."

You could hear a pin drop. Gwen held her breath. She had no idea if things had gone well enough for this to work yet. She knew the King wanted his daughter to have a love match. But he also wanted to keep his word.

After a long silence, the Earl spoke in a voice that was soft and cold as ice. "If you are not going to correct your daughter, my Liege, perhaps you would like me to take on that husbandly duty in advance of our nuptials."

The King's eyes looked troubled. Gwen couldn't tell if the Earl's remonstrance had angered him, but he surely wasn't best pleased with Ava's declaration. "My daughter, you have had years to choose a match for love. Why now? Why her? Will you not reconsider?"

The shock on the Earl's face at this gentle plea surprised her. Did he not know that the King wanted his daughter to have love? If Gwen knew, surely all the lords did.

"I will not reconsider, Father. As for your questions... No one else braved a dragon to save me, Father. No one else risked their life to protect me. She shielded me with her body and gave me the Oath so I would not be unguarded! Why her, you ask? How could I choose anyone else?" Ava had moved while speaking, striding decisively to stand by Gwen. They took each other's hands, presenting a united front. "I would choose her over any lord in the Kingdom. I *have* chosen her, and I would do so over and over

104

again, each and every day for the rest of my life. She is my soul mate, Father. Just like Mother is yours."

"And if I say no?" The King looked curious, now, and his question was gentle.

"Your papers will not get signed. I will not marry when my heart belongs to someone else. I don't think you would want me to." She took a deep breath. "Your choice, Father, is between me marrying the woman I love and me remaining unmarried for as long as you're alive."

"You can be made to sign." This was the Earl. "My Liege, are you going to allow your wilful, headstrong daughter to make a mockery of your word? Of your will? You have told her she is to marry me. Make it so."

Ava tensed. So did Gwen. The King did not like being spoken to like this, but the Earl commanded far too many troops to upbraid him as he deserved. It would only take a handful of the larger duchies to take his side and the King might even be outnumbered. This was the whole reason they needed to carry on this farce, rather than Ava simply refusing to wed with no replacement suitor.

"True love makes a mockery of us all, Lord Reginald." The King's voice was almost warm. "Would you really take a wife whose heart belonged to another? I would not. And I would not wish it upon you." His voice grew stronger, his decision made. "I release you from your word concerning marriage to my daughter. She is no longer available. I think you for your service, my Lord, and wish you luck in securing a match more worthy of your heart."

"Your armour is quaint. Would it protect against a spear thrust, do you think?" Lord Reginald's tone was conversational as they all strolled to their horses after lunch.

"I do not know, my Lord," Gwen replied with as respectful a tone as she could muster. "It holds up against a hundred-pound longbow, and it will repel a dagger thrust. I haven't had cause to test it against more chivalrous weaponry."

"A plate that turns aside a determined dagger should fare admirably against a blunted lance. I believe King Harald is hosting a tourney to celebrate the safe return of his daughter. Would you care to test your arm against mine in the joust?"

Gwen didn't need the brief shake of Ava's head to tell her not to accept this invitation. "Thank you, my Lord, but I must decline. I have never fought from horseback; nor have I fought for amusement. I fear I would either be no sport at all or else risk injuring you."

"A pity. Perhaps I will instead see you in the grand melee?"

"All things are possible, my Lord."

A horse had been provided for Ava, meaning an end to their time riding double. While Gwen was sure her horse appreciated not carrying them both anymore, it did reduce their opportunities to talk without fear of being overheard.

On one of their brief interludes where everyone else was engaged in their own conversations, Ava quietly spoke. "I was expecting some degree of chaperoning upon our return. Luckily for us, you are capable of reading – and the guards aren't."

"What, none of them?"

Ava hesitated. "It's possible one or two might know their letters. And I wouldn't want them taking notes I passed you to Father anyway, so we'll try to be discreet. But be ready for my missives."

Gwen smiled. It seemed their games weren't over just yet.

The day was drawing to a close when they reached the walls of the Capital. Trumpeters lined the route from the city walls to the castle, and the King and Queen waved regally to the onlookers. Gwen was trying very hard to avoid gaping like the village girl she knew she was. She had at least seen the city before now, but she had never seen it like this, with what seemed like the whole population on the streets to welcome home their princess.

While most of the attention was focused on the royal family, every so often she saw someone pointing at her, talking animatedly to the person next to them. Ava rode in close beside her and held a hand out to her; Gwen dropped the reins to a single hand and took hers. They squeezed briefly and smiled at each other before dropping their hands back to their horses, who seemed more comfortable riding slightly farther apart.

When they reached the castle, they handed their horses over to stable hands. Gwen was pretty sure she could tell which one was Will – the young lad looked barely old enough to shave, but he was as devoted as she'd described. Gwen went to take her own bags, but a serving woman with an air of authority about her intervened.

"Now, now, my Lady, your bags will be taken to your rooms in perfect order. You're a guest of His Majesty, and that means leave the bag holding to us, hmm?" The smile she gave was matronly, but kind.

"I don't even know where I should go, good mistress." Gwen had no idea how to address a senior servant in a castle, but she did her best. The serving woman did not correct her.

"You'll be shown your rooms once His Majesty has finished with you, my Lady." And she bustled off, presumably to see to affairs in another corner of her domain.

When Gwen turned around, there was Ava, smiling at her. "Gwen, darling, I'm so glad to have you home with me." She took her hands, smiling, but there was worry in her eyes. "We're too late for the homecoming banquet to be tonight, so there will be meals in our rooms. I've asked Father, but he said I couldn't have you come to mine. I'm so sorry, my love."

Gwen took her cue from the princess. "Ava, my beloved, I will miss you terribly, but we will see each other tomorrow." She put all the love she could into her gaze. Gwen thought briefly of kissing her but dismissed the thought – if it were a good idea, Ava would have already done it.

Just when it looked like maybe Ava was going to kiss her after all, suddenly Deidre appeared at the end of the hall. "Princess Ava! You're home! And you –" here she turned to Gwen. "I never did catch your name, but I'm so glad you brought her back safely."

"It's Gwen, Lady Deidre." Gwen tried for a bow. Apparently knights always bowed, whether they were men or women, and Ava wanted her to appear like a knight. "Your help was invaluable. Thank you for pointing me in the right direction and telling me what to look for."

Deidre looked around furtively. She'd never make a good spy. "We'll need to find time to talk properly, then, Gwen. For now, just let me say I'm so glad you were able to rescue her. Good night."

Damn. She quite obviously suspected something, and while she appeared to approve it could still be a problem if she let something slip. Gwen bade her goodnight and followed the others as they headed for their bedchambers.

She woke the next morning feeling strangely uncomfortable. The bed was better than any she had slept on in her life, and there was a wonderful smell coming from the tray the serving woman had brought into her chambers. She watched the woman set her fireplace and light a fire for her, trying to work out what was making her ill at ease.

Of course. Ava wasn't sprawled on top of her. Strange – she'd slept alone her whole life without problem, but in one short week the little princess had made her so used to the feel of waking up together that she felt odd and unsettled without her. She tried not to think too hard about that – their upcoming marriage could wind up an awkward place if she let the princess know she held unrequited feelings for her.

New clothes had been laid out for her while she slept. They were well tailored, trousers made of fine wool and an expertly fitted linen shirt. Her own cloak had been laundered while she slept, and her boots brushed and polished. She wouldn't look like she was dressing above her station, but she would look well-presented, and she would fit in at court.

She dressed, ate, and went out to find the princess.

As soon as she stepped outside her room, she found a flaw in her plan. She had no idea where the princess was, or what was expected of her. There was a guard stationed outside her door – was this normal with guests? Or was this because everyone believed she'd taken liberties with the princess?

"Hello," she addressed the guard informally, not sure of his rank. "Would you be able to take me to see Princess Ava?"

"Good morning Miss Carter." Gwen had almost become used to people inflating her rank when they weren't sure of her, so being addressed correctly felt odd, but welcome. "The princess will call for you when she wishes to see you."

"I see. Am I restricted to my rooms, or may I wander around the castle grounds?"

"You are not permitted to head up to the Royal Quarters. Aside from that, the castle is yours to explore. You are a guest, Miss Carter, not a prisoner."

"But if I go exploring, how will Ava find me when she wants me?" Gwen deliberately used the princess' first name without honorific, wondering how the guard would take it.

"If you tell me where you're going, I can make sure any missives from Her Royal Highness make it to you. Otherwise, you are free to remain if you wish."

There weren't any books in her rooms, so she didn't feel any real urge to stay. "Could you tell me where the library is? And perhaps also where the archery butts are? I assume I could borrow a bow for some practice – mine is home with my brother."

"Practice bows never shoot straight, miss – you'd be better off making a new one yourself. But the short-range butts are down on the east wall of the courtyard. If you want to practice over

110

distances longer than a hundred paces there are other butts to the west, outside the city walls."

"And the library?"

He gestured to his right. "Follow the corridor around the corner and take the second branch to the left. You should be able to smell the books soon enough. If you get lost, most anyone can point you in the right direction."

"My thanks. I might loose some arrows this morning, and if Ava still hasn't found me, I'll go to the library later today."

"Whatever you like, Miss Carter. I'll be here when you get back."

She found the butts easily enough, and she hadn't forgotten her way around a longbow. While it took her some practice before she could hit the centre of the target reliably with her borrowed bow, it was nowhere near as poorly made as the guard had led her to believe. The bow she had borrowed felt like around ninety pounds draw weight, and by the end of her three-hour session she was getting groupings the size of her fist at a hundred paces.

No word from the princess, though. She tried not to worry.

After lunch she went to the castle library – alerting her guardsman where she was going before she went. Just in case Ava wanted her.

She found texts on philosophy, history, and legends of the Realm. The books were fascinating to her, and she wondered if the librarians would allow her to bring them to her rooms – but they could not entirely distract her from the fact that the princess hadn't wanted to see her today.

She knew the grand love story they were trying to project was all fakery. She knew that. She tried to tell herself that her concern over not hearing from Ava was merely that maybe their devotion to each other might be questioned if they didn't seek each other out all the time. That they needed to look desperately in love for a while longer yet. She tried not to think that maybe she was feeling a little bit hurt that Ava genuinely didn't want to see her.

When she returned to her room, a surcoat of rich silk brocade was laid out on her bed. It fit her perfectly. She dressed in it for the feast and felt a fabulous fraud.

At the Royal Banquet, Gwen was seated in a position of honour, on the right hand of Princess Ava. She wished she knew why the princess had been avoiding her today.

"Your Highness," she said formally, bowing when she saw her.

"Gwen, my love," Ava had almost flinched at the formal address, but the warmth in her words made Gwen want to hope. She stood to greet her with a kiss to each cheek.

"I've missed you today." She took Ava's hands in her own and wished the look of longing in her eyes required more in the way of acting.

"I've missed you, too. Today has been…" she trailed off, searching for the right word or phrase. "It's been very trying. I would have preferred to have had you by my side."

Gwen felt a somewhat reassuring warmth at that, but she was still feeling vulnerable. It probably didn't help that she had not been permitted to seek Ava's company herself – she did not like feeling powerless in any situation.

She tried to bury those feelings of vulnerability and inadequacy. They wouldn't help anyone. "Would you like to talk about it, my sweet?"

Ava hesitated. "Come get some fresh air with me?"

"Of course."

They slipped out of the banquet hall, hand in hand. "Quickly. We'll walk in the palace gardens – Father will send someone to check on us when he sees we're missing, but I don't think he noticed us leave so we might have a few minutes."

They got to the gardens and strolled together through the rose bushes. "What's on your mind?"

Ava grimaced. "Father is willing to go ahead with our wedding, but he needed to be cajoled into it. He's scared Forquitte will foment rebellion because I've insulted him – the whole point of playing up the we're-so-in-love angle is to make sure that won't work! But Father doesn't believe it's enough. He'll go ahead with the betrothal, but he wouldn't do up documents for us to sign tonight. While he still badly wants to see me married off before more trouble can emerge, he wants you to look like a better match for me first."

"How do I do that?"

"A few ways. One you're already doing – wearing better tailored clothes of better materials makes you look more like you belong here. Another is that he plans to bestow a knighthood and some lands on you – he can't make you a Baroness or higher without it looking exactly like it's to make you a proper marriage candidate for me, but a knighthood for service to the Realm is reasonable."

Gwen wasn't quite sure how to take that. She didn't need lands in her own name if she was about to become Ava's consort, but she trusted the princess' judgement. "Alright. Anything else?"

Ava took a deep breath. "Yes. You need to win something at the Tourney. It doesn't have to be the joust – and I still strongly advise you not to take part in that, by the way. I'm worried about you getting injured in the grand mêlée, but we'll sort something out. We need you to be a champion."

"Rescuing the Princess from a dragon isn't enough, eh?" Gwen had a teasing tone in her voice, but honestly, she was worried.

"It's enough to give you a title. A title plus a championship gets you seen as worthy of winning my heart. Which everyone knows you have anyway, so a betrothal at that point works."

"This is what you and the King worked out today?"

"It's the best I could get out of him. He's glad I chose someone! He's willing to try to make it work. The Earl is just a thorn in our side right now, and I need to play this very carefully."

They'd stopped walking in the middle of the roses, and were facing each other, their bodies almost touching. Gwen took Ava's waist in her hands. "Someone might see us," she offered as explanation. The truth was, she just wanted to hold her.

"Yes," murmured Ava. "We must always act like someone might see us." She pressed her body forward, closing the last inches between them until they touched.

"Will I get to see you tomorrow?" Gwen could lose herself in those eyes.

"Yes." Ava was on her tiptoes, now, her breath playing against Gwen's lips as she spoke. "Go to the centre of the hedge maze after breakfast. We need to plan." Her lips touched Gwen's.

Her blood caught fire. There were no other words for it. She pressed her lips to Ava's, pulling her in closer, trying to keep her mind clear. Ava was calling the shots, here, so Gwen couldn't just pull her to the ground and touch her under her dress…

Gwen's mind was getting carried away from her. She swallowed her moan, revelling in the feeling of softness under her lips, under her hands. Ava's hands were at her shoulders, her neck, under the edge of her shirt. Her lips parted, and their tongues met softly. The kiss was sweet, sensual, and needy.

Gwen wanted to deepen the kiss, but Ava kept it right there, setting her nerves on fire with no relief in sight. It was sweet torture. Gwen didn't know if she wanted it to stop right now, or to never stop at all.

"Your Highness! The King is looking for you! We can't start the banquet without you." The voice wasn't familiar to Gwen.

Ava broke the kiss unhurriedly and turned her face to the intruder. She didn't let go of Gwen. "Thank you, Lady Margaret. We'll be back in a moment."

The woman looked a little embarrassed. "I'm sorry, your Highness, but His Majesty asked me to be your chaperone until you returned. You'll have to come with me, I'm afraid."

Ava sighed and let go of Gwen's shoulders. She stepped back took her hand instead. "Lead on."

They returned to the banquet.

Chapter Seven – The Royal Court

She hadn't slept well. She kept having vivid dreams, and waking to find her bed empty, her sheets damp with sweat and tangled around her legs. By the time the serving woman came in with her breakfast and the day's clothes, she'd already bathed in the basin and was reading a book of natural philosophy that the library had graciously loaned her yesterday.

After breakfast she made her way to the gardens, and the centre of the hedge maze. She sat down to wait.

Several minutes later she started wishing she'd brought her book with her. They'd agreed to meet after breakfast, but there was no formal hour when that would be. She was just beginning to think she should go back and find her book when the princess appeared, a smile lighting up her face.

"Hello, you," Ava's voice was low and playful. "Fancy seeing you here."

"Of all the hedge mazes in all the castles in all the Realm, I had to walk into yours?" Gwen suggested, smiling. Seeing Ava made her happy. Best not to think too deeply about that.

"We shouldn't be disturbed here. I suspect the whole 'chaperone' thing is for show; my Father certainly hasn't instructed anyone to accompany me on walks in the garden. But I'll change the excuse from time to time anyway, just to be sure."

"Okay. What are our aims, here? You've told me I need to be a champion, but I don't even know the rules of the tourney. Back home, we just played knights with sticks when we were kids and kept up our archery practice three times a week, as the law demands."

"Ah, yes. Speaking of knights – we'll need to see Father an hour before lunch. Dress formally and wear your sword. Can you meet me in the quiet corridor near the pantry afterwards?"

"Of course, but can I ask why?"

"Well, this week we need to set tongues wagging. My specific aim is to make sure so many people see us together that Forquitte's pride wouldn't let him marry me even if I weren't marrying you. Servants gossip, and they tend to embellish stories, so I figured it would be easiest to start our scandalous antics there." Her eyes were gleaming. She already knew that Ava enjoyed these games, but the more they played the more it seemed to thrill her.

Gwen found this whole thing more terrifying than thrilling. She wasn't fearless the way Ava was – though part of it was that for her, there was danger on both sides. Don't act well enough and their scheme falls apart; act too well and she might disgust Ava, losing a friendship that had quickly become priceless to her. Ava only had to worry about the first.

"Alright. We're meeting right before lunch to be scandalous. Got it." Gwen tried to grin in as carefree a manner as Ava did. *This is all a lark; we're friends making people think we're more.* Her grin felt forced. *But if it doesn't work, Ava has to marry a monster, and I'm either banished or dead.*

"Excellent. Now, the tourney. There are four events – the Joust, the Single Combat on Foot (that's blunted swords, if you're wondering), the Archery, and the Grand Mêlée." The way Ava said it made it clear she knew where the accents went. "You've never practiced with a lance, so we're not entering you into the joust. You seemed pretty confident in your ability with a sword, though – and I've heard that you're good enough with even a borrowed bow that people are talking about you as a possibility for that."

"I'm better than average with the bow, though I wouldn't call myself champion material. I'm the best in Farrowdown with a longsword; I think I like my chances best in the single combat." An idea occurred to her. "Would it be possible to send for my bow from home? If I need to try to win the archery, I'd prefer to make my odds as good as possible. I don't think it will be enough, though."

"Single combat is blunted weapons and metal armour. You win by forcing your opponent to their knees. You won't be the only woman in the ring, but most of your opponents will be men. Have you fought in full plate before?"

"No. I wear boiled leather because it's lighter and lets me move more easily." She paused, reluctant to admit the next part. "And because it's cheaper. I don't have the money to buy a properly fitted suit of plate armour, but my leather fits like a second skin."

"That's two things we need to sort out this morning, then. We need to send word back to your home and have your longbow brought to you, and we also need to get a suit of plate armour fitted to you. There isn't time to have one made perfectly to your measurements, but there are men as tall as you and you're closer to a man's shape than most women are. We should be able to have one fitted well enough for you to start training in it tomorrow."

Gwen wrinkled her nose. "The other problem with plate is that it makes the wearer smell. I've been doing fine bathing in the basin in my rooms, but that won't cut it for the mix of metal, grease and sweat from acclimatising myself to plate armour."

Ava smiled her wicked, dimpled smile. "Luckily for you, my plan for tomorrow involves a trip to the Royal Baths."

A little more than an hour before noon Gwen found herself summoned to the Audience Chamber by a herald in a white tabard. She followed him and found King Harald waiting with a selection of the nobility. There was Queen Constance, of course, and Ava. Lady Deidre was there, and Gwen recognised Lady Margaret from last night. The Earl of Lubrey was in attendance, which did not make her feel as comfortable. There were five others she didn't recognise, all dressed in finery that suggested high birth.

Gwen bowed deeply to the King. "Your Majesty, how may I serve the Realm?" Ava had told her this was a safely formal way to respond to a summons.

"Your service to the Realm is why we are here, Gwendoline Carter of Farrowdown." King Harald's eyes creased in a smile, and Ava was beaming at his side. "We cannot grant accolade to an unlanded freewoman. To remedy that, I bestow upon you the estate of Essen, a small vineyard of eight acres along with the families living and working on the land. Now, Gwendoline Carter of Essen, hand me your sword and kneel."

119

Gwen drew her sword carefully and presented it to the King hilt first across her forearm. She knelt before him and bowed her head.

King Harald tapped the flat side of her sword on her right shoulder. He passed the tip over her head, flipping the blade as he did so to tap the other side of the blade on her left shoulder. "Now rise as Sir Gwendoline Carter of Essen, Knight of the Order of the Dragon."

She knew she'd be 'Sir' rather than 'Dame' — knighthoods awarded for military service always carried the masculine honorific. She hadn't known about the Order of the Dragon, however. When she stood and accepted her sword from the King, he also pinned an insignia on the right of her surcoat. It was in the shape of a gladius, point down, with a coronet around the top, where the hilt met the blade. The coronet looked very similar to the one Ava was wearing now.

"For the final part of your reward, Sir Gwendoline, we must retire to the treasury." The King was still smiling in a benevolent way, and most of the onlookers looked similarly pleased. The sole exception was Lord Forquitte, whose stony face might look appropriately dignified were he not surrounded by celebration.

As they walked, Gwen tried to get close to Ava, but there were too many people wanting to talk to her, and too many wanting to talk to the princess. She gave up and made her best effort to be sociable and charming to the lords and ladies around her.

Gwen had to admit she was impressed. She hadn't known the Royal Treasury contained so much wealth. It wasn't like a pirate's horde, or a dragon's for that matter; there were no gems and jewels flowing out of open chests, or anything of that nature. What there was were neatly labelled sacks of coins, with denominations and total value written on the sides, along with stacks of gold and silver bullion. Gwen knew enough about the worth of such things to know that the knee-high stack of gold bars, roughly the size and shape of a crate of arrows, was as valuable as everything else in the room put together.

"The reward my heralds announced," the King began once they were all inside the room, "for the safe return of my daughter to me, was whatsoever her rescuer may carry from this room using nothing but the strength of their two arms." He turned to Gwen and gave her a fatherly smile. "A strong young knight such as yourself can no doubt carry enough to make you as wealthy as many Barons in this Realm. Whatever you choose, it is yours – provided you can carry it without dropping anything before the end of the hall."

Gwen eyed the piles of gold. She could probably stack a dozen bars in her arms and be sure none would drop in the thirty yards or so she had to carry them. And their strategy didn't appear to rely on the grand gesture right at this moment, so perhaps it wouldn't hurt to have the gold as a backup plan. If she ended up marrying the princess it would just wind up back in the vault, but if she didn't it could well be enough to set her little brother up for life.

She looked around the room. Everyone was smiling. Including the Earl. Ava's smile looked a little bit worried. *Damn it, Gwen, you really* do *have it bad if you can't bring yourself to look after your own interests even as a backup plan.* She took the three steps to stand in front of the princess and smiled adoringly down at her.

"Whatsoever I may carry from this room using only my own two arms." Her smile broadened, and she touched Ava's cheek. "Well, I know what I value most in this room." She bent slightly, one arm under Ava's knees, one behind her shoulders, and swept her into her arms. Ava's arms came around her neck, and she smiled up at her as Gwen carried her princess out of the room and down the corridor. As they passed through the door the silence broke with a smattering of applause, which died away quickly. It was apparent no one quite knew what to make of Gwen's interpretation of her reward.

Gwen set her down gently just beyond the end of the hall, and they stood there, forehead to forehead, nose to nose. Ava's arms were around her neck, and Gwen's around the smaller woman's waist, holding each other close. They stood like that, nuzzling noses together, not kissing but still with a quiet intimacy, until the others came around the corner and found them.

She waited a breath after the King came in sight, for the tableau to establish in everyone's minds. Then she stepped to the side, stood tall, and addressed King Harald. "Your Majesty, your daughter has asked me to marry her. I have said yes. I now ask your blessing on our union. We would prefer to marry with your blessing than without, but I intend to marry your daughter whether you will or no."

There were a few shocked gasps. Gwen didn't know whether word hadn't reached them yet of Ava's proposal, or whether they were just shocked that she would address her King so boldly. Ava was standing by her and hadn't interrupted, so she assumed she hadn't done anything monumentally stupid yet. There was still time, though.

King Harald had lost his fatherly smile. He didn't look angry, not quite, but there was a tightness around his eyes. "Sir Gwendoline, my daughter and I have discussed this. I will give my blessing or otherwise after we have finished celebrating her return. In the meantime, be patient. Eat, drink, be merry and enjoy the festivities. They are in honour of your heroism, after all."

They had all returned to their quarters to freshen up before lunch. Gwen splashed some water in her face and put her sword away before heading off to find the quiet corridor near the pantry.

She arrived to find Ava already there. Her face lit up and she rushed to meet her. Gwen caught the smaller woman around the waist as she launched herself into her arms, the impact spinning the two of them around. Ava's lips found Gwen's, and there was nothing gentle or subtle about the kiss. She was holding Gwen's face in her hands, her tongue demanding entry. Gwen's mouth opened reflexively, and she moaned as she felt Ava's tongue enter, intoxicating her with her insistence, requiring her submission. Gwen was only too eager to obey, her hands wrapping around Ava's body, one hand behind her shoulder pulling her in tightly, the other gripping her arse, grinding their hips together.

Ava broke the kiss just long enough to moan "Oh yes, darling, yes, just like that, you know *exactly* what I like," in a needy voice that was low but carried like a stage whisper. As soon as she'd finished, she was kissing Gwen again, pressing her body up so there was no gap between them anywhere. One of her hands left Gwen's face and travelled down her shoulder, pausing to drag a finger over her neck before dropping down to her breast. Gwen gasped as the small hand squeezed gently. Her nipple had hardened into a spear point, driving into the princess' palm. Ava rolled her hand around and moaned again.

She felt a small leg hook hers, and she took the hint, driving her thigh up between Ava's legs in a possessive gesture. The answering grinding motion, and the accompanying groan, made her wish they had privacy for this. Made her wish they'd be doing it even without the audience.

She heard a high-pitched gasp behind her, and Ava broke away, looking suitably embarrassed. Gwen turned and saw two scullery maids with their hands over their mouths in twinned shock. They disappeared before she had a chance to say anything.

Ava made a heroic effort to stifle her giggles. "Well, I suspect that by the time our chambermaids have heard of this, you'll have had half your hand in me, and I'll have been screaming your name in the pantry for all to see."

"Only half? I'm disappointed." Gwen managed deadpan for about two seconds before giggling herself. She was glad they could joke together afterwards. Even if she took it altogether too seriously while she was in the middle of it.

They spent the afternoon together, with a chaperone. Ava took her to the royal armoury to get fitted for full plate armour, which Gwen found both odd and familiar at the same time.

The arming jacket was a padded gambeson with chainmail patches sewn onto the areas where the joins in the plate armour created vulnerabilities. It was there to prevent skin from rubbing on the naked steel, but it also provided additional armour protection. The plate itself was far lighter than she had been expecting. While the steel was thin, the concave shape provided enormous strength from blows from outside, much like the shape of an egg afforded more protection than you might expect for the chick. Plate and gambeson between them were only around half again the weight of her boiled leather, though the fit of the suit she tried left her with significantly less mobility than her leather afforded her.

The arming jacket fit her surprisingly well straight off the rack, but the smith bustled around her taking measurements for the plate itself. "I can have you a full suit that will fit you like a dream, Sir Gwendoline, but it'll take a month or more. A plain set of armour good enough to protect you during the tourney can be ready tomorrow afternoon – providing none of the apprentices take the morning off sick."

Ava responded for her. "We'll take both, thank you Master Smith. She'll need to get used to moving in plate, so please let us know when the plain set is ready. As for the custom fit, we would like to commission a suit fit for a Royal Consort. Please make sure it is completed to the highest standard."

The smith looked surprised. "Fit for a consort, your Highness? Of course. Of course. That level of workmanship and decorative detail will add time, you understand. It might be two months, or even three before it's done."

"You have three months. I have every faith in you." Gwen loved hearing Ava sounding so aristocratic. It was so different to how she sounded when they were alone.

The next morning, Gwen went to visit the bowyer, fletcher, stringer and arrowsmith. Back in Farrowdown there was only the arrowsmith – he made the bodkins (that is to say, the arrow heads), but each archer made their own bows, and fletched their own arrows. Gwen wasn't interested in a new bow, since hers was on its way, but she did want to make some arrows she could be sure would fly true, and some spare strings for her bow might come in handy as well.

She spent a couple of hours turning staves into rounded arrow shafts on a jig. She then fastened goose feather fletchings with a whipping of linen thread. She affixed the fletchings with slightly more twist than the castle fletcher did on his – she always found her arrows flew straight and true for longer if they had more spin.

By noon she had a dozen fletched shafts ready to attach bodkins to. The ones she had practiced with had been warped, as old practice arrows tend to be. Especially ones used by many different archers. She had a much better feeling about how these would perform when she had her own bow again.

After lunch, word arrived that her simple suit of plate was ready. She went to the armoury to try it on, and while she was doing so the Master of Arms happened by.

"Sir Gwendoline. I hear it's your first time in full plate?"

"Yes, Master Dennings." She had heard his name spoken yesterday and hoped she had got the correct form of address. "I've always worn leather in the past."

"The squires have their practice shortly. Would you care to join them? It's the young boys right now, but the Sergeant instructing them is quite patient."

"I'd appreciate that. Thank you, Master Dennings."

She slipped in with the young lads. There were six of them, aged between fourteen and sixteen. She knew squires could be as old as twenty or even twenty-one, but the older boys weren't here today. The Sergeant had them doing simple drills, moving forward and back, blocking imagined strokes, and swinging at the air in a group. Gwen was grateful for the opportunity to get used to the feel of moving in plate. To her relief, it felt a lot less restrictive than the poorly fitting suit she had tried on yesterday. It still wasn't as easy to move in as her leather armour.

After a time, they moved from swinging swords at the air to using the practice dummies. They still danced in and out, pretending to ward off blows before bringing their own to bear, but now it was possible to know their strikes were hitting where they ought to be. Gwen was relieved that she was on target for the most part, though she was slightly disconcerted that some of these beardless boys were able to move more swiftly in their plate armour than she could.

They had just finished with the training dummies and had been paired off to spar with each other when Lady Deidre arrived. "Sir Gwendoline, Her Royal Highness Princess Ava requests you attend upon her in the Royal Baths at your earliest convenience."

Armour doffed, Gwen followed Lady Deidre through the halls of the castle. She had never been to the Royal Baths before.

"I have to say, Sir Gwendoline, that a bath sounds like a magnificent idea." Deidre wrinkled her nose. "You smell like an armoury."

Gwen gave a lopsided smile. "I did warn Princess Ava that that would happen, my Lady."

Deidre's laugh sounded polite. "Perhaps her timing wasn't entirely coincidental, then." They walked a few more paces in silence before Deidre began talking once more. "Has she warned you she intends you to be… shall we say, intimately groomed?"

Gwen gulped. "Yes, but she never said exactly what that entails."

"Well, she's bringing a razor and shears. The razor is most likely for your legs, but the shears…" Deidre's smirk looked highly amused this time. "Let's just say I doubt she plans to cut the hair on your head, my good knight."

"Ah." Gwen felt a little uncomfortable having this conversation. "Will we at least have the bath house to ourselves?"

"More or less." Her smirk had not lessened any. "Queen Constance knows what her daughter has planned and has asked me to be your chaperone this evening. Given your reputation for strength of voice, I can probably afford to turn my back and give you some semblance of privacy."

Gwen's cheeks burned. Her ears burned. Her neck was turning crimson to join them. The temptation to protest that they had not in fact *done* anything was strong, but she managed to resist. She should be happy that Deidre no longer appeared to suspect them of putting it on. Best that everyone believed the two of them were enjoying each other's company. Vocally.

"Your knight, sans shining armour, your Highness," announced Deidre as they entered the room. Ava was seated beside an enormous sunken marble bathtub full of steaming water. She was wearing a silk robe, apparently with nothing underneath. Beside her were the grooming tools Deidre had mentioned, along with soap and scented oil. Several towels were laid out across the cold stone, with others folded neatly nearby.

"Excellent, Deidre." Ava stood gracefully to greet them. "Thank you. We will be fine from here – I wouldn't want to keep you from your important business."

Deidre coughed. "I'm sorry, your Highness, but your royal Mother requested that I remain in the room with you to make sure that some degree of propriety is kept. I've brought my needlepoint and will not need to pay close attention to your grooming if privacy concerns you."

Ava rolled her eyes and addressed the ceiling. "Honestly, Mother, what do you think can happen that hasn't already?"

"I think she feels the need to pretend she's keeping you on a short leash, your Highness, even though the whole Realm knows you've wandered astray." Deidre answered the rhetorical question. "If anyone should ask me, yes, I made sure your virtue was exactly as intact when I left as when I arrived."

"You wouldn't need to stay in the room for *that* to be true." Ava's direct comment had Gwen's cheeks flaming again.

Deidre sighed. "Yes, your Highness, we know, but we're pretending not to, and we're taking great care to imply without lying. You know the game."

"Politics." The word was a grumble. For a woman who enjoyed her own schemes so much, she seemed to have a hard time accepting that others also liked to play these games. She gave herself a subtle shake, and turned to Gwen, smiling. "It's a delight to see you, my darling, even if we can't have the privacy I would have dearly liked."

Gwen stepped into her personal space and gave her a demure kiss on each cheek, her hands resting lightly on the princess' hips as she did so. "It's always a pleasure to see you, my love." The endearments flowed easily off her tongue, now. They didn't even really feel like a lie.

Ava took her face in her hands, rubbed their noses together softly, then pressed a chaste kiss to her lips. "Shall we wash the smell of metal from you, darling? And then we shall see about a proper grooming."

"As you wish."

The process of washing the smell of metal from her was at once heavenly and torturous. Gwen revelled in the feel of Ava's hands on her skin, soaping her back and making her feel clean and wonderful. But at the same time, every time one of Ava's hands brushed over anything remotely sensitive, she could feel her body light up with desire that she desperately tried not to show.

"You're beautifully muscled, you know." Ava's voice sounded admiring and, not to put too fine a point on it, slightly lustful. "Your back is strong and hard, and I've never seen a woman as broad of shoulder as you."

Maybe it would have been alright to show just a little of her desire. But she had never been very good at half-truths. "Thank you. All archers build strong backs. I'm glad you like it, though." She wondered if she should compliment Ava – but she wasn't facing the smaller woman, and it would feel a little forced.

"Mmm. How could anyone not?" She could feel the small fingers ghosting over her skin. It made goosebumps rise in their path. She turned to face Ava, who didn't lower her hands.

The soapy fingers gliding over her ribs and under her breasts made Gwen gasp. Ava's grin was beautiful in its wickedness; she'd never tire of seeing it. "I prefer smaller women, myself." Her hands started wandering over Ava's stomach, now. She trailed them up, mimicking the other woman's movements, tracing a line under her breasts. Breasts which perked up noticeably at the touch. "Your slender waist and beautifully flared hips would attract stares even if you were the lowliest born scullery maid. You're beautiful, Ava."

Gwen cupped her hands under Ava's breasts. Her soapy thumbs traced circles around the beautifully hardened nipples. Ava moaned and pressed her body in closer.

Deidre's cough broke the moment. "Do I need to throw a bucket of cold water over the pair of you?" And it did feel like a broken moment – Ava was blushing as hard as Gwen as they sprung apart, and neither could meet each other's eyes for a long second.

Ava recovered first, glancing up to meet Gwen's blushing gaze. She grinned and winked. *Alright, so she's letting me pretend that I'm not seriously – and obviously – aroused, here.* Of course, Ava had shown signs of physical arousal, too; it was likely she thought Gwen's was purely a physical response to touch, the same as hers. Nothing to worry about.

"I think you're smelling nice again, now, darling. Let's make you beautifully groomed as well." Ava's dimples flashed. She took Gwen's hand and they climbed out of the gorgeous marble bath together.

They sat facing each other on the towels. Ava took Gwen's legs one by one, rubbing them with soap and then shaving off her hair. Gwen had never thought her legs were particularly hairy – though she usually only compared herself with the men she associated with, and not highborn ladies who had enough time to pretty themselves up regularly. Ava wiped the soap residue off her legs with a cloth. It felt wonderful.

The shears were small, dainty, and as sharp as the razor had been. "I'll need you to spread your legs, my love. Don't worry – Deidre won't look." This last was directed at the lady in question, who waved the hand not holding her needlework in acknowledgement. She didn't turn around.

Gwen spread herself open, acutely aware of how swollen she was. And wet. She'd only been out of the bath for a few minutes, and already she felt like she was oozing all over the towel. Ava stared for a moment before beginning work with comb and shears. Gwen couldn't read the look on her face.

Once her hair was uniformly short, Ava picked up the razor and the soap again. She looked up at Gwen's face quickly and spoke low and without any jest. "Are you alright with me doing this? You look worried."

"I've never done it before is all. Yes, I'm alright with you doing it. But…" She glanced at Deidre, then back at Ava, and shrugged helplessly.

Ava seemed to understand and nodded. She also glanced toward Deidre before saying, clearly and lovingly, "Don't fret, my love. You're beautiful."

Her hand started to slowly spread the soap lather through Gwen's folds. Gwen closed her eyes and breathed deep and slow. She couldn't stop herself twitching, but maybe it would be okay. Ava's hand felt so good, though. Her fingers slipping through Gwen's own wetness, soaping up everything below her mound, and all around the creases of her thighs. She opened her eyes again, and saw Ava staring intently at her, mouth open. She looked as aroused as Gwen felt. *Gods but Ava is good at this. If I didn't know it was all a ruse, I'd never believe it.*

Ava closed her mouth and looked up, her fingers still playing very lightly around Gwen's sex. She blushed before speaking. "Well. I think you're lathered enough. Let's get you shaved." Her hands didn't tremble at all when she picked up the razor, for which Gwen was exceedingly grateful.

When she was finished, Gwen was groomed exactly the way Ava kept herself – a small, neat patch of short curls, otherwise bare. This time when Ava wiped her down with the cloth it was all Gwen could do not to groan. Her eyelids did flutter shut on their own.

Ava touched up her own grooming in no time at all while Gwen was still feeling a little blissed out from the whole adventure. She put away the razor and shears and opened the bottle of scented oil. "I'll oil yours if you oil mine?" The offer sounded almost shy.

"Of course, my sweet." Gwen's voice sounded hoarse, even to her. She thought she heard Deidre mutter something about buckets of cold water, but she seemed mostly to be talking to herself.

They each took a handful of scented oil and lavished it upon the other. At first, they rubbed each other's legs, which felt wonderful, but Gwen's mind was full of the anticipation of the final part of the grooming ritual. Rubbing oil into the freshly shaved parts of each other's sex.

"Ready?" Ava whispered, looking like she had a plan to steal honeycakes. Her eyes were alight with mischief, and her hands were covered in oil. Gwen nodded once, her mouth dry.

Their hands met each other's bodies simultaneously. Gwen couldn't decide whether the warm, soft, smooth feeling of Princess Ava against her hand was the best, or whether it was Ava's hand against her newly smooth, sensitive skin. She'd never considered before that hair could dull sensation – it didn't grow on

133

the most sensitive parts, so she'd never thought of it. But every touch on the newly bare area felt like fireworks, and it was all she could do not to rub herself fully and totally against that beautiful hand.

It was just as challenging to keep her own hand within the bounds of what she thought was acceptable. She slid her fingers very slightly between Ava's folds. She'd been so carefully trying to avoid going deep enough to touch her clit, but there it was, swollen and pulsing. The instant her finger touched it, Ava's hips jerked, her hand clenching enough to rub against Gwen's own overheated centre. Gwen was gone, spasming and jerking through her climax. Ava's motions were twitchy and irregular, too, her stomach muscles tightening and relaxing in an off-beat staccato.

She froze. There was no one watching. She couldn't pretend to be acting everything up for the sake of rumours. There was just her and Ava, and she'd just come in the Princess' hand. Ava also froze, staring in horror at her. Neither knew what to do.

Just then Deidre's voice cut through again, sounding peevish. "I really do have a bucket of cold water here, you two. Don't make me use it!"

Their horrified looks melted into giggles. Somehow, everything was alright again.

Chapter Eight – Forging Fury

The next morning, she decided to take her arrow shafts and see if the arrowsmith could show her how to affix the bodkins. She told the guard outside her door where she was going and headed out.

To her surprise when she arrived at the forge a young woman was working the anvil. She was short – only slightly taller than Ava – but broad of shoulder with wiry muscles, and she swung her hammer with a precision that suggested she'd been doing it most of her life. Ava waited for her to finish shaping the arrowhead she was working on.

When the woman finished, she quenched the arrowhead and held it up to the light, turning it to check that the point was in line with the socket. She noticed Gwen in the doorway. "Well met. Name's Catherine Thatcher, and this here is my forge." She placed the finished piece neatly in a pile of others and took her gloves off. "Who might you be?"

"Gwen. Gwendoline Carter, if you please, but I prefer Gwen. I was hoping for lessons from the arrowsmith – do you have time for me?" Gwen took care to show she understood that she was speaking to the master smith. She'd met a handful of younger masters in their trade, and not one of them took kindly to being assumed to be a forge hand.

"I don't have room for an apprentice right now." She looked Gwen up and down. "Though you look too old for that anyway. I might have time to show you a thing or two today, if you've the strength to swing a hammer?"

Gwen held herself up straight. "I'm not looking to master the trade, Mistress Thatcher. For today, I was hoping to learn how to fit bodkins to my shafts." She held her shafts out for inspection.

Catherine glanced at them. She didn't appear impressed, but she wasn't sneering at them, so Gwen felt they must at least pass muster. "You'll need to cut shoulders into the end where you want the bodkin to fit. Have it tapered slightly," she picked up another arrow to show how the head fit snugly onto the shaft. "But remember to file it slightly too large to begin with, bringing it down slowly until it fits. If it's too large you can file it further down, but if it's too small there's no way to put the sawdust back on. It should be tight enough that you need to twist it to get it off, even dry."

Gwen did the first two under Catherine's eye, before she seemed satisfied she wasn't going to destroy the place. Catherine went back to forging arrowheads while Gwen completed the shoulders on the remaining ten shafts. When she was done, the smith showed her how to use a dab of glue and a metal pin to ensure the heads didn't come off when retrieving arrows from the target.

"You've a steady enough hand. Fancy a lesson in real forge work?"

Gwen smiled. "I'd love to."

Catherine handed her a pair of gloves, and showed her how to work the bellows, and what colour the coals should be for heating the bar stock. When it came time to pound flat the section to bend into a socket, she snorted with laughter at the way Gwen was holding her hammer. "Not like that, Gwen. You'll wear your forearms out within the hour if you try hammering iron with *that* grip."

Gwen couldn't see how her grip was different from the master smith's, and said so.

"Here, let me show you." Catherine stepped into her space, holding the hammer steady with one hand while she adjusted Gwen's grip with the other. The changes were subtle, but she could see that it would use different muscles to bring the hammer down at the correct angle.

"My darling! I've been looking for you everywhere," Ava's voice rang loud through the smithy. "Did you forget you were to come to court with me this morning?"

Gwen gaped. She was certain she'd told Ava she was planning on finishing her arrows this morning. Other people certainly knew where she was.

"Your Highness," Catherine curtseyed deeply. "It's an honour to have you visit my forge."

Ava's gaze contained a touch more aristocratic hauteur than Gwen was used to seeing. She looked regal, beautiful as a stained-glass window and cold as the heart of Winter. "Of course. Your arrows are excellent. But I must take my beloved – we are required elsewhere."

By now Gwen had her gloves and apron off, and Ava took her hand. She pulled her with surprising force for such a small woman, and Gwen found herself stumbling into the princess' arms. Ava kissed her, fast and fierce, before leading her off in the direction of court.

Gwen was thoroughly confused.

"So…" began Gwen when they were out of sight of the forge. "I don't recall anything about court today. What's going on?"

"Our plan, darling." Ava sounded terse. "We've scandalised the servants; this morning we're getting caught by some courtiers. I know just the place – the biggest gossips from my father's court all leave the same way when Father dismisses them. But we must make haste, or we'll miss our chance."

They hurried on in silence. It seemed Ava didn't want to talk. Gwen had no idea what had upset her. Then again, she didn't know how the princess had spent her morning before now – it could have been anything.

"Here." Ava's voice still had a hard edge to it, and she positioned Gwen where she wanted with more force than usual. "I'll take the lead. You just try to make it look like *I'm* the one who sets your loins on fire, got it?"

"Got it," said Gwen. Ava sounded angry at her personally, but it wasn't the time to try to work out why. Now was the time to let Ava do as she wished, and to cry her appreciation for the whole world to hear.

Ava pushed her up against the wall, knocking her feet into a wider stance with one small foot, and pulling her down for a kiss with a handful of her hair. Her free hand quickly positioned Gwen's two on her hips, and then began rapidly unlacing her shirt.

138

For once Gwen had no trouble remembering that this was fake. The ferocity in Ava's touch, in her kiss, felt more like anger than like lust. The feel of her pressed to her was lighting Gwen on fire, true, but it was a very wary fire. She didn't know what was coming next, and the apprehension didn't feel like the pleasant kind.

She did her best, moaning into Ava's kiss, but there was a part of her that was turning the princess' words around in her head. What did Ava know? Was she angry because she knew Gwen wasn't faking it? Did she feel used because Gwen was enjoying her too much?

Gwen had worked herself into a state of near panic when she felt Ava's hands rip her shirt open. She was just barely aware of footsteps approaching down the corridor when Ava switched positions. Her hand was now on Gwen's breast, her mouth had taken the other nipple, and her free hand had plunged between them.

She was already arching up in response to the assault on her breasts when she realised that the other palm was now pressing hard into her centre. Ava leaned in, twisting her nipple with cruel ferocity, sucking so hard on the other it was almost a bite, and rubbing fast and furiously through her trousers. The gaggle of courtiers appeared around the corner, and Gwen came.

Right on cue.

Shame flooded her even faster than pleasure had. That wasn't love. It wasn't tender. It felt cruel, and the negative emotions filled her even as the positive physical sensations spread through her body. The shame and self-disgust she felt seemed to be feeding off the throbbing ecstasy filling her, both growing with each beat of her heart.

She tried to look blissed out in front of the nobles. She succeeded in looking embarrassed. She didn't even try to look at Ava.

As soon as she was able, she fled to her room.

She'd been crying so long that she had no more tears left. Her eyes were puffy, her head hurt, and she didn't know if she could keep doing this any longer. The sun had gone down hours ago, and still she lay on her bed, face down in her pillow, and sobbed.

A noise at her window made her look up. Two small hands gripped her windowsill, and there was a scrabbling from below. A blonde head came up, along with an elbow hooked over the ledge. Gwen rushed over and helped her princess in. Despite everything, she didn't want any harm to befall her.

"How did you..." she began, and Ava pointed out the window. Gwen looked and saw a wide ledge a couple of paces down. "Oh."

"You've been crying," Ava began. She sounded shocked.

Gwen shrugged and looked away. "You were angry. And you hurt me."

Ava looked a little contrite. "I'm sorry. I brought some salve for your bruises." She reached for Gwen's shirt, but Gwen pulled away. Ava offered the small jar instead.

Gwen ignored it. "I wasn't talking about those. I've had worse bruises walking into a door." She took a deep breath, not sure how to express how she felt without giving everything away. "While we were on the road, that second inn. Do you remember telling me you didn't see me as your whore? That you didn't want me to feel like I was?"

A mix of comprehension and slight horror filled Ava's eyes. "Oh. Is it because I touched you directly? Rather than being careful off to the side? But after last night —" She cut off abruptly, her cheeks flaming bright red.

"Not... exactly." Gwen didn't know how to explain properly. She tried anyway. "Last night got a little out of hand, yes, but we were both in it together."

"I wasn't the one sneaking off with another woman this morning. *I* was fully there." The anger was back.

"What in the name of the Gods are you talking about?" Gwen's temper flared. "This is exactly what I meant! You were angry at me, and you took me anyway. I feel used. You took me with no care, no attempt to make me feel like it was okay, like I *mattered*. I felt like your Gods-be-damned whore."

They stood in silence for a long moment, each woman in her own anger. Gwen could see Ava was furious with her, but couldn't for the life of her work out what she'd been talking about. She tried, though. Even through the anger, she tried to understand. Even while so damned *enraged*, she cared about the little princess.

Eventually, Ava spoke. "This morning. At the forge. That smith had her hands on you." She muttered so quietly Gwen had to strain to hear.

She blinked. *That* was what had her upset? "Oh. She was showing me how to hold a hammer. I never even considered that it might look like something else to an onlooker."

"She had her arms around you, Gwen! She was standing too close to you, too intimate. Any *onlooker*, as you put it, would have thought she was claiming you as hers!"

Gwen scratched her head, confusion cutting a hole through her anger. "I still don't think they would have. We were wearing full protective gear. No one would think I was cheating on you."

"It looked like the two of you were a bit too cosy," Ava's tone was angry, yes, but also hurt. "We can't afford for anyone to think either of us is cheating on the other. You have to give me your word you won't be seeing anyone else. Promise me."

"I swear, Ava." Gwen smiled, pushing her own hurt away. She could almost fool herself into believing her princess genuinely cared. "I'm not a complete idiot. I'm never going to cheat on you."

"Thanks. I swear, too, by the way. I'm not asking you for anything I won't give myself."

"I appreciate that." Gwen hesitated a second, before deciding that this was too important not to say. "Next time, though… if you're that angry, please don't touch me for real. It made me feel awful. Either talk to me first, or stick to pretend, okay?"

Ava had the grace to look ashamed of herself. "I promise. I really am sorry – can you forgive me?"

"Of course." Gwen folded her into a hug, feeling a lot better about things.

"Oh, and Gwen?"

"Yes?"

"Tomorrow, same time of day, corridor on the other side of the throne room." Ava gave a slightly nervous smile. "I want it fully convincing, as real as you're willing to go. But tomorrow, I want you in charge."

"As you wish."

Dragon Queens

Ava had stayed long enough to apply salve to Gwen's bruises. They were worse than she'd realised in the moment – her breasts looked mauled. But it was the tender contrition that was more healing than the ointment itself. It was a balm to her soul to feel cared for again.

She hadn't stayed the night, of course. Gwen felt a little sad about that, but she knew they'd be watched a lot more closely if they snuck around for overnight visits. And, as she watched the servant bustling in with her breakfast and fresh clothes for the day, she knew they would have been caught. She smiled to herself at the thought. *Everything else we've done, we've* wanted *to be seen. But just spending the night cuddling like we did on the road? Oh, no, wouldn't want people knowing we were doing* that.

She was just finishing breakfast when the guard stuck his head in the door. "Delivery for you, Sir Gwendoline."

"My thanks." She took the long object wrapped in linen, knowing exactly what she'd find underneath. She unwrapped it carefully. Her bow, seven years old and made of yew, slightly longer than she was tall and kept carefully waxed. Unstrung, it looked almost perfectly straight.

Three hempen strings were wrapped separately. The silk ones they used at the Capital were better, but these would do for today. She retrieved one, hooked one end over the top of the bow and let it fall loosely to her hand. She carefully threaded the bow around her legs and settled the string on the string nock at the bottom. Bracing the belly of the bow behind her hip, she leaned her weight into it and slid the top loop up until it settled into position. Gently releasing tension, she stepped out of the bow, satisfied.

She drew the bow empty, reacquainting herself with the feel of her own longbow, being careful not to loose it without an arrow.

143

Letting the tension out slowly, she decided to take it and her dozen new arrows down to the butts for some practice.

She had a couple of hours before their next engagement. Might as well spend it productively.

She approached the throne room with some trepidation. Seeing Ava ahead calmed her soul but set her heart racing even faster. She'd been told to make it convincing, to go as real as she was willing to go. She hoped Ava meant that. Because if not… this could be unpleasant.

They rushed towards each other, their momentum leaving both women slightly off balance, rocking in a circle as they embraced. "When's showtime?" Gwen asked.

"We should have a minute or two. Keep holding me?"

"Of course. Are you particularly attached to this dress?"

Ava giggled. "I have others."

"I love the laced-up bodice. But I have grave fears for its longevity." Her voice purred in Ava's ear.

Ava's eyes fluttered, and she gave a very small gasp. "My poor gown. Its sacrifice shall be sung about through the ages." Gwen grinned like a wolf. Bringing herself back to some semblance of seriousness, Ava spoke again. "I think I can hear them coming. Are you ready?"

Instead of replying, Gwen fixed her mouth on her throat, nibbling and sucking gently. *So soft*. Ava's pulse was rapid and strong, playing on her lips. Gwen dropped her hand from the back of her head once she was satisfied the princess would keep her head back, neck exposed. She took a fistful of cloth on either side of the laces and paused.

Now. She could hear them, talking amongst themselves, barely hidden around the corner. Courtiers always walked slowly when in groups, but they'd hear this. She firmed her grip and pulled hard. The fabric ripped along a line to the right of the laces, clean from neck to waist. The tearing sound was one of the more satisfying noises she'd ever heard, and she let her teeth scrape the princess' elegant neck.

Ava's groan rumbled low and needy. *Good Gods, where did she learn to act this well?* Gwen pushed her torn bodice aside, gently taking one small yet deceptively weighty breast into her hand. She rubbed her palm across the nipple, enjoying the feel of the nub hardening beneath her touch. Her other hand gathered the princess' skirts up, running her fingertips up her inner thigh.

She paused briefly when she found dampness between Ava's legs. *So it wasn't a fluke that other time. She really* does *find these performances thrilling.* Ava's cheeks reddened, and she started to pull away slightly. Gwen cupped her centre and pulled her in firmly, biting down gently where her neck met her shoulder. Her answering moan was a balm to Gwen's soul.

Gwen had just begun to gently rub her through her undergarments, revelling in her heat and motion, when the approaching steps suddenly stopped. She continued briefly, to be sure that all saw them like this – her mouth on Ava's neck, her hand on Ava's breast and her other hand beneath her skirts, moving rhythmically. Quickly enough to appear natural, she stopped, removed her hands, and covered Ava carefully to protect whatever modesty was left to her.

"Can your Highness not wait until an appropriate time? Pursuing your pleasures in the public eye is unseemly, Princess."

This was a foppishly dressed man of middle years. His hat was bright green velvet, his doublet and hose were red and black, and he clearly saw himself as important enough to rebuke the princess publicly.

"Oh, do give over, your Grace," said a younger woman in a simpler dress. So, a Duke. But she didn't know who this young woman was, either. "Can't you see they're in love? And it's not like they can get away with fooling around in their own bedchambers now, is it?"

Ava's blush was adorable. "Thank you, Lady Maria. Lord Egbert. My Lords and Ladies. I would love to stay and converse, but I must retire to my rooms and see to my dress." She slipped away, amused glances following her.

Gwen sketched a bow and was just about to make her own excuse when the King's booming voice stopped her.

"Sir Gwendoline. A word in private, if you would be so good."

"I don't appreciate the two of you attempting to force my hand." The King's voice was stern, but low, and his attendants were far enough away not to hear. Nevertheless, Gwen chose her reply with caution for onlookers as much as for King Harald.

"I am sorry you see us as so calculating, your Majesty." She wasn't going to apologise for their actions themselves; that would send entirely the wrong message. "It is difficult to control our affections around one another."

"You presume to speak for my daughter?" His tone was light, but underneath there was steel.

146

"No, my Liege. You asked about the two of us, and so my answer was in kind."

"Well then." He sighed. "In truth, I am pleased she has finally shown an interest in marriage – though I would be lying if I said you were my first choice of suitor. I intend to honour her wishes, but I would appreciate being left more room for diplomacy. Your antics could make calming Lubrey harder than it needs to be."

Her wishes. It wasn't lost on Gwen that the singular was deliberate – the King wasn't being subtle about his loyalty to his daughter. She wasn't sure why he was emphasising it – perhaps he did not think she knew? "Ava is of the opinion that the rest of the Court is more likely to be on our side if they see just how utterly in love we are. She feels the best way to defang the Earl is to be sure he has no allies who believe him to have been personally insulted." Her voice was soft, only for the King's ear.

"And you say the two of you aren't calculating." He raised an eyebrow at her. "My daughter is an excellent tactician, but the battle she plans for need not be fought at all. Better for Lubrey to have no wish for rebellion than have him take up arms against his King, even if he does so alone."

"As you say, your Majesty."

The King sighed. "As I say. And yet, you will still follow my wilful daughter's lead and make a most aggravating spectacle of the two of you, won't you?"

"Would you rather me disobey my future wife?" Gwen let a hint of confidence enter her voice.

King Harald sighed again. "I suppose not."

That afternoon Gwen trained in her plate armour again. The squires this time were slightly older, and the excited talk between rounds was of Duke Holyoake's imminent arrival. Apparently, the man was bringing his daughter, rumoured to be plain of face but the sole heir to the largest duchy in the Realm. The consensus among the young men as they trained was that any man should court her like she was the most beautiful woman in the world. The true beauty they courted would be her huge tracts of land.

Holyoake was coming at the express request of King Harald. Listening in on the conversation, Gwen learned that his wife had died in childbirth, and the Duke had grieved long and never remarried. This was the first time he had left his manor in years. Speculation was that he was being invited in order to marry him off again.

Gwen had her own suspicions. Perhaps an eligible young lady with sufficiently large tracts of land might mollify the pride of a powerful lord. The idea of him amassing so much additional power made her uneasy, but the Earldom and Duchy together wouldn't quite match of the power of the King.

She hoped he would be satisfied. She feared he never would be.

She bathed before dinner and wore a simple tunic and hose when Ava appeared once more at her window. She smiled, and helped the beautiful woman in.

"My Princess. To what to I owe the pleasure?" Her formality was in jest, and Ava clearly knew it.

"How many times do I have to tell you to use pet names, Gwenny dear?" She smiled and put her hand on Gwen's forearm. "Maybe I just wanted your company?"

"Well, it doesn't sound like you're angry about earlier, so maybe you did." She paused, but figured repeating the same level of affection Ava gave was safe enough. "Your company is certainly welcome."

"I'm glad." Ava fidgeted slightly. "What did Father want to talk to you about?"

Ah. So not just her company, then. Gwen was glad she hadn't said anything too revealing. "He wanted us to be more circumspect. Says he understands the display makes rebellion more likely to be entered into alone, but that he's working on stopping the Earl from rebelling at all and thinks us rubbing his nose in what he isn't getting won't help that."

Ava rolled her eyes and threw herself onto Gwen's bed. It was a most excellent flounce. "If we didn't rub his nose in it a little bit, he'd still think he had a shot with me. Making sure he knows he's never going to be my consort is more important than Reginald's over-inflated ego."

"True. It seems like a fine line to walk, but I trust your assessment of how to walk it."

"Did you tell Father that?"

Gwen laughed. "I didn't have to. He correctly surmised that I would take your orders over his every time."

Ava's smile was warm. "You would, wouldn't you? You'd disobey your King for me."

"Well, my star is well and truly hitched to yours, Ava dear. And he doesn't outrank you by *that* much."

The princess' laugh was like bells chiming. "He outranks everyone, darling. But I'm glad you're loyal to me."

There was a comfortable silence. Gwen sat next to Ava on the bed, just enjoying her company. Ava's eyes were warm, amused. There seemed to be something going on behind them, though. "A penny for your thoughts?"

Dimples flashed. "I should think my thoughts were worth more than a penny."

"As you say. Are you going to tell me what you were thinking?"

Ava pulled her cheeks in, considering. "I spent the afternoon with my ladies-in-waiting."

"And?"

"And… they have opinions. About knights."

"Of course they do. Care to share them with me?"

There was a long pause. Ava seemed to be struggling to find words. Gwen felt it best not to press too hard, but she waited attentively. "I… may have mentioned that I let my jealousy get the better of me with that arrowsmith."

Gwen knew better than to name the woman. "And your concern that I always appear faithful to you led them to opine on the fidelity of knights in general?"

"More or less." She fidgeted, sitting on the very edge of the bed. "They said that knights have… certain urges. One might almost say certain needs." She looked more uncomfortable than Gwen could ever recall seeing her.

"They tried to tell you I'd feel compelled to stray? Am I understanding this right?" Gwen was somewhat affronted. "I've given you my word, Ava. I'm not going to embarrass you. I won't promise not to pursue friendships, but I'll be careful how it appears, and I will never cheat on you."

"That's just the thing." Ava still looked uncomfortable, but she seemed to have made the decision to see this through. "You've promised not to cheat on me, but I'm not... well, we're not... um..." She trailed off, blushing.

Gwen quirked a half smile. "We almost are, some of the time. Really, Ava, you do set up the most outrageous pranks." She could feel herself blushing, but it was worth it to see the princess relax a little.

"I couldn't ask directly, of course, but I get the impression that 'almost' doesn't really cut it." She coughed, still somewhat embarrassed. "My ladies are most convinced that a knight who doesn't have his – or her – needs met is guaranteed to stray, no matter how nobly intentioned."

"Am I to take it that you feel the need to continue our extravagant displays during the months of our betrothal, then? To convince your ladies that I have no need to stray?"

"Well, that's part of it. But it's not everything."

"What else?" Gwen was confused.

"Umm... Gwen... what if they're right?"

"What, you think having my own sword tapped on my shoulders renders my word of honour moot?" Gwen wasn't sure whether to be amused or offended. "I've said I won't cheat, and I won't."

"I believe you. But... what if they're right about knights having needs? What if asking you to be true to me when I'm not... meeting your needs... is wrong?"

Gwen shifted slightly. She thought she could see the shape of where this was going, and she didn't trust how much her heart lurched in hope. Because it was just as likely it should be lurching in fear. "What are you getting at?"

Ava took a deep breath, clearly steeling herself to say what she was planning. "What I'm getting at, Gwen, is that if you do feel needs, I don't want you taking them anywhere else. I know you've already promised not to stray, but I also want your word that if certain... urges... arise, you won't hide them from me."

Gwen boggled. *Is Ava offering to...? For real?*

Ava continued in a rush. "I'm not promising I'll always say yes no matter what you ask. But I *am* promising that I'll never judge you for asking, and I'll always thank you for bringing that sort of problem to me rather than trying to deal with it elsewhere. Please? Will you promise me?"

Gwen released her breath in a rush. No offers, then – just a request. Okay. "I will, Ava, as long as you promise me the same."

Ava blushed and gave a nervous laugh. "No one ever said princesses had those sorts of uncontrollable urges, you know."

"I don't care. If I'm making an embarrassing promise to you, I want you to make the same one to me, got it? If either of us get uncontrollably inflamed, we bring it to the other, and no judgement is issued. Are we promising that?"

The princess considered this. "Yes," she said at last. "I think we are."

The sun rose on the day before the tourney. Gwen ate a healthy breakfast, but her nerves were rising. She was good with a sword, but she'd seen the older squires train, and she wasn't as certain as she had been. And back home there was always one or two of the old men who'd been loosing arrows their whole life who could beat her with the bow.

She decided a bit of practice was in order. She took her bow and arrows down to the butts, and for a solid three hours she was one with the target. Her groups weren't the stuff of legends – no split shafts, and only a few that touched – but she had her eye in and would make a good showing. She set up an apple as a target and managed three arrows in it before it fell apart.

She had no idea what the competition would be. She'd taken part in several in her life, all of them different. Practicing for consistency seemed the best bet. At least the sword would be more predictable.

When she was finished and walking away with her unstrung bow and arrows, she was approached by none other than Lord Reginald Forquitte.

"Sir Gwendoline," he hailed her. His cheerful tone did not match his hard eyes.

"My Lord," she replied politely. "To what do I owe the honour?"

"You stole my wife." He sounded conversational. "I should think you'd be more careful."

"She was never yours, my Lord." Gwen tried hard to keep the anger out of her tone. "And I feel no need to walk armed in the castle grounds."

"Oh, physically careful? Yes, you should be that." He sounded mocking, his smile never reaching his eyes. "You've entered into the single combat tomorrow. Many of my knights and their squires may be under the misapprehension that doing you an injury would please me. You should be very careful indeed in the ring. But I was referring rather to your delicate female heart."

Gwen bristled. Being taller and stronger than most men meant they tended not to express opinions on the frailty of her sex within her earshot. But of course, the Earl had no fear of her. Quite possibly he knew the comment would vex her. "I must confess I have no idea what you mean."

"Oh no? Then let me instruct you." He wasn't bothering to hide his contempt. "You are not the first, nor the last, nor even the latest of her conquests. Never fear me trying to win her back – I have no interest in soiled goods, least of all goods used by so many hands." His sneer grew deeper, and he wrinkled his nose in disgust. "And not just hands. Do you wish a list of her playmates?"

"No, my Lord." She considered her next words. "It is my understanding that petty gossip is beneath the dignity of my current rank."

The Earl's nostrils flared as he heard the insult. She had only barely veiled it well enough that he could not demand she be punished for it. "I see I should also be concerned for the health of your delicate female brain." He turned on his heel and strode off, every step affronted.

Gwen watched him for a moment before returning to her room. His parting shot was weak, but she didn't like that he was attacking Ava's reputation. She didn't know what to do about it for now, though.

Best go have some lunch. Thinking was easier on a full stomach.

She trained with the sword alone that afternoon, banishing thought with hard work. The day wasn't warm, but plate armour complete with gambeson could make a woman sweat in a blizzard. Her strikes were landing true on the practice dummy, though she didn't feel able to lift her elbows high enough for her preferred blocking techniques. Still, the tourney was tomorrow – there wasn't much she could do about it now.

After she had completed her session and changed out of her armour, a page appeared. The girl looked around 8 years old and was out of breath from running. "Sir Gwendoline! Sir Gwendoline! Her Highness requests you in the royal baths! She said to be quick about it, too!"

Gwen smiled. "At my earliest convenience, perhaps? Or without delay?" She knew how Ava liked to sound in her missives.

"No, Sir Knight! She said to get you right quick. She said I was to help winkle you out of that tin can if need be!"

"I'm out of the tin can already, and on my way. Well done – you'll make a fine squire one day."

The girl beamed and trotted off.

When Gwen arrived at the baths, Ava was pacing around looking agitated. Deidre was with her, presumably as their chaperone again.

"Some crooked nosed knave has been making up wild stories to sully my reputation." Ava was clearly holding her temper by a thread. "I wanted to see you first in case you were of a mind to believe any stories you might hear."

"Let me guess – stories making you out to have had multiple lovers? Both before me and since, if I were to hazard a guess." Gwen was calm and tried to indicate her lack of concern for the tales.

"You've heard them already? Surely you know it's not true?"

"Relax, Princess. Forquitte is trying to make it look like you're the one not worthy of him, rather than vice versa. He hadn't even bothered to make up names for these supposed partners when he ran his sorry tales past me earlier. He's full of hot air – is anyone stupid enough to believe his lies?"

Ava relaxed slightly. "I wish you'd brought it to me as soon as you heard, but as long as you're treating them like the worthless fables they are, we should be alright."

"He has names, now," Deidre spoke up. "I'm one of them, which is absurd enough to be laughable. The knight who is claiming to be one is the Earl's man, so it's no surprise to confirm that's where these rumours started."

"A knight is telling these lies for himself? It's one thing to claim to have heard vague rumours; claiming events that never happened is a lie his honour can't recover from." Gwen felt some anger about this. She'd thought her new rank carried dignity and respect. Apparently, knights did not feel obligated to treat women well at all.

"Well, you'll get to meet him in combat in the third round, provided you both win your first two." Deidre sounded a little satisfied at that. "You're half a head taller than him, so my money would be on you in that fight. Sir Barnaby's his name. I'd be delighted if he were a little sore after tomorrow."

"Speaking of combat," Ava wrinkled her nose. "You smell like a blacksmith's armpit. Strip – the bathwater is hot, and the perfumed soaps will help with the smell of armour and sweat."

Naked and in the bath together, Gwen wasn't focussed on the beautiful body of the princess. She was more concerned with how upset she was.

"Would you like me to wash your back?" She offered once she'd washed most of her own stink off.

"Please," Ava replied gratefully, turning her back and pulling her hair out of the way. Gwen soaped up a cloth and began very gently rubbing it over her back, pausing to apply slightly more pressure every time she got an appreciative murmur from the princess.

"Is there anyone taking this nonsense seriously?" Gwen asked softly. "Or are you just upset that anyone is willing to say it at all?"

Ava sighed, leaning back into her fingers. "I don't know. It's too soon to have asked many people. My ladies-in-waiting found it hilarious the instant Deidre's name was mentioned, of course. Father won't believe it, but he might act rashly once he realises all the knights and squires pushing this rumour belong to the same Earldom."

"He's been trying to avoid unrest. If others took this seriously, would it make it more likely they'd join Forquitte in rebellion?"

"No. Not over this, at least." Ava looked slightly troubled. "Politics is tricky sometimes. It will help if you win tomorrow."

"The sword?"

"Anything. Sword, bow, grand mêlée, as long as you're a Champion your presence at my side will quell any perceived loss of legitimacy these rumours stir."

Gwen sighed. "So winning is still important, even with Forquitte no longer pursuing you."

"It always was, Gwen. But yes, I need you to win."

They were quiet for several minutes. Gwen let her mind go blank of everything but the feel of Ava's muscles gradually losing their tension under her hands. It felt satisfying to know she was giving her that small measure of peace.

"Will you wear my favour tomorrow?" Ava asked suddenly.

"You mean a ribbon or something?"

"I was thinking a scarf. Purple with thread of gold. So no one can mistake who gave it to you."

"I think everyone knows I'd never wear anyone else's, Ava," Gwen smiled. "Still, if you want to make a spectacle of it, why not bestow it on me between events? Maybe after the sword, before the bow?"

"Hmmm. That might well work. Favouring you as a gallant victor; or to encourage you in the next. Both work – but make it the first if you can, Gwen."

Gwen laughed. "I'll do my best, Ava." A thought occurred to her, and she became more serious. "Forquitte said to watch myself tomorrow. He said his knights and their squires would be trying to injure me to curry favour with him."

"He said he set his lackeys on you?" Ava's anger was sharp.

"Not in so many words. I don't know if he ordered it or not, but he's not hiding the fact that he's happy they'll do it."

"Hmmm. The sword should be fine – it's got a lot of rules and it's only one opponent. But I'm not sure I want you in the grand mêlée if his toadies hope to hurt you. They could cause you some small amount of mischief in the sword; a group of them at once could outright kill you in mass combat." Ava had turned toward Gwen now and was frowning.

"I suppose I'd best try to win the earlier events, then." She put on a brave tone, but she was worried.

Ava nodded pensively. For several moments they soaked in silence. Then the princess broke it. "Gwen?"

"Yes?"

"Remember you made me promise to tell you if I had needs?" Ava didn't sound right, but Gwen's traitorous heart started pounding like a drum anyway.

"Yes?"

"I need you to hold me." Her voice was small.

"Oh, Ava." Gwen pulled the smaller woman into her arms and held her gently. Trying not to notice the feel of their bodies pressed together was futile, but Gwen succeeded in pushing it down and not showing anything. Ava needed her, and that was that.

"I can't bear to think of anything happening to you." The small voice was muffled by Gwen's shoulder. "If it did, it would be all my fault. You could have left me with Father and then ridden off rich if I didn't drag you into this."

"I won't let anything happen. I have no intention of letting the Earl's goons corner me. And at the end of tomorrow, one way or another, we'll make things official."

"You promise?"

"I promise."

Ava didn't let go. Gwen held her until the water grew cold.

Chapter Nine – The Tournament

The morning of the tourney had arrived.

Gwen was nervous. She'd gone down to the armoury well ahead of her first fight, and then paced up and down beside her suit of plate for ages in front of an amused armourer. Wouldn't do to tire herself out by carrying the weight all morning.

She knew she was the official reason for the tourney. Well, the return of Princess Ava, but Gwen was all over that story, so she still felt the pressure. She didn't want to see the grand speeches and ceremony ahead of the events, nor did she particularly want to watch the joust. Forquitte was taking part in the joust; part of her wanted him to come off his horse, which would be worth seeing, but she suspected he'd win his early rounds handily, and she did not want to watch that.

When the knights and squires came in, she started putting her plate on. The other knights. It was hard to think in those terms, but she should. Maybe she should get herself a squire, too. But then, she was about to become Consort instead, so maybe she shouldn't. She wouldn't know how to train anyone properly, anyway.

You're babbling, Gwen. Stop it. They'll smell your fear.

Calming herself down, she roped one of the younger squires into helping her with her plate. The older squires would be competing alongside the knights, but the younger lads were just here to help. One younger lass, too, as it turned out.

She began warming up. She knew only the very basics about the sport – it's for nobles only – but the rules were straightforward enough. The swords were provided by the Castle and were so blunt as to be basically clubs. Rounds would be five minutes long unless a combatant was knocked off their feet. If you're off your feet you're deemed defeated. From what she'd heard they almost never went the full five minutes; the ones that did tended to end with whoever was judged the victor going on to lose the next round due to exhaustion. It's single elimination – first loss and you're out.

"Sir Gwendoline? You're up next." It was the same small girl as yesterday.

Gwen raised her visor and smiled. "On my way."

The crowd roared when she was announced. Most people come for the joust, but everyone wanted to see her fight. She tried not to think about that. She had enough to be worried about already.

Her opponent was an older knight named Sir Osbert. They met in a cheery fashion, visors up, saluting with swords raised. Osbert had come in with Duke Holyoake, and his greying moustaches rose in a smile. She knew little about him, but he seemed far friendlier than any of the knights she had met who travelled with the Earl of Lubrey.

The adjudicator signalled for the bout to begin. Gwen circled to her right, sword raised. Osbert came in with a slash, and Gwen was too slow with the parry. She felt a solid blow on her left shoulder –

one that hard wasn't going to affect her ability to fight, but she didn't want to take too many of them.

She re-evaluated her tactics. She had only had two lessons in swordplay wearing full plate. Osbert was aging, but he was still a knight who had done his drills a thousand times over. She didn't think he was faster than her, but he knew what she was doing the second she started circling and she didn't have the experience to anticipate him in the same way.

Decision made, she charged in. His sword lifted to defend a wild swing, but she let one hand go and barrelled her shoulder into his cuirass. Her right foot stepped in behind his right ankle as she did so, and his step backward turned into a fall. From there, all she had to do was hold her feet; her arms flailed wildly as she staggered forward over him, but she managed to remain upright while he was on the ground. It was the least elegant thing she'd ever done in her life, but she considered a win to be a win.

The adjudicator raised a flag bearing the insignia of the Order of the Dragon. Gwen raised her visor and heard laughter from the ground below. "Well done, Sir Gwendoline! Unorthodox, and my son will know to watch for it, but jolly good show nonetheless." Osbert had his helmet off and looked genuinely delighted. "Care to give an old knight a hand up?"

She passed off her sword to a waiting page and stepped over to help him up. "Thank you, Sir Osbert. What is your son's name?"

"Landan. He's twenty years old, and due to earn his knighthood next year, though he hopes a good showing here will convince the King to bring it forward." He smiled good-naturedly. "Well, convince the Duke, really – I've never known the King to ignore the advice of his vassals on such matters."

"You're clearly proud of him. I hope he gets his dreams."

Another smile, this one fond. "Thank you, Sir Gwendoline. I hope you get yours, too."

Deidre approached her between bouts. "Sir Barnaby's out. He got an absolute trouncing in the first round by some wet-behind-the-ears squire and left the ring limping. Well done on yours, Gwen."

She smiled, glad Deidre wasn't sticking to formal address right now. "I'm glad. Would have been nice to be the one doing the trouncing, but that utter ronyon being dispatched by an unknown boy will make his words worth even less."

"Girl," Deidre corrected.

"Pardon?"

"The wet-behind-the-ears squire. You're not the only woman competing, Gwen."

Gwen laughed. "Excellent! Dispatched not by a boy too young to shave but by a girl too young to wed. Please tell me she's smaller than him, too?"

"They looked of similar size in armour. I can find out the girl's name if you like?"

"Don't trouble yourself. If she's any good, we'll hear of her again. And if she isn't, well, Sir Barnaby's humiliation will be complete."

Deidre smiled and changed the subject. "Have you seen your next opponent yet?"

"Sir Osbert said it was his boy, Landan. I haven't seen him."

"Tall, gangly, and young. Might be taller than you, even – though his shoulders are narrower. Handles a sword well, though I freely admit I'm no expert on such things."

"I thought I handled one well, too. Either Osbert is an expert despite his age, or I've been underestimating the competition." Gwen felt a little troubled. She knew she was better with the sword than the bow, but an actual fight in full plate was far more taxing than she'd anticipated.

"You're fine, Gwen. You're not properly trained, but that just means they don't know what you're going to do. And you've half again the muscles of your next opponent, so brute strength may just win it for you."

"May just leave me too exhausted to move for the third, too."

"True enough. Here – you're up. Good luck!"

It was after.

She didn't feel humiliated so much as educated. The boy, Landan, was far quicker than his father – and Osbert had held a grace in his movements that belied his years.

She'd started off trying to swing with enough strength to break through a block. After one parry ended up with his sword against his cuirass and him backing up a step, he stopped trying to deflect head-on. After that, he just simply... wasn't there.

Oh, he still parried somewhat, but he was barely altering the path of her blade while stepping to the side, so she hit nothing but air or ground. And his counterattacks, though not heavy, hit the exact same spot on her shoulder over and over again until she struggled to lift her sword.

When she realised that was happening, she had switched tactics just as she had in the first round. But where Osbert was caught off-guard, his son saw it coming. He stepped aside, pivoted on his sword, and tripped her as she charged.

As soon as the fight was called, he was there helping her up. His smile as he congratulated her on her strength and courage was radiant. She had no trouble returning the compliment, praising him for his speed and dexterity.

And now, she was out of her armour and testing her battered shoulder. It seemed a lot stronger free of its casing – the feeling had returned quickly, and she hoped her arm would be at full strength again by the time the archery started.

The same little page girl she'd seen a few times already rushed up to her. "Sir Gwendoline! Sir Gwendoline! Princess Ava wishes you to present yourself to the royal box before the archery starts!"

Gwen smiled. She knew that, but it was good to be reminded. "Thank you, little one. Say, what's your name?"

The girl's eyes went wide. "Elfrida, Sir Gwendoline."

"Alright, Elfrida. Tell Ava I'll be there."

The girl nodded once and scurried off.

The knight who eventually won the sword was a man named Sir Edmund Dwerryhouse. She didn't know a lot about him, save that he was slightly older than she, and that he spent a lot of his time training squires – any who wanted instruction, not just his own. He seemed decent enough. She didn't begrudge him his victory. Landan had made it to the semi-final, making his father proud.

She approached the royal box between events. Her first sight of Ava made her stumble, her breath catching in her throat. She'd seen the princess in dresses before, of course, but the emerald green velvet gown she was wearing had a magnificence she hadn't expected.

"Gwen! Darling, you're here." Ava rose and glided toward her as if on wheels. Gwen had never seen her turn on noble grace like this.

She couldn't help it. She dropped to one knee in front of her princess and bowed her head. "Your Highness, I live to serve." This wasn't strictly proper, but hopefully it would pass.

"My Knight," her heart thundered at Ava claiming her as *hers*. "I would have you wear this token of my affections." She held a narrow scarf, a pattern of gold peacock feathers on a vibrantly purple background. Gwen raised her right arm for the princess to ceremoniously tie it on. "Return it to me when you are Champion."

"I will, my love. I swear it." Gwen wasn't sure if she was going off script. They hadn't discussed specifics. She stood slowly and saluted, fist over heart.

Ava's smile was dazzling.

Gwen's heart was in her throat when the archery event began. The first round was splitting the wand at one hundred paces.

She felt she had a chance with this one. From what she could see, the nobles around her had bows too light to maintain accuracy at this range. There were one or two with sturdier limbs, though, so she didn't want to get too cocky. Cockiness had got her nowhere with the sword.

Splitting the Wand involved stepping up and aiming at a narrow wooden staff, standing upright a hundred paces away. The staff was smoothly cylindrical, and slightly slimmer than her wrist. Points were awarded for any arrows that stuck in the wand. If any arrow split the staff perfectly down the centre, the archer responsible would win the event. If not, it ended after ten arrows each and victory was awarded on points.

The adjudicator called them one at a time from the left to right. Gwen was a little over halfway down the line. Her anxiety rose with each name called.

"Sir Gwendoline of Essen – loose!" By the time her name was called, her nerves were too tightly wound to keep the tip of her arrowhead steady. Instead, it made figure of eights in front of her as she attempted to find the calm she needed.

She loosed. She watched the arrow fly straight and true to a section of the earthen butt three paces left of the wand. No one else had hit it yet, either, but her miss was one of the worst so far. She took a deep breath and tried to clear her head.

No one managed to hit the wand on their first attempt. One man to her left got a solid hit on his second; a young lass managed to make the wand wobble, but the arrow didn't stick. She needed a heavier draw to embed it at this range, but her aim was good; she should be a fine archer one day.

Gwen cleared her mind once more. Her name had just been called.

She raised her bow. The arrowhead held steady as she held her peace tightly inside. She loosed.

168

The arrow flew through the air, spinning gently on a path to the wand. She saw it strike, but on the curved side where it glanced off without sticking or splitting. No matter. She had her eye in now.

Other archers were getting their eyes in, too. On the next round four more archers managed to strike the wand, though none landed a solid enough hit to score a point. It was Gwen's turn again. She caught a glimpse of Ava's favour tied to her arm and felt a surge of determination flood her.

She knew before she loosed the arrow. She didn't even have to look. She lowered her bow and smiled at the crowd before it hit.

There was the creak of splitting wood. The crowd roared. Ava got to her feet in the royal box and Gwen felt her heart rise, lighter than a feather.

The second round was the Popinjay. A stuffed bird, possibly a pigeon, was hung from a horizontal pole protruding from the top window of the clock tower. Archers were arranged in an arc facing the tower; all had one arrow and could loose at will. Any who missed, or who had not used their arrow within the allotted time, would be eliminated as the bird was inspected. This would repeat until only one archer remained.

Gwen eyed the target sceptically. The target was big enough given the range – they were standing a mere fifty paces from the base of the tower, which was perhaps another twenty to thirty paces in height. She did not think the low draw weight on the bows of her competitors would impede them as much in this event as in the last. What concerned her was that everyone was loosing their arrows at once. All their arrows were clearly marked, so that wasn't the issue. The problem was that if someone else hit the popinjay, it would swing out of position. The string it was suspended on was five times the length of the bird.

She decided she wasn't likely to be the fastest to draw, given the weight of her bow, so she would wait several seconds for the first volley to pass. She held her arrow nocked, bow at rest, waiting for the adjudicator.

A loud voice boomed over the field. "Archers at the ready!" They all lifted their bows, but none drew their arrows back yet. "You have one minute! In your own time – loose!"

A dozen arrows immediately rained down on the tower. One took the popinjay cleanly. Two others looked as though they would have, but the bird was swinging. The rest fell wide, striking the stones of the tower anywhere from a foot away from the target to several paces clear.

The second volley had fewer arrows, and none hit the bird. Gwen eyed those around her – she wasn't the only one waiting for a stable target. She raised her bow and began to draw the string back but let the tension out as three others drew more swiftly. One more arrow hit the popinjay.

She waited for the swinging to stop. A couple more arrows bounced off the stones near the bird as it slowed down but didn't make impact. "You have half a minute remaining!" The adjudicator boomed, and several more archers attempted to hit the bird. One made contact, though the arrow did not look well seated in the bird. She waited again.

As the bird came close to a stop, she raised her longbow once more. One other archer raised his bow, but she was committed. The two arrows flew through the air, and both took the bird at once. The poorly seated arrow was knocked out of the bird by the impact.

170

She heaved a sigh of relief, and her mind began to drift. She was aware of the final bowmen sending arrows at the bird, but she knew hers was unlikely to be pushed free.

Seconds later, the voice came again. "Archers, that is time! Bows down, please. If you have not loosed your arrow, it is now too late."

Two more arrows went flying as he spoke, but they fell short. Two others un-nocked their arrows and began the process of unstringing their bows. Once the adjudicator was satisfied no more arrows were flying toward the tower, he gave the signal to retrieve the bird.

A new one was strung up as the pierced one was brought down. Five archers had hit the target – one Baron and four knights, one of whom was Dame Allura Foxe. Gwen realised she had no idea what got you knighted with the honorific Dame – it was something she'd have to find out.

Since there were only five remaining, they reverted to taking turns. At the end of the second round, the other three knights had missed their turn, but Gwen's and the Baron's arrows had flown true. Her nerves were beginning to reassert themselves. She knew that while she could hit a target that size at that range most of the time, it wasn't a guarantee – especially with the shape of the popinjay.

The final target was raised. Gwen was to go first. She raised her bow, drew back, and released the arrow.

She watched it clip the wing, but fall out, tumbling down the side of the tower as the bird swung gently. Now it was all up to the Baron. She hadn't even caught his name.

He raised his bow – it looked the weight of the first one she made at age 14. She shook her head. Light or not, he clearly knew how to use it. He drew the string back to his cheek with no effort and loosed his arrow.

Her heart pounded in her chest as it flew. It looked so close, it could go either way.

The arrow clattered on the stones, an inch from the head of the popinjay. Gwen breathed again.

"Ladies and gentlemen! With a partial hit on the third bird and no opponents hitting cleanly, the winner of this round is Sir Gwendoline!" The crowd erupted.

She didn't need to listen to the rest. With two rounds to her, there was no need for the Clout Shoot.

Gwen was Champion of the Bow.

She hadn't watched the grand melee, though she heard two men had sustained injuries severe enough they might not walk again. She was glad she hadn't had to take part after all – she'd made a brave show to Ava the night before, but in truth the event terrified her.

The Champion ceremony passed mostly in a blur. She noticed that Duke Holyoake had won the joust – she was just glad it wasn't Earl Forquitte – and the knight who won the melee was one from the Capital named Sir Gareth.

Ava had presented the prizes, as the tourney was officially in honour of her safe return. When she handed Gwen her prize – a solid gold statue of a bow as long as her hand, fully drawn with a ruby broadhead arrow – her smile was dazzling. Gwen heard her name her Champion, and her voice was like honey poured across her soul.

There had been a brief moment to change into fine clothes, and now it was the banquet. Gwen was seated at Ava's side, the other champions sharing the top table. The Duke sat on the other side of the King, in pride of place as Champion of the Joust. Gwen still felt overwhelmed, but at least she was now overwhelmed at her princess' side.

"Are you alright?" The question was pitched low, and Ava was smiling broadly, the concern in her voice not showing up anywhere on her face. Gwen figured she was supposed to look on top of the world. She matched her smile to Ava's.

"Mostly, but also tired and not sure what happens now."

Ava laughed. "Now? We eat."

"Alright, but I've done what the King said I had to. Is it enough? Am I enough?"

The princess' smile was tender, almost loving. "Oh, Gwen. You've always been enough. I knew you were the right person to do this with as soon as I met you."

To do this with. Gwen's insides knotted up as she realised she hadn't even been thinking of their arrangement as a ruse today. It wasn't as if she'd forgotten that they'd decided to marry without being in love; it was more that their friendship was the closest thing to love Gwen had ever had in her life.

She managed a reply. "But what about your father? Am I enough for him? He has to choose me as a worthy wife for you, too."

"My mother and father adore you. And yes, now that you're officially a champion, we'll be formally betrothed." Her tone was reassuring, but the sparkle in her eyes looked slightly out of place.

Gwen thought perhaps she saw it all as a game and was delighted to have won. It looked like the thrill of victory.

"When?"

"Tonight. I suspect he will announce it after the main course. The signing is an informal ceremony but knowing Father he may make it grandly ceremonial anyway."

Gwen nodded without saying anything more. Food was now being served.

After they had eaten their main course there was a little time to talk.

"I had a feeling you'd win the bow, you know," Ava said softly.

"Really? Because after the beating I received in the sword I wasn't so sure." Gwen had a self-deprecating smile on her face.

Ava laughed. "I've never known anyone not castle trained who was as good with the sword as they thought." A very slight pause, and she continued. "And I've never known anyone who *was* castle trained who was as good with the bow as they thought."

"Really? Why?"

Ava's smile looked thoughtful. "Young boys who grow up around knights train with the sword incessantly. I've seen boys from the country come in thinking they're amazing because they could hit their friends with sticks, but it's nothing like swinging swords while wearing plate."

Gwen coloured. That sounded altogether too much like her. "We used to wear padded coats and try to hit each other with trimmed branches we couldn't make bows from. I'd always win.

Even when I was fifteen, against full-grown men. I thought I was amazing."

"And maybe some of those full-grown men didn't want to hurt a teenaged girl. Oh, I have no doubt you won legitimately when you were older, but perhaps the gap wasn't as wide as you thought?"

Gwen shrugged, still a little red. "You could be right. My mother was always fierce – none of the men from Farrowdown would have wanted to provoke her wrath. That might explain how I did so poorly with the sword – but I still shouldn't have won the bow. I know six men and two women who could beat me back home. Half of them could beat me even if I had the luck I had today."

Ava's laugh was fond. "Did you not hear the second half of what I said? Men who train in castles think they're better with the bow than they are. They spend all their time in plate training on horseback and with a sword. The tiny amount of time they have left to train with a bow they only see other half-trained noblemen and they think they're good."

Gwen nodded slowly. "By law we have to train with the bow three times per week."

"Yes, because should war break out all the townsfolk will be formed into archery units. But knights would fight on horseback, and never need use their bows in anger."

"So the people I used to compete against in archery back home are better than most knights with a bow?"

"I should hope so. If they aren't, we'll be sitting ducks should Varoux decide to invade."

Gwen smiled. She'd been wrong, but it all made sense, and it seemed to be working out. Before she could say anything more, trumpets sounded a fanfare.

King Harald rose to his feet and clapped his hands twice. The room fell silent, and everyone looked towards him.

"My Lords, my Ladies, friends and honoured guests. Tonight we celebrate my daughter's safe return to us, and we celebrate our fine Champions of today's tourney. As wonderful things should always be celebrated in threes, it seems fitting to declare that one of our esteemed Champions is my daughter's beloved. Tonight, we would like to invite you all to be witnesses as they formalise their betrothal. Scribe?" A skinny man barely any taller than Deidre scurried over, bearing a rolled-up parchment, ink, and a quill. King Harald spoke softly, for Gwen's ears alone, "My daughter tells me you know your letters. Please tell me she is not mistaken."

"I can read and write, your Majesty," Gwen said, her voice just as low. She glanced at the King, who looked mildly relieved before he resumed his air of pomp and dignity.

The parchment was unrolled in front of Ava and Gwen. She glanced over the clauses briefly as Ava signed with a flourish, but there was no time for checking more than that the document was what had been said – a formal betrothal. Ava handed her the quill with a smile, and Gwen signed. Her signature wasn't as beautiful as Ava's, but the whole thing looked good. Moreover, it looked legal.

They'd done it.

As soon as the parchment and writing tools were cleared from the table, Ava tugged her hand gently. She got the message immediately and fell into a sweet and beautiful kiss. She had a momentary sad thought that there were likely to be fewer opportunities for this sort of thing over the next few months.

She just wished she could persuade her body that this was all only an arrangement. The tingling of her lips and the gooseflesh on her arms were really *not* appropriate for the sealing of a business deal.

They retired to their own rooms after the banquet finished. Gwen was glad for a little time with a basin of warm water and some soap – it wasn't as good as the baths, but it allowed her to remove the stink of the day.

She was towelling herself dry in her undergarments when the princess made an appearance at her window. She smiled, wide and genuine, as she helped her over the ledge. "Ava. It's wonderful to see you."

Ava's return smile showed her dimples. "You as well. You're smelling much nicer."

Gwen waved her hand vaguely at the basin. "I didn't think I could sleep if I stank like an armoury."

"Good choice, good choice." Ava hesitated. Her eyes darted to the side, and her lips moved silently as though she was trying on words for size. "My ladies-in-waiting were talking earlier. They all seem sure that each of the champions will be in a fine mood tonight."

"Seems reasonable," Gwen replied, not sure what about that took so long to get out. "We did just have exciting victories, after all."

Ava blushed a deep scarlet. *What on earth is embarrassing about that?* "So... you *are* in a fine mood, then?"

"Of course I am, Ava," Gwen was really confused, now.

"And you're in such a fine mood… with me?" The blush was flaming now.

Oh. Maybe she wanted to be reassured Gwen wasn't upset? The only thing she could think of that she might be upset about was the melee that crippled two men. It was unfortunate for them, but not entirely unexpected and she didn't know the men. Opting for general reassurance, she made her tone tender. "Yes, Ava. I'm in a fantastic mood with you."

Ava's breath hitched, and her eyes widened. Gwen had only a second to wonder before she was leaning in, holding onto her undershirt, and kissing her thoroughly. Gwen's mouth opened slightly at the contact, moaning softly, her hands snaking around Ava's tiny waist, and the princess deepened the kiss.

The princess' hands tightened briefly in her shirt, scrunching the fabric into balled fists before attempting futilely to push it up – as if it were possible to remove her clothes without breaking the kiss. Gwen pulled her in closer, trapping her hands between them, her own hands moving from Ava's waist.

One hand moved down to hold a perfectly shaped hip right where it began to flare into her gorgeous arse. The other moved up, behind Ava's shoulders, pulling her in close. Their kissing became more heated, more desperate, tongues stroking each other, and moans swallowed on both sides. Gwen could feel Ava's chest rising and falling erratically and knew her own was no better.

Ava tore her mouth away and stared at Gwen, fire blazing in her eyes. "Clothes. Off. Now."

Gwen nodded mutely and released the pressure holding their bodies together. She deftly unlaced Ava's bodice and had begun gathering her skirts up when Ava's hand stopped her. She looked up in surprise "I thought we were removing clothes?" She didn't add *I want to be removing clothes.*

"*Your* clothes." Ava's hands were back pulling at Gwen's shift. She stopped her, shaking her head.

"Not just mine. If we're doing this, we're both doing it."

It was Ava's turn to look surprised. Gwen had no idea what was shocking to her about a request for parity, but then, nothing about this evening made sense. She was just going with it. Ava's surprise turned into a wicked smirk, and she nodded. "Okay. Both sets of clothes off, then."

Removing their clothes was rushed and inelegant, but Gwen had never been more excited in her life. She knew she wasn't going to last and was vaguely aware she should feel embarrassed about that, but as long as Ava felt the same excitement she didn't care. And Ava was the one who had started this.

Their clothes strewn around the floor, they pressed their naked bodies together. Ava's small form melded perfectly to her larger one, breasts under breasts and legs entwined. She steered them toward the bed, resuming their kiss at a slightly less feverish pace. She knew her arousal was showing; she could smell it. She could also feel the start of a drip easing its way down her thigh.

She pushed the princess down onto her mattress and slid her thigh firmly between Ava's legs. She heard the gasp as her wetness met Ava's thigh; it was hard to concentrate on that when her head was spinning from the arousal she felt coating her hip. She let out a deep and heartfelt groan, closing her eyes and grinding her hip deliberately firmly against Ava's soaked centre. Ava's matching "Oh Gods…" was drawn out and beautiful.

Gwen took a perfect nipple into her mouth, and sucked gently, rolling her tongue around it. The luxury of being able to do this without fear of interruption was intoxicating, and she started rocking her hips slowly, rubbing herself against Ava's thigh while she drove her hip directly against her clit. One hand supported part of her weight on the bed while her other hand cupped Ava's other breast. She was in heaven, but knew she had to be careful, or this would end before she'd satisfied her princess.

Ava shuffled down the bed a little, shifting off Gwen's hip but maintaining contact with her thigh. She lost her nipple with a soft 'pop' and gave Ava a questioning look, her hips never stilling. "I want to touch you," was all the answer she got. Gwen nodded, understanding. She wanted to touch, too.

Ava's hand slid down to Gwen's wetness. Slipping between them, her fingers slid past her clit before stopping just outside her entrance. They both groaned. Gwen felt her eyes try to close in pleasure, but she forced them open to see the desire clouding Ava's perfect features. She saw Ava's head tilt back against the mattress, lids heavy with want, as Ava's hips began to mirror Gwen's movement. Her neck was so beautiful, so exposed, and Gwen was powerless to resist the pull. She pressed her open mouth softly just above her collarbone, sucked gently and bit down.

The princess' moan was almost a scream. Her hips bucked frantically, and copious quantities of liquid poured onto Gwen's thigh. Ava's fingers curled, and as she felt those fingertips began penetrating her Gwen slid her thigh out and pushed down, taking them in fully. As Ava regained control of her limbs, she controlled her fingers too, pumping in and out rapidly while rubbing Gwen's clit firmly with her thumb.

Gwen wished she could draw out this perfect feeling, but within seconds she was seeing lights flash as her muscles spasmed, and pleasure rocketed through her body. It felt like everything good in the world was radiating out from Ava's hand.

She could feel her wetness leaving her in pulses and filling the princess' palm, which would have bothered her a lot more had Ava not just finished coating her thigh with the same. Happiness bubbled up within her, and she fell to the bed beside Ava, her panting sounding almost like giggles of joy. Her princess smiled indulgently and turned to face her, stroking her cheek with her dry hand.

"So, my beautiful champion. Has your fine mood been satisfied?"

Chapter Ten – The Aftermath

Gwen froze. "My... my what?"

"Your..." Ava hesitated, her smile slipping. She licked her lips. "Your fine mood? You told me you were in one."

"I... well, yes, but why would a good mood go away because... And why would one need to be satisfied?" Gwen was babbling, but she was in panic. She didn't even want to put words around what she was panicking about in case it made it real.

"Not a good mood, a..." Ava's eyes widened. "You didn't know what I was asking?" Her voice was faint. She looked queasy.

Not half so queasy as Gwen felt. "I thought you were talking about being happy about winning! I didn't think you were asking if I were a... a dog in heat." She swallowed, tasting bile.

"But you responded! When I kissed you. I thought you wanted..." She looked flustered. "I didn't think I was taking advantage of you. And I never called you a dog."

"Not arguing about the 'in heat' part, though? And of course I wasn't going to reject you. I thought you wanted –" She cut off abruptly, unable to form the words.

"Oh, for Gods'..." Ava crossed her arms. "I wasn't implying you were in heat. Battle lust is different. Everyone knows that."

"Battle lust? What in the Realm do they teach you in the Capital?" Gwen was gobsmacked. She was vaguely aware she was being churlish but couldn't stop herself. It was better than thinking about how badly she'd taken advantage of her princess. Better than admitting she hadn't questioned that kiss because she wanted it so much.

"Alright. Alright." Ava held her hands up, halfway between placating and frustrated. "You weren't overcome by lust. You just responded to me because you didn't want to have me feel rejected. Where does that leave us?"

Gwen shifted very uncomfortably on the bed. She tried to pull a sheet over her nudity. "I don't know. I suppose it leaves me apologising and wondering if you'll ever be able to forgive me for the whole kerfuffle." She didn't meet Ava's eye.

"Well," the princess replied thoughtfully. She looked more grounded, somehow. Gwen wondered how she'd calmed so quickly. "Am I at least correct in my assumption that you enjoyed the way things turned out?" At Gwen's horrified expression she added, "Until we got into our brief bout of existential angst, of course?"

Gwen gaped. "How can you ask that?" She knew her discomfort was written on her face. "What sort of a monster would I be if I enjoyed intimacy that you only gave because you felt you had no choice?"

"What do you mean, had no choice?" Ava still sounded calm, but her eyes flashed briefly. "Do you think I'd offer myself like that out of desperation? Am I not allowed to simply want you to be happy?"

"However bad I think I am, I know I'm less awful than Lord Forquitte." Gwen was mumbling now, not wanting to follow that thought to the end, either. *How much difference is there between intimacy offered under duress and that same taken by force?* She shuddered.

"Oh, get over yourself, Gwen." Ava rolled her eyes. "Can we try to get past this like adults, and shelve the self-pity for a moment?"

"What?" Gwen didn't know what to say to that. She was worried about Ava, about doing the right thing by her – how had the princess taken that and thought she was worried about herself?

"I can see you're finding it hard to admit you enjoyed it." She straightened her shoulders, not at all concerned about being naked, but clearly steeling herself for something anyway. "Would it... would it help at all if I admit I enjoyed it first?"

Gwen gaped. "You... you did?"

"Honestly, Gwen. Don't you have eyes?" Ava's tone was a little softer; it softened still more as she continued. "Yes. I enjoyed it very much. More than I thought I would. And now... can you tell me you enjoyed it too?" There was a vulnerability in her voice.

Gwen paused, shut her eyes, and took a deep breath. Then another. "Yes," she admitted finally. "It was... wonderful." There. She'd laid her soul bare for her. Ava had done it first, but... *No. There is no 'but'. She's braver than I am.* That's *what she meant by self-pity.*

Ava smiled, clearly relieved. "Well, then. We may have ended up there from a misunderstanding, but we both enjoyed it, so where's the harm?"

"I..." Gwen cleared her throat. She hadn't got her wits about her yet, clearly. "I guess nowhere? As long as I didn't hurt you."

"How would you feel about doing that together a bit more often?" Ava's blush was pink, but she looked a lot calmer than Gwen felt. "After all, neither of us is going to be doing it with anyone else any time soon. And we *did* both enjoy it."

Gwen sized up the offer, trying to think it over so she wouldn't stutter through her response. It *had* been rather nice. And she'd like to do it again. "Yes." She said, decisively. "Yes, I think that would be a good idea. When would you like to try it next?"

Ava's smile spread slowly, giving the most beautifully wicked gleam to her face. "I don't know. Are you busy right now?"

They lay together, skin to skin, kissing languidly. There was no rush. Gwen felt like there should be, but there wasn't. She forced herself to take it slow. Besides, the kisses felt nice. More than nice. The feel of Ava's tongue gently stroking her own was setting a dull throb between her legs.

She ran her hands gently up and down Ava's sides. She couldn't decide which felt nicer – her hands on Ava, or Ava's hands on her. It didn't matter. It was all wonderful.

Their legs entwined, and while she knew some of what she could feel between Ava's legs was from earlier, she could swear she felt some fresh wetness slicking their thighs. The thought thrilled her, and she compulsively tugged Ava's body tighter into hers. She could feel her own wetness pulsing out with each throb. She wondered if Ava was as fascinated by her arousal as she was Ava's. An hour ago she wouldn't have dared think the question.

As their wetness spread across their thighs, mingling between them as they moved, Gwen started wondering what her princess tasted like. The thought thrilled her – she didn't know if she dared ask. The longer they kissed, the more they stroked each other's bodies, the more fixated Gwen became on what she wanted next. The slickness of Ava's core excited her, and her kisses got less languid, her moans more intense.

Ava broke away first, panting. "You're thinking something." She said, her eyes bright and her tone challenging. "Tell me."

Gwen wished she had that level of self-assurance. It was sexy as hell. She tried her best to project a confidence she wasn't feeling. "You. I'm thinking about how wet you are –" a very slight pause that she hoped Ava didn't notice – "and how much I want to taste you."

Ava's eyes flashed, and her lips quirked in a half smile before she resumed her challenging gaze. "You do, do you? I think we can grant that wish. Provided I'm in charge."

"Of course. Your wish is my command." She hoped that sounded smooth. Her heart was thumping in anticipation, her mouth was watering, and her arousal was beginning to pool beneath them on the sheets. By all the Gods, she wanted her mouth on this woman.

"Good." Ava took control, pushing her down onto her back and straddling her waist. She kissed her once more, deeply and hungrily, before moving up her body. She took her hands and pinned them to the bed above her head, leaving Gwen in no doubt who was in command.

Gwen could only groan as she lay pinned helplessly under the smaller woman. Ava's scent filled her nose as she edged closer, the seconds stretching into eternity. Gwen suspected she was going slowly on purpose to torment her – the anticipation was the most beautiful torture.

"Last chance to back out." Ava's grin was wicked. Her glistening folds were inches from Gwen's mouth. She started rocking her hips back and forth ever so slightly as the trapped woman stared. "No? Don't say I didn't warn you."

Her hips surged forward, and Gwen met her eagerly. Mouth open, she drew her tongue through slick folds, moaning in ecstasy as Ava's taste shocked her senses. Her hips started jerking involuntarily, trying to gain purchase on empty air, and her hands tugged ineffectually against Ava's grip, wanting to hold her thighs as she feasted.

The princess' groan was deep and sensual, her hips and thighs moving as she rocked herself on Gwen's face. Gwen was so lost in her own pleasure that she scarcely registered how much Ava was enjoying her devotions – but what little got through thrilled her. She dragged her tongue through Ava's folds again, pausing at her opening. Stiffening her tongue, she entered her.

Ava's groan became a cry of pleasure, and her movements shifted. Instead of rocking back and forth she began pressing down, trying to take Gwen's tongue as deeply as she could. Gwen met her pressure as best she could, pushing deeper and flexing her muscle in all the ways she could think of. The taste on her tongue aroused her more than she could imagine, and the ways her princess responded to her ministrations made her heart soar.

When her tongue grew tired, she stopped digging deep and instead concentrated on the ring of muscle around her opening. Ava seemed to especially enjoy being licked low on her entrance, so she concentrated her attentions there, rubbing her perineum lightly with just the tip of her tongue. Ava gasped, and rocked forward, and –

– all of a sudden she wasn't licking smooth muscle but crinkly, her tongue sliding over Ava's puckered rear. Ava shouted out in pleasure "Yes! Oh, Gods yes! Right there, please, please don't stop!" – And Gwen didn't stop. She ran her tongue over the area again and again, adding more pressure as the princess bucked against her, screaming profanities, and pleading with her for more, please more, oh Gods more, and…

"Inside. Please, Gods, I need you inside me," Ava was panting, and she released one of Gwen's wrists, only to grab it again and forcibly move it down to her opening. "Inside. Now. Please, Gods, please I'm…"

Her words devolved into unintelligible gibberish, screams and moans conveying her need, and Gwen slid her fingers inside as the tip of her tongue broke through the tight barrier, and –

The force of Ava's climax blew her away. She could feel convulsions through her body, squeezing her tongue, squeezing her fingers, wetness flowing in bursts as spasms rocked the princess. Her screams were just sound, her body jerked as though every muscle was contracting as hard as it could but with no rhythm or pattern to it. Gwen gained control of her other hand and brought it down to rub Ava's clit gently, guiding her through her orgasm and bringing her back to earth. As soon as the twitching settled, indicating that extra pressure would be pleasure more than pain, Gwen pressed down. Her wrists were at an awkward angle, but she managed to curl her fingers upwards.

A couple of very short thrusts later she withdrew her tongue, ran it in a tight circle around Ava's sensitive rear, and then pierced her again. Ava screamed as she came again, riding the waves of fresh ecstasy before she had recovered from the last.

This time it was all too much for Gwen. She twisted her thighs together, providing just enough friction to her hypersensitive clit for her to join her princess in sweet, pulsating release.

When they finally recovered enough to move, Ava shifted down the bed to cuddle up close. She kissed her gently, with closed mouth.

Wow. My beautiful, sweet princess enjoys taking control. Good to know. Gwen grinned and held her tight.

They'd been holding each other long enough for their breathing to subside and their hearts to return to something approximating normal. Ava broke the silence. "Wow."

"I'll say," said Gwen, smiling.

"Really?" Ava pushed herself up off Gwen's chest to look at her incredulously. "But I haven't had a chance to… to make you happy yet." Ava's blush was positively adorable.

"Ah. You didn't notice me being happy, then?" Gwen's grin spread from ear to ear.

"Are you missing euphemisms again?"

Gwen laughed. "Not this time. I… joined you the second time." She could feel her cheeks heat, but she was too happy to care.

"So you didn't mind… um…" Ava didn't get any less adorable the more she blushed. "When things went south?"

Gwen snorted. "Did it look like I minded? I loved how excited you got. I loved doing it." She paused, wondering if she should bring it up now or leave it until it came up naturally. She decided to get it out of the way. "I'd rather you not do… that… to me, though. If that's okay?"

"Why wouldn't it be? I'd be happy to, of course, but if you don't want it, I won't." Ava's blush faded somewhat. She seemed more comfortable with this. Maybe Gwen's uncertainty reassured her.

"Oh good." Gwen offered a relieved smile.

"May I... taste you... though? If I promise to stay in bounds?"

"If you want to. I'd like that." Gwen felt shy, but hopeful.

"Now?" Ava's smile also looked shy and hopeful.

"Now would be wonderful."

Ava pushed Gwen down onto her back again, and their lovemaking began anew.

Three days later, Nicholas arrived.

"Nicholas! How have you been, baby brother?" She ruffled up his hair, but at fourteen he was getting near as tall as she was.

"Gwen! All the better for seeing you! The news that reached us is true, then? You've scored yourself a princess?"

Gwen rolled her eyes. "We're betrothed, yes. Trust you to make her sound like some prize rather than a living breathing woman."

"Well, I haven't met her yet. I will though, won't I?" At Gwen's nod he continued. "Besides, word is you did win her as a prize – for defeating the dragon and then beating all the King's Knights in single combat. Oh please tell me that's true." His eyes were as pleading as a puppy's.

"None of that is even close to the truth. Where do you hear all this, anyway?"

"Down the pub." He didn't look the least bit embarrassed, despite being nowhere near old enough to go rumour hunting in pubs. "And really, none of it?" The pleading intensified.

"Fine, there was a dragon, but I just snuck in and stole her away – I never fought it – and I lost at the sword. I did win with the bow, though."

"Really? Wow. Sounds close enough to me." His boyish grin was disarming.

"I take it mother chose not to accompany you?"

He shuffled his feet, looking awkward. "No. You know what she's like."

She sighed. "I do. I love her, and I don't regret sending all my money to support the two of you, but sometimes I just wish…" She let her sentence trail off.

"Yeah. I know." He looked uncomfortable for a second more before offering up "I actually thought she'd be different since it's the princess."

"Yeah, well." She shrugged. They stood in silence for a moment, lost in thought. "Have you considered what apprenticeship you'd like? One of the perks of marrying Princess Ava is that my brother gets to train wherever he likes." She gave him a fond smile and a friendly shove.

"Haven't really had time to look around yet. I'd like to go into something like being an armourer or weaponsmith, but I reckon finding a master I get on with is as important as the specific trade I go into."

Gwen nodded. "Seems fair. I'll take you around to meet everyone. Might show you off to folks in a wider range of trades, too, if that's okay – you've got a decent mind on you, for all you tend to fall back on your muscles."

"Only compared to you, sis." He grinned. "You rely on your muscles 'cause your brains got beaten out years ago."

"Hey! I can read and write with the best of them." She feigned being affronted. This was an old jest.

"Ahh, Gods love ya, sis." He hugged her tightly.

"Gods love you, too – because sure as taxes, no one else will," she said, in completion of the ancient ritual of siblings. She loved her brother dearly, and he knew it.

The next night there was a scrabbling coming from her closet. Gwen cast around the room for some kind of weapon, settling on a poker from the fireplace. Iron bar in hand, she carefully opened the cupboard door.

Ava was startled, but grinned once she was over her surprise. "What were you planning with that, Gwen dear?"

Gwen lowered the poker, smiling, and took her princess into her arms. "Well, I had no idea what was making the noise. You've always come in through the window before."

"Yes, and since I've still been here the next morning a couple of times, Mother started taking an interest."

"You think she's less likely to notice you're here if you hide in my closet?" Gwen was confused.

"No, silly," Ava laughed. "She showed me the secret passage connecting our rooms. We can come and go as we please."

"She did? You mean to say your mother, the Queen, is enabling our... frivolities?" She knew her mouth was hanging open, but she just couldn't fathom a mother being okay with them, let alone helping them out.

"Well, we're betrothed now, and she remembers what that's like. Besides, she knows we're doing it anyway, and she made me admit how I was getting to your room." Ava grimaced. "Mother was not pleased when I told her I was clambering on outside ledges. She thinks I'll fall and break my neck."

Gwen pulled a face. "I can't say I'd be happy, either. A secret passage does sound safer than the window ledge."

"Want to follow me back to my room? We've spent every night in yours so far."

Gwen smiled. A part of her was worried that she was actually falling for this brave, intelligent, and beautiful young woman. That wasn't part of the deal. They used endearments for each other, sure, but no one ever said anything about actual feelings. Still, the deal seemed to have become genuine friendship mixed with mind-blowing sex, and she'd take that any day.

"Lead on, my love."

They'd spent almost every night together the past two weeks. Waking up with Ava sprawled on top of her was never going to get old. Even better than waking up entangled was doing so with a pleasant dull ache between her thighs that spoke of the previous evening's activities. She had a deep contentment settling within her, mixed with feelings for her princess that she didn't think too hard about.

After all, if she didn't name them, they couldn't be a problem.

Some mornings they'd carefully returned to their own rooms before servants arrived with food and clothes, but they'd been caught a number of times. Just cuddling, but cuddles first thing in the morning suggested earlier pastimes. Gwen felt more awkward getting caught when the events hinted at were real than she had when it had all been pretend. Still, the notion that they couldn't get enough of each other was firmly planted, and they eased off the public displays somewhat.

Only somewhat. Ava had warned against complacency; she explained that if they stopped altogether as soon as their betrothal was complete then it would look a lot like they'd only been pretending to be in love before. And while the Earl had moved on to seek other marriage candidates, he was still the sort of man who would return and make trouble if he felt insulted. And he was definitely the sort of man to take Ava pretending to be in love with a woman so she wouldn't have to marry him as an insult.

So here they were, two weeks into their betrothal, hiding in the rose garden and kissing. Gwen didn't mind one bit. The feel of Ava's lips against hers never failed to stoke her fires, and she hiked her princess' leg up over her hip, stroking the skin under her dress softly. She was just beginning to wonder how far she could push things when a voice interrupted her.

"Hey! That's my sister, you know!"

They sprung apart, both blushing, restoring their clothes to something approaching order. Neither had counted on Nicholas being the one to catch them. Ava regained composure first and answered him. "I'm well aware. Pretty soon she'll be my wife, and I'm fairly certain wife beats sister." Ava arched her eyebrow questioningly.

"Yeah, well, don't the two of you have a room you can do that in?" He looked adorably awkward and grumpy.

194

Gwen took Ava's hand and spoke up. "It's hard enough losing the chaperone outside. Trying to do so in the privacy of an indoor room would be near to impossible."

"What are you doing out here anyway?" Ava asked. "I heard you got an apprenticeship with the arrowsmith, and I'm given to believe she can be quite strict on apprentices being where they're supposed to be."

"Mistress Thatcher gave me the afternoon off." Nicholas beamed, obviously proud of something. "She said I'd done really good work and could rest my growing muscles by spending the afternoon with the Keeper of the Scrolls. He thinks I've got potential as a seer – but I don't want to give up a proper apprenticeship in case he's wrong. I was just on my way to the library when..." He paused and blushed slightly. "When I interrupted the two of you."

"My little brother a seer? That's awesome, Nick. Whatever did you do to impress him so much?"

"Master Avery let me have a look at some of the old prophecies. They were heaps interesting! You know the tradition that slaying the dragon gets the hero half the kingdom and the daughter's hand in marriage?"

"Of course I do. From the sounds of it, it's what you think I did!" Gwen laughed. "You mean that tradition really is linked to an old prophecy somewhere?"

"Sort of. But people get the order wrong."

Ava showed a sudden interest. "How so?"

"Well," Nicholas began, "It turns out the prophecy isn't talking about rewarding a hero for defeating the dragon. Rather, it's giving conditions that must be met before the dragon *can* be defeated."

"And what are those?" Gwen asked, curious despite herself.

"Well, the hero has to have married the princess. And the King has to have given him half his kingdom already. There was a bunch of other stuff, but it seemed to say that the Hero had to have been lowborn, and a love match." Nicholas brightened suddenly. "You know what's really interesting? Old Common defaults to female form and pronouns when it isn't important. So the princess might actually be a prince for all we know."

"And the King might be a Queen?"

"Could be – I don't think Old Common even had different words for the two, only for the reigning monarch verses her consort. Oops, his – we're talking about Old Common and I'm slipping into the default feminine again." He laughed, obviously delighted by this difference.

"I can see why Master Avery thinks you're special," Ava said smoothly.

"He said being able to instantly recognise the direction of causation in old prophecy means I could well be a seer. He says lots of folks read them and assume the gifts come after defeating the dragon. I'm the first untutored boy he's had who got causal inference right without needing to be told." Nicholas beamed with pride.

"That's awesome, brother; you always were good with languages." She smiled fondly, and he beamed back at her. "Go – we can't keep you from your prophecies!"

"Thanks, Sis. Have fun – but not too much!"

He sped off.

Gwen and Ava watched him go. Once he was out of sight, they turned back to each other, and resumed their kisses and gentle

196

touch. After all, they still needed to be caught by random passers-by. Not that Gwen needed the excuse.

Best not to think too hard about that, really.

A few days later Gwen had finished her archery practice and was at her fitting appointment. Clothes befitting a knight who was about to become the heir's consort required several fitting sessions, it would seem. It could have been painfully dull, but the tailor and her three apprentices bantered amongst themselves too merrily to ever get boring.

Elfrida the page girl came barrelling in as they were finishing up. "Sir Gwendoline! Sir Gwendoline! Her Highness summons you to the royal baths!" The child was mildly out of breath, but she beamed with the pride of a job well done.

"Really, Elfrida?" Gwen's amusement was plain for all to see. "Then of course I shall have to go to her. Tell me, how do you always end up being the one carrying messages for my fiancée? Did you do something terrible?"

"Yep!" The girl's chest puffed out so far her feet appeared in danger of leaving the floor. "I beat all the boys in arm wrestling, that's what I did."

Gwen laughed heartily. "That'd do it, alright."

"As you summoned me, my Princess, so am I here." Gwen gave her most extravagant bow, poking fun at Ava with ridiculous faux formality. A few short weeks ago Ava would have been aghast at that, telling her she needed to relax all formality and use cutesy names. Now, though, they knew each other so much better, and the playfulness could feel a lot more natural.

"Oh good, I needed my back scrubbed." Ava held her nose as high in the air as she could manage, turning her hand in a slow circle, an exaggerated royal wave.

"I live to serve, your Highness." Gwen walked smartly over to the loofah and soap, laid out with the towels.

"Oh, stop that." Ava rolled her eyes, but the affection in her tone wasn't forced. "Are you well? I've been busy the last couple of nights, and you were asleep when I came to check on you."

"I'm well, Ava. It must have been late – I tried waiting up last night." She didn't want to say so, but it warmed her heart to know her princess had come for her, even if it was too late to do anything. "You can always wake me up if you like?"

"It seems a crime to wake a sleeping beauty."

Gwen laughed. She'd been called handsome, and even striking, but no one had ever described her as beautiful before. "I see you've ditched the chaperone?"

"Mother isn't being as insistent as before. And Father tends to follow her lead. Officially, we've got one, but right now? I'm all yours." Ava's dimples were showing. How could her smile look both innocent and wicked at the same time?

"Mmm. That sounds divine." Gwen eyed her up and down, allowing her lust to rise to her eyes. "I assume you had plans in mind when you summoned me?"

"Why yes, as a matter of fact I did."

"And they are?" Gwen loved that Ava had grown more confident in asking for what she wanted. They'd grown more comfortable with each other in many ways, even as they were still discovering new things about each other's bodies.

"Cleanliness." Ava's tone was decisive. "It's next to godliness, you know."

"So I've heard." It was all Gwen could do not to laugh. She suspected that what they were about to get up to wouldn't be very godly at all. Well, maybe one or two of the less reputable Gods.

"You're going to clean me. Thoroughly."

"Clean isn't the same word as wash. How thoroughly were you thinking?" She had a fair idea, but she didn't want to be wrong. Besides, it was hot hearing her spell it out.

"Extremely thoroughly."

"For the purposes of...?" Oh yes, she was going to enjoy hearing this.

"Making me clean enough to slide your tongue into. Tonight. I want you behind me, your tongue as far up my back passage as you can possibly make it go." Her eyes flashed. She knew Gwen liked her to state what she wanted. In detail. "So right now, you are going to use those beautiful fingers of yours to make sure I'm... shall we say, clean enough to eat?"

"Oh Gods." Gwen gulped audibly. It was more or less what she'd expected, though she'd thought Ava would be slightly less explicit in her explanation. "Your wish is my command, my Princess."

They had stripped naked and entered the bath together. They'd done this several times by now, but Gwen always found the experience of soaking in warm water with Ava almost spiritual in the contentment it engendered.

"Would you rather start with kisses, or by washing each other's backs?" She wasn't nervous. Well, not the way she had been when they first started doing this.

Okay, maybe she was still a bit nervous.

"Washing backs. Then kisses. I'll start." Ava grabbed the loofah and some soap, and Gwen turned her back. Those small hands running over her body made her feel like the queen of the world.

After several minutes, it was Gwen's turn to wash Ava. She still felt awed whenever she was allowed to touch the beautiful young woman. Maybe it would be best to start their touches while they weren't looking each other in the eyes.

For now, she contented herself with soaping up her princess' back, one hand holding the loofah and the other following with fingers. The feel of her soft, smooth skin under her fingertips made Gwen feel reverential, like she was worshipping one of the Gods themselves. She could feel her own heartrate and breathing pick up, even though she would have thought she'd be used to this by now.

Perhaps I'll never get used to it. Wouldn't that be nice?

Ava's waist was small, curving out smoothly in both directions. Gwen couldn't resist reaching around slightly as she washed, brushing her soapy fingertips against the underside of Ava's wonderfully rounded breast. The princess' sharp intake of breath did not sound at all displeased with her.

After she had thoroughly washed Ava's back, including around her collarbones, breasts and hips, the princess turned and looped her arms casually around her neck. Letting go of the loofah, she wound her own arms around the smaller body, and smiled at her betrothed.

"Kisses?" Ava suggested, making no move but smiling like the cat who got the cream.

"As you wish." She returned the smile, then dipped her head to press her lips against Ava's. She tugged the smaller body in close to hers, pressing one hand to the small of her back and the other between her shoulder blades. The closeness of that position, the merging of their breasts into each other, the soft brush of their stomachs and the hard press of their upper thighs, all served to set Gwen's senses reeling. She moaned softly, and Ava took advantage of her parted lips to deepen the kiss.

One of Gwen's hands came up and found a perfect breast, her palm brushing lightly over the hardened nipple as she enjoyed the subtle weight of it. They moaned in unison, and the stroking of tongues became a dance between them.

Gwen had no idea how much time had passed when Ava pulled back, breathing heavily. It could have been seconds, or it could have been hours, and either way would have been wonderful.

"I think I'm ready now." Ava's eyes left no ambiguity about what she meant, and Gwen didn't press her to spell it out a second time.

Gwen gently turned Ava by her hips. After the briefest resistance, the princess accepted the direction and turned her back. Gwen held one hand firmly on Ava's lower belly, providing stability as she used her foot to nudge her legs apart. Her other hand applied soft pressure to Ava's upper back, encouraging her to lean over the edge of the bath. Gwen hadn't taken control like this before, and the feeling of Ava following her unspoken directions willingly was as much a turn-on as when the princess took command of her.

She pulled her up onto her tiptoes, using light pressure to direct the motion. Ava's hips were now clear of the water, and her torso angled downward to the marble edge of the bath. Gwen soaped up her hands and stroked gently around her lower back, hips, and upper thighs. Sliding her hand between, she spread her legs slightly wider until her fingers could move freely. The water was taking some of the soap away, but there was enough around to slide easily into the crease at the top of one thigh.

Gwen was taking her time, enjoying the way Ava responded to her touches. Every time she moved her hand, the princess would shift her weight, trying to make contact, but Gwen stayed tantalisingly out of reach. When she finally moved just enough so that the very tips of her fingers played along the cleft between her princess' cheeks, Ava let out a moan so heartfelt it sounded ripped from her very soul. Gwen paused, holding her firmly with one hand while the other trailed fingers ever so gently up and down her sensitive flesh.

"More, damn you Gwen," Ava panted the words out. She sounded frustrated, but in such a good way.

The steadying hand moved from her lower stomach, down to cup her sex lightly. Gwen could feel heat radiating from her, and her swollen clit protruded just far enough to graze her palm. Ava gasped. This wasn't what she'd asked for, but she wanted it.

Ava's hips began rocking against her hands. The light, teasing touches were too difficult to maintain, so she didn't try. Two fingers around the front slid into the wetness, one on either side of her swollen centre, and at the back she went from teasing along a crease to slipping between perfectly rounded cheeks.

Well, she did say she wanted me to clean her back here…

The princess' gasp had become a series of guttural moans as she undulated in Gwen's hands. She picked up a little extra soapy water on the way through, maintaining the pretence that this was all about hygiene.

"Oh Gods, if you keep this up I'm going to..." Her words trailed off into groans, but the point was clear. Gwen tried to slow the motions, wanting to keep her princess in this state as long as she could.

Her fingers found the crinkled skin that she was supposed to be washing. She found some extra suds, and her slippery fingertip slid inside to the first knuckle. Ava's groan turned almost anguished, and it was all Gwen could do to keep them both still as she got used to it – she wasn't quite ready for this to be over.

Widening her fingers up front, she pulled her fingertip out, slid the soapy water around the outside, and slipped back inside a little deeper, being ever so careful not to push past what Ava could comfortably take.

"Gods, Gwen, do you have any idea what you do to me?" Her back was arched, her fingertips white from gripping the side of the bath.

"Do you really need me to answer that?" Gwen slid her finger a little deeper, beckoning very slightly with the tip. The groan she received in return sent shivers up her spine and dampness down her thighs.

Judging her to be ready, she let her front fingers close again and began stroking slowly. Pumping very gently with her other hand, she worked her way in until her knuckles met resistance. She stopped trying to control Ava's movements, and instead stepped closer so her own body was pressed against hers as she bucked wildly against her.

Ava tensed up, and she could feel the spasms gripping her finger. She pressed her centre hard against Ava's hip and joined her as she came.

When the stars had stopped flashing and they were both back to some semblance of reality, Gwen very gently disentangled herself. She was grinning like a fool, and she took the opportunity to kiss Ava tenderly on the mouth.

"Well, really, Gwen," Ava laughed when she had her wits about her again. "Just how long do you think your tongue *is*?"

Chapter Eleven – Betrothed

It was later. Ava was sprawled happily across her chest, as she often ended up on evenings such as this. She twitched her fingers slightly, and Gwen felt delicious aftershocks shiver through her. They had not untangled yet.

"Mmm. I could get used to this." Ava's murmur sounded extremely content.

"Is this... what you expected? When you asked me to marry you?"

Ava laughed softly. "No. I suspected we could be friends. And I'd never really expected to marry someone I could be friends with, so that seemed like a nice bonus. But I didn't expect... this much friendship." Her blush was adorable.

"You didn't think you'd be friendly with your consort? Rumours of palace intrigue are usually exaggerated when not entirely made up, but I'd heard that King Harald had given you several years to choose your own spouse." She hesitated. "I don't know a lot, but history books suggest heirs are usually promised before they're old enough to wed; sometimes years before."

"Yes, Father gave me some time to choose for myself. But the people – mostly men – he considered suitable candidates were..." Ava paused, casting around for the right word. "Not people I wanted to spend my life with."

"Like Lord Forquitte?"

"Oh Gods, Reginald was the worst of the lot of them. I feel sorry for whoever he does end up marrying – word is he's now chasing Holyoake's heir. I should have realised I'd end up promised to him if I didn't choose for myself in time; he's the most powerful bachelor in the Realm, and the royal family must marry for power." Her lips twisted sardonically.

"How did you know I wouldn't be as bad? I mean, as the average noble. Not the Earl. I know the odds of being as bad as him were pretty low." She smiled, showing Ava she wasn't being too serious.

"A couple of reasons. Firstly, your motivations were pretty simple. You wanted money to support your mother and brother. I could give you that without compromising anything that mattered to me. Secondly, you swore the Oath without hesitating for a moment. You were willing to put your life on the line for me when you didn't even know me; it made me fairly confident you wouldn't abuse any rights you gained as my spouse." Ava smiled at that, showing her dimples the way she always did when wicked thoughts occurred to her. The smile vanished as she continued. "Finally, of course, I was out of options. My chance to take an average noble instead of Reginald had passed – I'd met all the eligible ones and hadn't picked any. I now needed to fall in love both spectacularly and publicly, or I would end up married to a brute who would make my life miserable."

Gwen nodded. Their earlier discussions seemed a lifetime ago, but it all fell together. "So you weren't holding out to meet someone you actually fell in love with?"

Ava's snort was derisive. "Gods no. Growing up surrounded by all of this killed off any childish impulses to believe in love. All the grand romances were much like ours – played up for politics. And honestly, I suspect ours is better than most of theirs in the bedroom despite also being faker than a rooster's egg." She paused for a moment, then continued in a slightly gentler tone. "Why? Did you hope to one day marry for love?"

Gwen's smile was rueful. "No. Not since I was still in skirts and pigtails. Once I took up bounty hunting my prospects became a lot more limited, but even with the full field open to me there was never a man worth giving up my independence for. And while it may be acceptable to marry a woman in the Capital, where I come from it really isn't."

"Would you have? If it had been?" The quiet sincerity in the question made Gwen pause and take a moment to consider her answer.

"Perhaps. A woman wouldn't have made me stay home cooking and cleaning and tending to a horde of children. But it was never an option, and it wasn't as if I ever fell in love with anyone anyway. I'd stopped believing in it; much like you by the sounds of it."

"I guess we should both consider ourselves lucky, then. The arrangement we have is much better than any marriage I could have hoped for – and it sounds like it's much the same for you?" The hopeful upward inflection at the end was slight, but it was there.

"Definitely. We have passion, and we have affection. What need have we for love?" Gwen's smile was cavalier. She hoped Ava couldn't see that she was lying.

They spent a lot of time together over the next few weeks. Gwen taught Ava how to make herself a bow, as well as the basics of fletching arrows. Ava's bow was laughably light, but the joy in her eyes when she finally managed to get six arrows into a pumpkin at thirty paces was very real.

At the same time, Ava was teaching her some botany – which plants had medicinal uses, and which ones were toxic; which ones were liked by various wild animals, and which could be used to keep vermin down. Ava also taught her some gardening skills, because plants that merely looked and smelled nice were valuable too.

Gwen thoroughly enjoyed her lessons. She knew the princess was highly intelligent, but seeing the depth and breadth of her knowledge was awe inspiring. Her gentle patience when it came to lessons was another thing that filled Gwen's heart. They knelt in the dirt together tending seedlings, and they stood over a mortar and pestle or a boiling pot together making ointments and tinctures.

The lessons with the seneschal on estate management and planning were less fun. But she needed to know these things if she was going to be useful to Ava as her consort. Some of those lessons she attended by herself, while others they went to together.

Finally, there were the days spent at court. Ava described these as 'practical politics' – she got to hear grievances from nobles and common folk alike, and watch the King dispense his wisdom. A large portion of the time his wisdom appeared to be just telling the feuding parties to come up with a fair solution between them or else he'd make life more difficult for both of them. When it worked, he got praised for his wisdom. When it didn't, he got praised for his strength. Ava told her that this part – raising the prestige of the monarch no matter the outcome – was the important one. Gwen thought it was important that people actually got justice when they came for it. Ava just laughed fondly at that and told her that the few monarchs who could achieve both at once were remembered down the ages.

Between all of this, they still found time to sneak off and kiss in secluded corners, and they woke in each other's arms more often than not.

They'd had another thoroughly pleasurable evening together, and Ava was lying sprawled across Gwen, as was her habit. Gwen found herself fighting down a touch of melancholy. True, life was wonderful in all the ways they'd discussed – but she could feel herself falling in love with the princess, and she knew that Ava didn't welcome that. Didn't even believe in it. So she fought against her feelings and fought down the sadness that accompanied that struggle.

She tried to think of the good things. There were plenty of them.

"Do you want children one day?" Ava asked suddenly.

Gwen blinked. Where had that come from? She herded her thoughts away from their wanderings and toward this new conversation. "I've never really thought about it. It doesn't matter, though, does it? We can't have them."

"Not without help, no." Ava had that patient tone she got when Gwen was being slow on the uptake.

"So... what? You want me to carry a baby for you?"

"No. At least, not our first." Ava shrugged, still mostly lying on top of her. "Any babe you bear wouldn't be our heir. It's a stupid law, but there you go."

"And any child you bear is next in line. Makes sense."

"Not quite." Ava looked a little amused. She seemed to take great joy in discovering things Gwen hadn't ever had to think about before. "If I bear a bastard, it'd be named Fitz and inherit nothing. Well, no titles – and my family doesn't have much personal wealth separate from the Crown. But if we're married and you declare the babe yours, it's legitimate and our heir."

Gwen considered this. "Isn't this something you should have brought up when you asked me to marry you? After all, it sounds like I have a lot of power, here. What would you do if I didn't want kids?"

"Not have them, I guess." Ava gave a small smile. "I had bigger problems at the time, and your answer wasn't going to change my plans. I want children, but I'm flexible on timeframe, and I don't want them more than I want *not* to have to marry Reginald. Besides, I think I told you before that I have cousins who can be my heirs if it comes to that."

"Okay. So who would you ask to help? And how deeply are we inviting whoever he is into our lives?

"Your choice. And not at all."

Gwen blinked, feeling slow. "What?"

"My consort choses her stand in. And he has no rights beyond the right to say no to you – which most men wouldn't, by the way. Angering the princess' consort is not seen as wise. As far as the law is concerned, it's you getting me pregnant and it's you who parents the child."

"I see." It was a lot to take in.

Ava seemed to sense how overwhelmed she was. "Hey, it's alright. We don't need to decide this right now. Let's just have a bit more time cuddling before sleep." Suiting her words, she nuzzled her face into Gwen's shoulder.

"It's just that you've given me a lot to think about, that's all. Cuddling sounds just wonderful to me."

She held her close until sleep overtook them both.

"Gwen! Gwen! Wait up!" Nicholas was wearing his heavy apron from the forge, and his hair was a mess, but he looked jubilant.

"Hello to you, too," Gwen said with a smile.

"It's been forever since I last got to talk to you. Don't you miss me?" His eyes were wide and innocent, like a puppy. The effect was somewhat spoiled by the fact that he was filling out with muscle and didn't look as much like a child as he had even a few weeks back.

"It's been little over a week. It was longer than that when I left Farrowdown."

"Yeah, but then you were fighting dragons and becoming the Chosen One. This time you're just learning boring administrative stuff. Nowhere near as awesome." His smile was teasing, a little brother trying not to show how proud he was of his big sister.

"I never fought the dragon, and what's with this 'Chosen One' business?"

"Oh. Um. Master Avery said I wasn't to say." Nick's blush was adorable, but also slightly troubling.

"He did, did he? Did he say why?" She was genuinely curious. Master Avery was a little eccentric, but not usually secretive. On the contrary, he'd talk your ear off if you gave him half a chance to.

"Something about prophecy being in flux. If I tell you too soon, you might make different choices and not end up being the Chosen One after all?"

"Would that be a bad thing? Heroes in stories usually end up in danger."

"Um. I reckon you'll be in danger anyway. If you're chosen, though, you have the favour of the Gods to shield you? I think. Something like that."

"Well, I guess you'd better not tell me, then." She smiled at him. Prophecy all seemed a little esoteric to her, and she wasn't entirely convinced even Master Avery understood it all that well. Still, she was genuinely proud of her brother.

It was only a couple of weeks to go before their wedding. Thanks to their time with the seneschal, Gwen knew exactly how much the grand event was costing. Of course, she also knew exactly how much gold was in the treasury.

Perspective was a strange thing – the cost of her silk brocade doublet and hose, along with its fashionable half-cloak, would have horrified her half a year ago. Now, it was among the smallest items on a list that just didn't seem quite real to her.

Especially not when she and the princess were currently in old clothes, kneeling in the garden and weeding around the medicinal herbs.

"Forquitte is in with the King now. Word is he's already married Jane Holyoake."

"Yes. Father asked if I wanted to be there when he greeted them. I didn't." There was no particular emotion to her voice, and her weeding didn't change.

"They weren't betrothed at the time of the tourney, were they? I know he was talking to the Duke about it, but I don't think I could have missed that. Besides, it was less than three months ago that he was claiming he was going to marry *you*."

"The three months is tradition for the royal family. The lower born, the shorter the wait. For an Earl and the heir to a Duchy it's two months."

"That seems weird. Still, I'm glad he's safely married off."

"He could still be trouble. And while Jane and I have never been close, I still worry for her." She paused, looking at Gwen a touch strangely. "Why does it seem weird, though? How long were betrothals in Farrowdown?"

"Betrothals are a thing of the nobility. I've never come across them before meeting you."

"Come, now. Are you claiming that people in your town married the day they decided to?" Ava clearly knew the answer to that.

"No, of course not. It takes time to arrange a wedding. Besides, there are –" She stopped, suddenly. "Oh. Did you mean the Banns of Marriage? Those have to be read two weeks before the date."

"The Banns, yes. An opportunity for someone to come forward saying one party or the other is already married, or is underage, or they're too closely related. Other reasons, I'm sure, but those are the top three. The higher the rank, the more important it is that such things are discovered before the wedding takes place, and thus the longer the traditional delay between betrothal and marriage."

Gwen loved the way she sounded when she was in full lecture mode. She didn't love her own ignorance on so many things, but Ava didn't seem to mind.

"I see. The most powerful Earl in the Realm marrying the heir to the largest Duchy seems like a bit of a big deal. Is the King concerned at all about so much power in one pair of hands?"

"Well, we may have some terrible traditions when it comes to acceptable behaviour of men versus women, but we're not completely in the dark ages. When Jane becomes Duchess, she will not cede power to her consort any more than he has ceded power to her on their marriage. Besides, Holyoake isn't even fifty yet, and is strong and healthy for his age. It will be some time before the titles consolidate into a single powerful entity."

"Really?" Gwen gave her a sceptical look. "Jane didn't look as strong-willed as you are, and you were concerned about Forquitte wielding your power by terrorizing you. Why do you think she's immune?"

Ava looked slightly troubled. "I don't. But a Duchess has a lot more ability to divorce and damn the consequences than a Queen does. She doesn't have vassals who will rise against her on his side – because he isn't one of them. Lubrey isn't a part of Holyoake's

214

duchy of Eastwall, it's directly under the Crown." She thought for a second, not looking happy. "She's got a rough time ahead of her, and I'd love to be able to talk to her without him, but I'm guessing she's decided that having an heir who will inherit both titles is worth the risks and horrors of being his wife."

"Either that or her father did."

"You may be right. She's only twenty; she's been married off close to as early as she can be. Her father will have had a hand in it. Mine may well have done, too." A mix of relief tinged with guilt crossed Ava's face.

"I was wondering. But then I also wondered if he would want a single vassal controlling two of the most powerful estates in the Realm."

"Well, it won't be his problem. It might be ours, though. I ought to strengthen my friendship with Jane Holyoake – we haven't spoken much recently, and she was still a child when I was coming of age, so we were never that close. We could also offer to take any child they might have in as a ward, should they wish outside tutoring."

Gwen nodded thoughtfully, resuming her weeding. "I heard some of the squires gossiping about Lubrey being beset by raiders in recent weeks. Do you think King Harald might send some of the Kingsguards to help secure his lands?"

Ava snorted. "While I have no sympathy for the man, his serfs need protection. They're a long way from the Capital, though – it's more likely Father will send gold to aid his vassal in raising his own men. There are whisperings of Ogres, which sounds unlikely, but we can't afford to leave him without aid."

"Whyever not? He's the most powerful Earl in the Realm, surely you're not worried that Lubrey might fall to mere raiders?" Gwen was confused, and knew it showed in her tone.

"There's no good outcome to letting him fend for himself." Ava's voice was gentle, instructing without reproach. "If he fails, the Realm shrinks. And if he succeeds, what need had he of the King? No, we send aid, and hold up our end of the grand bargain. I suspect they're working out the details of how much aid is needed and what we should be sending in return as we speak."

"I can see I still have a lot to learn." Gwen gave a rueful smile.

Ava's return smile was fond. Reassuring. "You have all the time you need."

Four days before their wedding, her mother arrived at the Capital.

Gwen and Ava were at the archery butts. Ava had graduated to a forty-pound draw weight, and after twelve weeks of practice could reliably get a group the size of her two hands together at fifty paces.

It was the page Elfrida who bore the news, of course. "Your Highness." She made a bow that was getting less rough, then turned to address Gwen. "Sir Gwendoline, Rose Carter is here to see you. She's waiting in the smallest audience room."

Gwen looked at Ava, who looked back. "Would you like me with you?" The princess asked. "Or would you prefer your reunion with your mother to be private?"

She never knew how the princess could add up the little things she said and work out what she needed. "I think I'd like to face her alone at first. She's here for the wedding, of course, so you'll have to meet her, but it can wait a few hours."

"May the Gods bless your meeting." Ava kissed her cheek lightly. The formal benediction calmed her, and she smiled.

"Lead on, then." Elfrida scurried off ahead of her.

"Mother," Gwen increased her pace when she saw her, and enfolded her in a warm embrace. She didn't know how this was going to go, but despite her trepidations she loved her mother dearly.

"Gwen, look at you." She held Gwen by the shoulders, reaching up to do so. Rose Carter was taller than most, but still half a head shorter than her daughter. "You look healthy. Happy. I'm glad."

"I'm glad you could make it. A woman likes to have her mother with her at her wedding." She smiled, broaching the subject with warmth. She wanted her mother to be happy for her.

"Yes, well." Rose's eyes drifted sideways for a moment before her smile reaffixed itself. "Anything to make my daughter happy."

Gwen knew she should leave it. Her mother was being nice, there wasn't going to be a scene, and she didn't need to reopen old wounds. She could pretend to take the kindness at face value, and trust that her mother would adore Ava when she met her. But it felt off, and she couldn't make herself let it go.

"Are you happy for me, mother?" She prodded, but gently.

Rose sighed. "You're marrying the princess, dear. I'm proud, but I'm also worried. Things are different here."

"I'm glad you're proud. Yes, things are different, but I'm learning. Being a consort is a job as much as bounty hunting was. I'm learning what I need to be a good right hand for Ava."

"Of course you are, my darling girl. You have a strong sense of duty, always have, and I can't imagine you doing less than your best. No, I'm worried that others won't do their best by *you*, my dear."

"What do you mean? The King and Queen have been nothing but welcoming to me."

"I'm sure. I've also heard rumours that you're already getting caught up in…" Her mother's lips twisted in distaste. "In the deviancy that is rife within the Capital."

Gwen sighed. Here it was. "You're fine with me marrying a woman, but not with me kissing her first? Am I understanding you correctly?"

"Gwen. Darling. I've always known you wouldn't marry a man. I've made peace with that. But I've also always known that the only place you could go where you could marry a woman was the one place whose morals were so low that no one would be worthy of you." Her tone was sharp.

"Wait, so is it the kissing you're objecting to or not?" Gwen was getting confused, and her mother wasn't helping.

"Kissing? Rumours have the two of you getting up to more than that. A few simple kisses I'd have no issue with. But I'm not sure I'm happy with you binding yourself to someone who doesn't see any need to wait out a few short months of betrothal! You've known her, what, three months?"

Gwen raked her fingers through her hair, wishing it was bound back in her usual plait. "There are good reasons for that, mother. There was… another interested party."

Rose scoffed. "Of course there was. Did she try to convince you to join the pair of them in bed?"

"Good Gods no!" Gwen was horrified. "We were just trying to make sure he knew she wasn't interested in him. By flaunting how interested she is in me. I'm sorry if hearing rumours about us embarrassed you, mother, but there were reasons."

"And her word wasn't enough? She couldn't just tell this knave 'no, I'm not interested in you'? Is this the story you believe? The story you want *me* to believe?"

"What other story could there be?" Gwen was confused, and defensive, and beginning to feel a little angry. "This knave is a powerful Earl, and no, he wasn't the safest to say 'no' to."

"If she's telling you the truth, she's made you a powerful enemy. Not exactly a loving action, is it? More likely, though, it's just a ruse to get you to accept moral weakness, and the *laissez faire* sexual mores of the Capital."

"Oh good grief, mother. A little bit of premarital fooling around – with the woman I'm betrothed to, I might add! Anyone would think we were having orgies in the palace garden." Gwen paused, took a breath, then added softly, "I knew about the powerful enemy before I agreed to marry her, you know. She warned me. I wasn't blindsided."

"Oh, Gwen, you're such an innocent in so many ways. The fooling around I wouldn't have an issue with if I'd found out in a way that suggested you were being discreet. As you say, you're going to be married to her soon anyway. But the flaunting of it! She's softening you up to accept other indignities later on. And I'm worried you're not going to notice until you've accepted more than you ever thought you would."

"It sounds like you have specific concerns, mother. Out with them." Gwen folded her arms, waiting.

"Alright. I think you're going to find one day she'll cheat on you, come home pregnant, and pressure you to proclaim the bastard yours. That's what I'm worried about."

Gwen laughed. "Oh, mother. We've discussed children. If anything like what you're suggesting occurs, it will be a man I choose. Or it won't happen at all if I don't choose. It's not going to come out of left field – she's given me all the power."

Rose's eyebrows raised. "Did she suggest using your brother as your surrogate?"

"Gods, no!" Gwen's face showed the disgust she felt. "Nicholas is a child. Ava didn't suggest anyone, but no, she's allowed to say no, and she wouldn't accept any boy within years of Nick's age. That's just gross."

"Well, I'm glad you're so sure she's no paedophile, dear."

"Mother! That's your Princess you're talking about! Not to mention my future wife. Can you at least try not to be so insulting?" She knew she wasn't holding her rage in. Right now, she didn't care.

"You're the one who insisted on knowing my misgivings, dear." Rose adjusted the flowers pinned to her hat. "Do you remember when Nicholas was barely walking? You would have only been a couple of years older than he is now. You got caught fooling around with the miller's daughter in the field out the back of the mill."

Gwen scowled. "I remember. You yelled at me until I thought you were going to throw me out of home. It was right after father died – before the money ran out and I had to earn enough for all of us."

Rose nodded slowly. "I was angry with you, yes. You should have known better. But I don't think you knew the whole story."

"I remember she wouldn't talk to me again after that. Angela, her name was. She avoided me the rest of the year and married the farrier's lad the next Spring." Gwen was surprised there was still bitterness within her when she spoke of that.

"Yes, yes, all that's true, but did you know that the miller wanted to take you out into the field and put an arrow in your skull that night? Did you know how hard I had to beg him to let you off with the scolding I gave you? The whole village hearing me rage at you was part of the bargain for your life, Gwen. He had to see you as a wayward child, one who was being disciplined, before he would accept that you weren't a beast who had defiled his daughter. A beast who needed to be put down."

Gwen's eyes and mouth made perfect matching circles. Her anger had melted into shock. She didn't realise she'd come so close to being on the receiving end of the brutal informal justice that sometimes happened in small towns.

Rose's eyes softened. "You really never knew, did you? Well, why would you have? I couldn't tell you at the time in case you didn't act like a chastised child. I'd assumed you'd work it out sooner or later, though. You never did?"

"How could I have? Angela and I never even did anything. We never so much as kissed. We were caught cuddling on the ground with slightly askew clothing from horsing around earlier. That was enough that her father wanted me put down like a rabid dog? No, I never knew." Gwen grimaced, feeling sick.

"Oh my darling girl. I'm so sorry." The compassion in her mother's eyes was too much, and Gwen began to weep on her shoulder. "The things I had to do to you to keep you safe..."

The next day Gwen's mother found them while they were reading together in the library.

They didn't often find time for it, but Gwen enjoyed discussing books with her princess. They would take a tome into a side room built for the purposes of academic discussion, and while they were talking about matters of philosophy she would feel connected to her. Ava always took her ideas seriously and seemed genuinely surprised by some of the things she said, but never belittled her or made her feel less for her untutored ideas. If anything, she seemed impressed by her thinking.

They were discussing the paradox of the hare and the tortoise – that in a race, the quickest runner can never overtake the slowest, since the pursuer must first reach the point whence the pursued started, so that the slower must always hold a lead – when Rose gently opened the door.

"Am I interrupting anything?" She asked.

"Mother! We were just discussing the nature of paradox. Please, come in."

"Your Highness," Rose curtseyed to the princess as she entered.

"Please, call me Ava. You're about to be my mother-in-law, after all." Ava smiled, her dimples making it look charmingly sweet and genuine.

"Ava, then. A pleasure to meet you at last." Rose's smile was slightly guarded, but Gwen knew she was doing her best.

"Oh! I'm so sorry. Mother, this is my betrothed, Princess Ava. Ava, this is my mother, Rose Carter." She wasn't sure if she had the order correct. There was so much etiquette around introductions, but it hadn't seemed the most pressing thing to learn these past few weeks.

Ava smiled at her fondly. "Yes, dear. We'd worked that out." She patted her hand, and Gwen felt a little foolish, but comforted none the less.

"Well, there are a couple of things a woman wants to know about the person marrying her daughter." Rose's face was friendly, but there was steel underneath.

"Of course. The Crown doesn't hide a lot from the public." Ava's smile faded somewhat, taking Gwen's mother seriously. "What would you ask of me?"

"The most important question. Do you love my daughter?"

"Of course I do. With all my heart." The seriousness in her voice, in her eyes as she met Rose's gaze, was almost enough to break Gwen's heart. She knew it for the lie it was, but her treacherous heart wanted it to be true, and Ava was a skilled actress.

Rose held her gaze for three long breaths, before nodding slowly. "Good. You will never meet anyone as loyal or as dutiful as my Gwen. I want to know she has your loyalty in return."

"She has. Absolutely." This one might not even be a lie. Not a deliberate one, anyway. Ava almost certainly did believe her devotion to Gwen was as strong as Gwen's to her.

"Will your family accept her? Will she be your wife in truth, or will others view this as a game?"

Ava looked confused for a second but recovered and answered as forcefully as before. "Of course she will be my wife in truth. She will be my consort, and all members of my family accept that. All members of the nobility will accept it, too. And to the best of my knowledge, common folk in backwater towns merely accept that royalty is strange at times. But everyone who accepts that I'm the King's heir will accept that Gwen is my consort. This is no game."

Ava's eyes flashed. She wasn't used to people questioning their relationship, and it seemed to affront her that it was Gwen's mother who was doing it.

"Her family has been nothing but welcoming to me, mother," Gwen interjected. "I told you that already. No one treats me as a pawn in someone's game."

"I had to hear it from her." Rose's voice was gentle. "You're a good girl, Gwen, but you're too trusting. I don't think you'd know the difference between genuine acceptance and the humouring of a wilful and wayward daughter."

The soft tone raised her hackles. She was never as sure as she wanted to be of how her mother saw her – was she a grown woman who had supported her family for over a decade, or was she a child who needed to be shown the correct path? Was she free to make her own choices, or did her mother still feel she had the right to set her on the one true path? Was her mother proud of her, or not? And why, after so long, were the answers still so important to her?

"Your daughter isn't as naïve as you think." Ava was firm, not accepting anyone putting Gwen down. "She's trusting, it's true, but she can tell where it isn't deserved."

Rose smiled. "I can see you care for her. I'm glad. Tell me, which of the Gods are you planning on saying your vows before?"

"By tradition, the royal family says our vows before Mother Earth or Father Sky. Gwen and I decided that it felt appropriate to kneel to the Goddess."

"Kneeling in the dirt in your wedding finery is a royal tradition, is it? You *do* do things strangely sometimes, don't you?" Rose looked amused, but not unkind.

"There's supposed to be some fine religious tradition about the purity of being close to the Goddess as you say your vows, but I've always been of the opinion that it's more about showing off how wealthy we are. For the wedding of the heir, wealthy enough to ruin clothes worth more than some people earn in a year. Everything always comes back to power and prestige."

Rose pursed her lips thoughtfully and nodded. It appeared Ava had won her approval.

Chapter Twelve – A Royal Wedding

Three days later they were married.

The Royal Wedding was a much briefer ceremony than Gwen had been expecting. True, it was substantially longer for Ava – she paraded around the city one last time as an unmarried heir, waving at her subjects while dressed in her finery and riding the most elegant of the royal coaches. Gwen merely had to be present in the grove of Mother Earth at high noon.

Ava's dress was a sight to behold. They both wore green, of course, as was the custom when saying vows before the Goddess. Ava's was the palest honeydew, with golden scrollwork so tightly embroidered on the bodice that it looked more gold than green. Her skirts were wide and her train long, allowing eight pages to hold it off the ground. She'd mentioned that they were her cousins' children – it seemed her airy claim that there were plenty of potential heirs without her procreating was perfectly true.

Gwen's doublet was a darker forest green, with climbing vines up the sleeves. She waited nervously at the edge of the grove, her brother wearing blue at her side. As her oldest male kin, he would be presenting her to the Princess to be her bride. Gwen found it odd that she was garbed as a knight but still given away; apparently it was more to do with rank than with spectacle.

"Breathe, Gwen." Nicholas had evidently noticed her rising panic.

"It's fine, Nicholas. I hear it's normal for brides to be nervous on their wedding day?" She smiled. They were at the edge of the grove, out of sight of the audience, waiting for Ava to make her grand entrance.

"Not sure about that. From what Mistress Thatcher tells me, that's mostly because men aren't always the most considerate on their wedding nights. And you're not marrying a man, so maybe you'll be alright?"

Gwen snorted. What was he learning at that forge? "I'm not worried about... that. I'm more worried that I'll make a mess of the ceremony, to be honest."

"How can you? I saw the outline on Master Avery's desk. It looked even simpler than ceremonies back home – and you're not even jumping over a broom, so there's no chance you'll fall flat on your face there, either." He glanced back over her shoulder. "Shh – here she is."

The sight of Ava took Gwen's breath away. The dress was even more magnificent than she'd recalled; the thread-of-gold most intricately embroidered on the bodice, but with dots and looser whorls all around the hem. Pearls climbed her sleeves and lined the edge of her train. Her hair was an intricate collection of small braids and loose curls that appeared freeform and precise all at once. Gwen was staring and couldn't make herself stop.

Trumpets blasted a fanfare to herald her arrival, and she walked to the front of the grove, attended by her small cousins. Once there, she turned and faced Gwen. The smile on her face was nervous, which helped settle Gwen's own nerves somewhat. She wasn't alone. They would get through this.

The music changed, and it was time for Gwen to be presented to the Princess. Nicholas offered his arm. "Shall we?"

She nodded and took it. Smiling at her betrothed, she approached the sacred trees.

Gwen's heart hammered as she listened to the Priestess of Mother Earth. She couldn't listen to the words. She'd respond when it was her turn, of course, but while they were just kneeling on the ground in their finery, she only had enough attention for Ava.

She didn't know exactly when it had happened. She thought perhaps before they started sleeping together, though she'd been in denial for most of the last three months. But somewhere along the way she'd fallen head over heels in love with this beautiful, intelligent, courageous woman. She didn't bother hiding it – she was supposed to look in love on her wedding day, after all – but she hoped Ava would take it as affection played up for the crowds.

For her part, Ava looked radiant. Joyous. Absolutely thrilled to be where she was, doing what she was doing. It could be read as love, if you were so inclined – to Gwen, though, it seemed more like triumph. Triumph laced with affection for her, of course. That was enough. It had to be enough.

"And so, Sir Gwendoline Carter of Essen, it is time." The Priestess intoned her words with full regal solemnity. "Do you swear under the sight of the Goddess to love, honour and obey

Ava von Tryptshire, forsaking all others and owing fealty to none but her, for as long as you both shall live?"

"I do. Under the sight of the Goddess, I so swear." Good. She hadn't messed it up.

"And you, Princess Ava von Tryptshire, heir to the Realm without Night." The intonation had not lessened any. "Do you swear under the sight of the Goddess to love, cherish and keep Gwendoline Carter, heeding her wisdom and caring for none so well as for her, for as long as you both shall live?"

"I do. Under the sight of the Goddess, I so swear." Ava's voice was high, strong, and carried easily out to all listeners.

"Then, by the power granted to me by the King and under the sight of the Goddess, I now proclaim you Princess and Wife. Be upstanding." The briefest of pauses as they stood, holding hands. "You may kiss your bride."

Ava's arms were around her neck, and hers were around the princess' waist. Their lips met softly, melting into each other in a sweet kiss full of promise and romance. They were playing to an audience, of course, but this felt different. Despite herself, Gwen couldn't help feeling that this was real. They'd made vows to one another, and while she knew Ava didn't believe in 'love' she nevertheless believed in keeping her word.

The kiss lasted for less than a minute. It felt far longer.

It was that night, and they were married.

The parading had been interminable but spending that time with Ava was still magical. They had ridden through the streets as a married couple, and it seemed the whole city had come out to cheer them on.

The banquet had been thankfully early. Her dance lessons had allowed Gwen to at least maintain some measure of dignity as they led the other nobles. While rank and precedent had meant Ava had filled the traditionally masculine role for a lot of today, the sheer mechanics of their height disparity dictated that Gwen dance the male part throughout the evening.

The banquet had been filled with nobles and other notables from around the Realm. Gwen had been introduced to seemingly hundreds of people, all dressed in their finery, and all keen to make a good first impression on their heir's new consort. Gwen's head swam from trying to remember so many names.

At last, they had bid their farewells to all their well-wishers, and made their way to their new joint chambers. Much larger than the rooms either of them had occupied alone, this sumptuous space was fit for... well, for royalty. The bed was enormous, canopied with carved wooden columns. The sheets were silk, and the fireplace marble. There were tapestries on the wall, and shelves with books to either side of the door. Gwen couldn't imagine that the King and Queen themselves could possibly have finer.

"And now," Ava said with a grin. "At long last, I've got you all to myself." Her eyes twinkled. "Mother has assured me that no one will be in to disturb us until at least noon. You're all mine."

Gwen smiled, liking the sound of that. "All yours, Princess. As I swore to be."

"Ah, yes, you swore to love, honour and obey. Do you think you can... obey?" Ava had been unbuttoning Gwen's doublet as she spoke, and her eyes held pure mischief.

"What commands would my Royal wife have of me?" Her fingers found the fastenings securing Ava's dress and began the short work of unfastening them.

"I like your enthusiasm, my dear, but wait," her fingers tapped Gwen's sharply on this word. "For instruction. Can you do that?"

"I live to serve, my princess." She stilled her hands, smiling. She was more than willing to play this game.

"Good." Ava purred. "Because tonight, my sweet, you *will* serve."

Gwen gulped as Ava pushed her loosened doublet and hose off to pool on the ground. Within a surprisingly short amount of time she found herself utterly naked.

"Stand very still." Ava stepped back, undressing herself in a most unhurried fashion. As her dress came off, she hung it neatly on a rack Gwen hadn't noticed until just now. Her undergarments were removed slowly. Not so much a tease as an assertion of dominance. Ava was in charge, and she set the pace.

Gwen couldn't take her eyes off her. Yes, she'd seen Ava naked before, but she'd never seen her so filled with raw power. She was intoxicating.

When Ava had removed her last item of clothing, she stood firmly, facing Gwen. A whole head shorter than her, she nevertheless dominated the space, the Queen of their domain. "Bed. I want you in the centre." She jerked her head to point imperiously with her chin. "Arms over your head. Go."

Gwen hastened to obey. She backed quickly to the large, canopied bed, and sat down, shuffling herself in until her hips were in the middle of the bed. She lay back and raised her arms over her head. The bed was huge, but she was tall, so her fingertips brushed the carved headboard.

While she was doing that, she watched Ava walk purposefully to the dresser. She perused the second drawer for a moment before withdrawing several long silk scarfs. She dropped most of them in a careless heap on the chair nearest the bed but carried one bright red length of silk with her as she followed Gwen.

"If things get too much, tell me and I will stop." Ava's voice was still commanding, but there was something gentle in her tone, too. "Do you understand? Can you do that?"

"I understand." She swallowed to get some moisture back in her mouth. "I can do that."

"Good. Because I'm going to tie you up. Tonight, my fearsome knight, you are mine." She began wrapping Gwen's wrists together as she spoke, winding the silk in a figure of eight motion before wrapping the centre like a bowtie. One end went through a hole in the carved wooden frame, and back through another. The knot was a simple bow, and Gwen noticed it was left deliberately within her reach. Ava was in control tonight, but she left Gwen the power to call things off without saying a word.

Ava's smooth side was enticingly close to Gwen's face as she tied the scarf to the bed. Gwen didn't even think before nuzzling her face into her lover's skin. The delicate musculature below her ribs was soft and warm, and the feel of her sent little sparks down her spine.

"Did I say you could move?" Ava's hand was in her hair, pulling her face away. Her expression was fierce, but not angry.

"No, Princess."

"No. I didn't. So why did you?"

"Because." Gwen swallowed and tried again. "Because you're so beautiful."

Ava smiled a little, before hardening her features again. "So you touched me for your own pleasure?"

Gwen lowered her eyes, bashful.

"Tonight, I am touching you for my pleasure. Not the other way around. Do you understand?"

"Yes, Princess."

"And will you obey? As you have sworn to do?" She looked like she was enjoying this.

"Yes, Princess. I will obey."

"Good." Ava drew her fingers slowly down Gwen's chest, the feathery touches leaving gooseflesh in their path. "Because I intend to enjoy myself immensely." Her fingertips just barely avoided Gwen's nipples, which hardened to points in their wake regardless.

Gwen could feel her arousal pooling between her thighs. The tight heat curling in her lower abdomen was sending pulses down lower, and as Ava's fingers teased, she felt her whole body awaken.

She groaned softly, pushing her chest up almost imperceptibly. Ava's fingers stilled until Gwen controlled herself sufficiently to return her chest to its resting position. When the princess was satisfied that she was being obedient, her fingers resumed their ethereal caresses. Gwen groaned once more but succeeded in keeping her body still.

"There's my beautiful knight," Ava's gentle voice approved. "Spread your legs for me. I want to see you."

Gwen obeyed, wantonly displaying herself for her princess. The mere air currents on her overheated flesh were enough to make her twist her body in need. She quickly regained control of herself and lay back down, awaiting Ava's pleasure.

The barely-there touch of her fingertips quested lower, over her taught stomach and across her hips. Ava's touch rustled the downy hair on her outer thighs, leaving more gooseflesh in its path. Gwen caught her breath in a quiet gasp when Ava's fingertips traced around to her inner thighs, stoking her lengthwise from her knees to the crease where her thighs met her centre.

"It's hard, isn't it?" Ava's voice was conversational, as her fingers stroked up and down once more. "To keep still. I can see it in your face. You want to move – to make me touch you more firmly, to make me touch you where you want to be touched. But you can't. You swore to obey, and I want you to stay still."

Gwen stayed still, but the groan she let out in response was heartfelt.

"I love how responsive you are." Ava's voice was barely above a whisper, and Gwen strained to hear. "I'm barely touching you at all, but if I gave you permission, I know you'd unravel on the spot." She shivered. "I love knowing I can do this to you. And I love knowing you *won't* come undone – not until I tell you to."

With those last words she pressed firmly up into Gwen's sopping wet centre, and Gwen cried out. Remaining still was all that was in her head. She had sworn an oath to obey, but resisting her climax was tougher than she would ever have thought possible.

"Oh, yes," Ava breathed. "That's right. Scream for me – but don't you *dare* come." With two fingers she entered her. And Gwen screamed.

She screamed, as though the vocal release could possibly replace the one she so desperately craved.

All her muscles were tight, rigid with the tension of holding off her climax.

234

Ava's fingers pumped in and out, slowly, inexorably. Gwen's muscles were so tight around her, but she was too slick for her grip to impede the princess in any fashion.

A third finger. Ava had added a third finger, and Gwen's rictus was set, her body rigid, struggling to obey. A fourth, and the tightness was more intense than anything she had ever known. Her body quivered on the edge; she was holding herself back by sheer willpower.

Ava's smile as she pushed in past her knuckles was pure lust. "There's my beautiful knight. Not long now. Just hold back a few seconds more..." Her thumb brushed Gwen's clit, and she screamed again, her soul pouring out of her throat as she felt her grip slipping.

Ava pulled out one more time, thrusting in hard, her thumb sweeping over Gwen's hypersensitive flesh. "Now, my darling. Come for me *now*."

And with that, Gwen exploded. The release was like every part of her was ripped apart in pure pleasure. She was dimly aware of Ava's mouth finding her clit, claiming her, sucking her in as her hand pumped furiously in and out. She had no mental energy for cataloguing her sensations. She was fire, and she was air, and she was light.

There was no time, as her body convulsed in pleasure. She thought perhaps she climaxed over and over again; but it could have been all one. She floated in pure ecstasy as her muscles worked themselves to exhaustion.

At last, as the waves of pleasure began bordering on pain, she came back to earth. Ava's touch had gentled considerably; she had not noticed it lessen. Her left leg was coated in wetness – Ava's, she was sure – but she couldn't remember how it got there. The lassitude filling her limbs spread through her body, and awareness was too difficult to hold.

The last thing she heard before blackness overwhelmed her was her princess' awed whisper.

"Oh, my darling, you are *magnificent*."

Chapter Thirteen – Prophecy

As promised, they were left alone until noon. They'd woken up several times through the night, satisfying their need for each other and falling back asleep only to repeat the whole cycle again a couple of hours later. By the time they were forced to face the world once more they'd had plenty of sleep – however broken – and were feeling well rested and relaxed.

As soon as the sun had reached its zenith, there was a polite knock on the door, followed by a guard sticking her head around. "Your Highness, your royal Mother has requested your presence and that of your consort in the main audience chamber as soon as you are dressed. May I report that you will be there?"

"What, no time for breakfast?" Ava's smile was as lazy as a cat's.

"There is a tray of food out here, your Highness. It is important that you both maintain your strength." Her voice gave nothing away, but a twinkle in her eyes indicated she'd been on duty long enough to hear at least some of their earlier activities.

Gwen blushed, but Ava was unconcerned. "Thank you. If you could send it in, you can go tell Mother that we will be there in… shall we say half an hour?" This last question was aimed at Gwen, who nodded.

"Very good, your Highness." The guard bowed and left.

They arrived at the audience chamber to a fanfare of trumpets. Gwen was nervous but tried to copy Ava's confident smile and easy stride. Her clothes felt far too fancy, with their embroidery and jewels on already heavy velvet, but she was the heir's consort, now, so she had to look the part.

There were several nobles milling around, having private conversations. Mostly high ranking, from what she could gather – she saw Duke Holyoake and Earl Forquitte, as well as two other Dukes whose names she couldn't quite remember. The other men and women milling around seemed to be of similar rank. Gwen tried not to stare.

The Queen stood as they entered, and glided over to them, kissing her daughter on each cheek before doing the same to Gwen. "I'm so glad you're here. The Keeper of the Scrolls has news and wanted you present before he announced himself – your brother is being a most useful apprentice, apparently."

Gwen was startled but managed to keep her reactions muted as Ava replied. "Of course. We're happy to hear what Master Avery has to say."

"Yes, Nick hinted that one of the prophecies might be coming to fruition. I must admit I'm curious." Gwen thought she sounded suitably formal, but the fondly amused look Ava shot her had her worried she'd misjudged.

They proceeded – and it did feel like a procession – to the royal dais, where the King bade everyone quiet to hear Master Avery's words.

"My Lords, my Ladies, we live in a time of upheaval," he began. "The dragon flies at night, taking sheep and cattle and terrifying villagers. Why, he took our precious Princess Ava before the daring knight, Sir Gwendoline, stole her back and won her heart. Ogres stir in the mountains, and there is rumour that another barbarian uprising is imminent. In short, we are in a time when prophecy comes to pass."

He paused, looking around the room, catching the eye of each lord and lady in turn and ensuring he had everyone's attention. He did. They all knew by now how Lubrey was beset by ogres.

"As luck would have it, we indeed have a prophecy made for this time. A hero has come to save us – or, should I say, a heroine."

Gwen stiffened. Her brother had called her the Chosen One a few weeks earlier, and this sounded suspiciously like what he had been hinting at.

"Would you care to hear the words of the prophecy? The language of the translation has been supplied by Sir Gwendoline's brother, Nicholas, but I can vouch for the accuracy and clarify any points where he has left the language too flowery."

The King motioned him on impatiently.

Master Avery coughed once and began to read. "And so it shall come to pass, that the Princess shall be taken by the Dragon, and a Hero shall save her. And Lo, that Hero shall be a Knight and Champion of Knights, gifted half the King's lands and his Daughter's hand in marriage."

Gwen could hear the excessive capitals clanging into place with the declamation. After a breath, he continued.

"And the Love between Hero and Princess shall be a shining Beacon to the world of all that is Good and True. But the Dragon still lives, and as the echoes of their Vows still linger in the Grove, the Hero must away to save the Realm."

Another breath. "And the Hero shall be armoured in the Love of the Princess. And she shall wear that armour as she faces the Dragon, and she shall return to her Princess with its head. For the Hero foretold is the Princess' True Love; all dangers to the Realm shall fall before her Wrath, as the Hero who is Chosen and Beloved rides forth to her Destiny."

This breath was accompanied by some nervous movement, and his voice faltered for a second before he picked it up again. "But be warned, ye false Prophet. She who claims to be Chosen and yet is not Beloved shall ride to her Doom; she shall burn in Dragonfire where the fires of Love burn not, and the whole of the Realm shall burn with her."

A silence stretched out as his words ended. Gwen glanced at Ava, who looked startled and a little frightened.

The King was the first to speak. "For prophecy, it seems remarkably clear. There are some points that you might be able to clarify for us, however?"

"By all means ask — I shall answer if I can." Avery bowed his head, still looking nervous.

"It sounds like the Realm shall burn if we get it wrong and send a hero forth who isn't the Chosen One. What happens if we have the Chosen One and do *not* send her out?"

"Your Majesty, if I am correct and this is the time prophesised, we shall be overrun within the year. I don't know which will get us first, but between the dragon, the ogres and the barbarians we are doomed."

"I see." He didn't say anything further.

Gwen spoke up. "If it's talking about me I'll go, but I have concerns." Her main concern was that Ava didn't actually love her, but she couldn't say that in front of the assembled lords and ladies. "Gifted half the kingdom and his daughter's hand in marriage – but the King has only given me a very small parcel of land, and Ava chose me herself; she wasn't gifted. Can we be sure I'm the one?"

Master Avery's smile was gentle. "Half the King's lands is not half the Kingdom – legend tends to garble prophecy. As it happens, King Harald has very little in the way of private property that is his and not owned by the Crown. The small parcel of land he gave you was exactly half of his personal holdings." He looked at Ava briefly and smiled indulgently once more before continuing. "And you were most definitely gifted the King's daughter's hand in marriage – though you are quite correct that she bestowed that gift upon you herself."

Her stomach sank. It didn't seem she could get out of this without revealing their deception. She just had to hope that there would still be a Realm for Ava to rule once the fires had run their course. "I see. Do we know the timeframe it is talking about? It can't be literal – the grove where we said our vows wasn't echoey at all. When do I have to be gone by? Assuming it *is* talking about me, of course."

"This prophecy isn't as specific as I'd like. Cross referencing other prophecies that have already run their course I would hazard that you have at least until tonight and at most until tomorrow."

The Earl of Lubrey spoke in a startlingly loud voice. "And why are you expressing any doubt, Sir Gwendoline? This is as clear as prophecy gets. The world knows of your *inspiring*" – the word dripped venom in his mouth – "love story, and Master Avery has explained how your paltry holdings equal the King's. What are you waiting for? You're the Chosen One. Go forth and save the Realm."

Gwen and Ava exchanged a glance. Ava's eyes were filled with fear and doubt, but her voice was steady as she spoke. "I can armour you, at least. The suit of plate I commissioned for you upon our betrothal has been completed; you should wear it just in case the 'Armour of Love' is a little more literal than most prophecy."

Avery's smile looked forced. "I doubt a suit of plate is what was meant, but protection can't hurt." He seemed to sense an awkward silence forming, and he was the sort of man to rush to fill it. "The funny thing about Old Common is that the parts where it talks about the Princess' love for the Hero relies just as much on the Hero's love for the Princess. It has to be reciprocal to count. A weird quirk of the language – but not anything the two of you need concern yourself with. The whole Realm knows how well you love one another."

Ava's eyes held panic, but Gwen was sure she was the only one who could see it.

"Yes, they do." There was no getting out of this. Her decision was made.

She was about to ride to her death.

Before going to the armoury, they stole a quiet moment together. No one begrudged them that – the prophecy seemed to suggest that Gwen would win, but she was riding into danger and away from her princess, so some time together before she left seemed appropriate.

"You can't go." The door had barely closed on them before Ava was holding Gwen tight, her face pressed into the taller woman's chest.

Gwen's arms wrapped around her Princess. "I have to. I just have to hope the Realm burning is recoverable."

"Sod the Realm and its fires." Ava's voice was fierce, if muffled. "You'll die. I don't want you to go."

She would. She knew she would. But she had to go anyway. "If I don't, Forquitte will raise the lords in rebellion against you – he's riding out as we speak to deal with his ogre problem, and his own troops are already gathered. The only way to explain that I'm not the Chosen One is to reveal our deception. They'll depose your father and kill you."

"Then we run together. This isn't what you agreed to. You never agreed to die for me."

"No. I signed on for a better life for my mother and my brother. If your family survives the fires, you'll give them that, won't you? You'll keep your word?"

"Of course I will. I'm still scared."

"Me too." And if the princess was scared that confirmed it. Her love wasn't reciprocated; she wasn't the Chosen One of prophecy. She was riding out to die.

They took pleasure in each other's bodies one more time before parting. Love or no love, there was sweetness and comfort to be had, and both drank it greedily.

After they were spent, they went and fitted Gwen in the finest plate armour the royal armoury's master smith could produce. It had taken three months, but the fit was perfect, and it gleamed with polish and intricate gold and silver inlays. A sword had also been commissioned – Ava hadn't told her at the time, given they only needed her height rather than her full measurements. All in all, she looked like a member of the royal family – and like she was armoured in Ava's love.

The irony stabbed at her heart. The armour she was going to be baked alive in would look good, at least.

She didn't take her own horse with her. He wasn't a pet – she'd never even named him – but she didn't want him dying in flames with her. She took a horse she didn't feel attached to from the palace stables. To the outside world, it looked like Ava was sending her with the finest steed the palace could offer. Good optics and all that.

She took two pack horses, so her mount didn't need to carry more than her armoured self. She was given plenty of supplies, as well as money from the treasury. She was planning to stay at some inns, so the money would be helpful. She left her bow, as she had last time.

It wasn't as though arrows were any good against a dragon anyway.

Come to think of it, a sword wasn't much good against a dragon, either.

The whole city gathered to see her ride off. It was later in the day than she would have chosen to begin such a journey, but there didn't seem to be much choice.

She and Ava shared one last public kiss before she rode off. People were expecting it. She tried to look confident. People expected that, too.

She followed the same path she had three months earlier. If people recognised her, they didn't show any indication. She knew news was slow sometimes, but she suspected people knew Ava was married. Maybe they didn't know who to.

On the fourth evening, she walked into The Barbed Tail. Dragon country. She dropped a shilling on the bar. "Wine, please."

The innkeeper looked up at the sound of her voice, surprise in her eyes. "Well, you've come up in the world, haven't you?"

Gwen's smile was rueful. "Perhaps only temporarily."

"Oh, aye, you've heard about the ogres, then?"

Gwen nodded. "Ogres, barbarian tribes and, of course, the dragon."

"All in a day's work for the hero who rescued the princess, eh? Did you at least get to marry the scrawny wee lass afore they sent you out to meet your maker?"

She knew there was no malice behind it, so she tried not to bristle at 'scrawny'. Ava was short and slender, but she wasn't *that* skinny. "We've been married for less than a week."

The innkeeper's eyes filled with sympathy. "And now her family think you're the answer to their prayers, aye? If you succeed, they get to claim you as their own, and if you fail, well, they don't have to worry about their precious princess being in love with a commoner anymore."

"Something like that," Gwen muttered. She tried not to dwell on the casual assumption that Ava was in love with her. If she really was, this all wouldn't be quite so scary.

"And what did her Highness have to say about all this?"

"She didn't want me to go."

An indulgent smile met this. "Ah? Then I suppose she really does love you. Not that it's much comfort, I'm sure, but you can at least hold on to that when you get roasted on your horse."

"Yes. I suppose I can."

Could she? Was the innkeeper right? But no, Ava would be more confident in her return if she loved her. Wouldn't she? Ava believed in prophecy, of that Gwen was certain.

Perhaps Ava did love her, and her worry stemmed from not thinking it was returned. It seemed unlikely to Gwen – after all, her own feelings were written on her every action – but it was all she had. A last, desperate, million to one chance.

But in legends those last desperate million to one chances worked out surprisingly often.

She held on to that hope. It was all she had.

The journey from The Barbed Tail out to the dilapidated castle took three days. It felt longer, but also too short. It occurred to Gwen that she could run away – she had some money, and the armour would fetch a fair price. But she'd given her word, and her word was important to her.

Besides, if she were ever caught, Ava would bear the brunt of her cowardice. She couldn't have that. *Does love make everyone so stupid, or is it just me?* She rode on, accepting her fate.

She left the packhorses in the thicket before approaching. Risking her own life was one thing, but the horses had no choice. She rode out across the field, sword drawn, head held high, the plumes in her helmet waving in the wind of her passage.

As she neared the castle, the dragon rose. It was a burnished reddish gold, the colour of the sunset. Its wings were wide, its tail long and its head elegant. It circled around her once before hovering impossibly before her, beating its wings slowly.

Her heart hammered in her chest, and her mind went completely blank in her terror. She alighted clumsily from her skittish horse, who bolted the instant her hand left its bridle. Wishing she could bolt with it, she raised her sword in a high guard.

The dragon opened its terrible maw, taking a deep breath in. There was an instant, just the barest stutter in time, where she could have sworn she saw the spark light in the dragon's throat. It was immediately replaced with a rapidly expanding lance of fire, billowing at the edges, and preceded by a solid wall of heat.

She staggered back as the flame engulfed her.

All she knew was heat. The light was so bright she couldn't see – even through closed eyes the red of her eyelids became white. The rest of the world disappeared as she surrendered to her utter destruction.

And then it was gone.

Gwen didn't know if it had been mere seconds or closer to an hour. It took time for sight to return; during this time she realised that the heat had passed without leaving pain behind.

She also realised she was still alive.

THE PROTECTOR APPEARS. WELL MET.

It was less a voice, and more a memory planted in her very bones. She couldn't have told anyone what the dragon sounded like, but the message was clear. It was greeting her as an equal.

"Well met? *Well met?* Do you always greet new people by roasting them in dragonfire?" She was struggling to understand what was happening. The terror was draining from body, leaving anger in its wake.

It probably wasn't wise to direct one's anger at a dragon. She did her best to rein it in while she tried to come to terms with what was happening.

I DO NOT USUALLY GREET HUMANS AT ALL. THINK OF THE FLAME AS A TEST — ONE WHICH YOU PASSED, PROTECTOR.

"A test? You flamed me as a *test*? What would have happened if I failed?"

YOU WOULD BE DEAD. The flat finality of that statement chilled her to the bone.

She considered this, still trying to regain her composure. "Why aren't I dead, then?"

BECAUSE YOU ARE THE CHOSEN ONE — THE PROTECTOR. YOU ARE THE ONE FORETOLD BY THE ANCIENT PROPHECY

"You know about the prophecies, too? But they said that if your flame didn't kill me I'd return with your head! I thought I was riding out to save the Realm from you." It occurred to Gwen belatedly that perhaps she should keep some of her own counsel, but she'd always had a tendency to speak her mind.

THE PROPHECY AS TOLD WITHIN DRAGONKIND MADE IT CLEAR THE PROTECTOR WOULD RIDE WITH ME. PERHAPS YOU WILL RETURN WITH MY HEAD AND ALL THE REST?

"But... but you were willing to kill me!" Gwen was gobsmacked. "And now you expect me to just go with you? Wait – dragons have prophecy?"

OF COURSE WE DO. DO YOU THINK US MONSTERS? The dragon ignored the first question entirely.

"I suppose I did. I don't anymore. I'm sorry." She felt herself deflate. This was all too much for her – and she had an itching feeling that she was missing something very important.

AH. YOUR PROPHECY DOESN'T TALK OF THE PROTECTOR, RIDER OF DRAGONS, DEFENDER OF THE REALM? THE ONE WHO BRINGS THE RUNAWAY PRINCESS BACK AND MAKES HER DO HER DUTY ONCE MORE?

"It talks of the Hero, beloved of the Princess, before whose wrath all dangers to the Realm shall fall. Is that the same thing?"

IT MIGHT BE. MY NAME WOULD TRANSLATE IN YOUR TONGUE TO SOMETHING CLOSE TO WRATH.

"Wow." Gwen was lost for words.

WHAT DANGERS DO YOU SEE THE REALM FACING? THE BIGGEST DANGER I SAW WAS A PRINCESS RUNNING FROM HER DUTY, AND YOU ALREADY DEALT WITH THAT.

"Um, the ogres are stirring. And the barbarian clans. I think the lands of Lubrey are having ogre troubles, but I'm not so sure about the barbarians. I didn't listen to the details – I never thought I'd be having this conversation." What was with her today? She didn't seem to be able to control her tongue at all.

OGRES AND BARBARIANS? CHILD'S PLAY. I CAN HANDLE THAT. CAN YOU HANDLE KEEPING THE PRINCESS TO HER DUTY?

"I think so. She only ran to escape a bad marriage."

I SEE. DOES SHE NOW HAVE A BETTER ONE?

Gwen pushed her doubts down. "Yes. Me."

GOOD. The approval in the Dragon's voice was evident, even though she still wasn't exactly hearing it. THEN THERE IS ONE MORE GIFT I CAN GIVE YOU. WE SHALL DISCUSS IT AFTER WE HAVE DEALT WITH THESE GNATS THAT CONCERN YOU SO.

The dragon landed gracefully in front of her and lowered its neck to the ground. The invitation was obvious, but Gwen still hesitated.

CLIMB ON. WE TRAVEL FASTER IN THE AIR.

"But the horses...?"

WE CAN RETURN FOR THEM LATER. OR YOU CAN LET THEM GO. THEY'RE ONLY HORSES.

Gwen nodded, accepting this for now. It suddenly hit her what she'd been missing – the dragonfire had engulfed her, but it hadn't burned her. She really was the Chosen One – the Hero, beloved of the Princess.

Princess Ava loved her.

The realisation crashed down on her like the boulders of a landslide. Her knees went weak, and she sat heavily on a piece of crumbling masonry. There was no other explanation – Ava loved her.

She scoured her memory as she sat in a daze, tears of emotion flowing down her cheeks. The signs were all there if you let yourself look – Ava's cynicism had been diminishing for weeks, and her protestations of not needing love had contained more bravado than they once did.

There was no single event she could find that proved it, but she couldn't pinpoint the moment her own love had become genuine either so that didn't matter. Her princess loved her.

Princess Ava *loved* her.

PROTECTOR? ARE YOUR LEGS CAPABLE OF HOLDING YOU? CAN YOU CLIMB ON?

"Oh – sorry. Yes, I can climb." She shook herself, stood up on unsteady legs, and climbed onto Wrath's neck.

They flew north by northeast for hours, until they reached the edge of the mountains. Gwen had seen maps and had some idea how far from the Capital she must be, but it seemed strange that she had doubled her distance from Ava in a few short hours. It had taken her a week to ride as far as she had. The dragon – Wrath – flew *fast*.

As they approached the first caves where the foothills met the true peaks, she felt Wrath's voice in her bones again.

OGRES ARE PRIMITIVE, AND NO DANGER TO ME, BUT YOU SHOULD BE WARY. YOUR METAL SKIN WILL NOT PROTECT YOU IF THEY SWARM YOU.

"I know that. What do you suggest?" She was bellowing into the wind and hoping that Wrath could hear her anyway.

MY VOICE-MAGIC LOWERS INHIBITIONS. THIS WILL NOT HELP AS THEY HAVE NONE. I SUGGEST YOU STAY MOUNTED AND DEMAND AN AUDIENCE OUTSIDE.

Well, that explained a thing or two. "That seems best. Can you talk with them as you do with me?"

No. Only the Protector can hear my thoughts. But I can lend you my roar — they will listen to you.

"Alright. I don't know what to say to them, but here goes nothing." It was true. She had no idea what to say. She would not normally have admitted that; she had no idea if Wrath was making her speak her mind or if she'd just chosen to.

You do. Find out what they want. If you cannot make alliance, threaten them with my flame. Ogres fear fire above all else.

"You're okay with me using you like that?"

Yes. Your prophecy said they will fall before me.

"I suppose it did, at that."

Wrath had slowed to a hover. Gwen had no idea how it – he? She? It felt weird calling the dragon 'it' – did that.

Dragons don't have gender like humans. If it helps, I lay eggs, Protector. I can also cause eggs to quicken. Dragons are not humans, but you can use whatever word you choose.

"You can read my mind?" Gwen was shocked.

Only the thoughts you verbalize. Try it.

You mean like this? It felt weird, directing verbal thoughts at Wrath like that.

Exactly like that. If it makes you too uncomfortable you can keep moving the air.

You hear all my thoughts, then? Not just the ones I think at *you?* She'd have to be more careful in future. At the merest suggestion of self-control her thoughts tried to wander back to memories of her princess. She tamped them down quickly.

IT'S LOUDER WHEN IT'S DIRECTED AT ME. AND I CAN ONLY HEAR THE WORDS — THE THOUGHTS YOU THINK TO YOURSELF ARE USUALLY MISSING MANY AND REQUIRE EFFORT TO DECIPHER. WOULD YOU PREFER I ONLY RESPOND TO THE THOUGHTS YOU SEND MY WAY?

Gwen thought about this for a moment. *No,* she finally decided. *You're going to listen in anyway; you can respond if you think it necessary. Shall we call the ogres now?*

YES, LET'S. Wrath, still hovering, raised their head and roared.

Chapter Fourteen – Walk Softly and Ride a Big Dragon

The ogre at the head of the 'welcome' party was nothing like Gwen expected. And exactly like she expected. She wasn't sure how that worked.

He was male, over seven feet, with canines protruding so far over his lower lip that they framed his blocky jaw like tusks. He didn't have the green tint of the stories, but his pallid pinkness evoked the same sickly aura. His shoulders were broad enough to make him appear short from a distance, and the thick animal pelts covering them were barbaric – but richly so. Thick strands of crudely carved jade around his neck completed the impression.

No, that wasn't quite right. The double-bladed spear, taller than he was and carried as a staff of office, was what completed the look. That and the warriors arrayed around him in a wedge formation. He was the head, but the others were clearly noble.

"Human on dragon. What you want?" The grammar was atrocious, but it was declaimed with the confidence and authority of a royal proclamation.

"I am Sir Gwendoline, consort to Princess Ava, heir to the Realm." She could do formal, too.

"Did not ask who. Asked what." This sounded impatient.

"I want to know why you are attacking travellers within the Realm. Travellers and trade caravans, among others. Raiding parties on defenceless villages. One party of Kingsguards did not return from this region, too. Why?"

The leader barked a laugh. "Because fun. Because sport. Because I say so. Now go."

"You see that I ride a dragon. If I go, I go leaving you in flames." She put every ounce of authority she could muster into the words and had the satisfaction of seeing worry cross the leader's face. "Now, answer me properly. Why now? You've always enjoyed the sport, but you haven't raided in years. Why have you begun again? Why *now*?"

"Bigman of humans, he come tell us, we can raid these lands. Some lands now ours, some slaves, some sport. He tell us where rich traders ride, where soldiers ride and how many."

"Does this big man have a name?" Gwen worked hard to keep her voice even. Commanding.

"His men call him Milord Looby."

"Looby? Do you mean Lubrey?" If Gwen had been asked to guess, her gut instinct would have been the Earl. But his lands were the ones being hit, which made no sense at all. Why would he give permission to raid his own lands?

HOW DO YOU KNOW HIS LANDS ARE BEING HIT? HAS ANYONE BEEN TO CHECK?

He's been asking for aid for the past month. The King has sent a small number of men and a large amount of gold.

THESE MEN THE KING SENT. WOULD THEY BE THE PARTY OF KINGSGUARDS YOU SAID DID NOT RETURN?

Her stomach sank as the ogre replied. "That's what I said. Looby. Now, will you go with no flames?"

"Only if you swear to stop your raids on humans. You must stop attacking people, you must release all your slaves, and you must send a messenger once a year to the Capital to tell us that you have not forgotten your oath. You will not hear from Lubrey again."

It wasn't words, but she could feel Wrath's approval rumbling between them.

"I swear. Word of Xorth. You go; take dragon with you."

Is the word of Xorth worth much?

NOT A LOT. BUT PROBABLY MORE THAN THE WORD OF LUBREY. WE MAY NEED TO COME BACK, BUT IT SHOULD BE ENOUGH FOR NOW.

"Alright. We will go. And we will remember Xorth's word."

They didn't exchange words. Not even conscious thought. Wrath just flew west towards Lubrey, taking Gwen to confront Lord Forquitte.

They had been flying for a little over two hours, the evening shadows darkening into dusk, when they crossed out of the wild regions and back into populated land.

Or, at least, into what should have been populated land.

Something's not right, here.

THERE'S A VILLAGE BELOW US WITH NO PEOPLE AROUND. I CAN SEE FARMS WITHOUT LIVESTOCK; THERE AREN'T ANY WAGONS. NO HORSES. Wrath didn't seem to be perturbed; they were simply reeling off facts they had noticed. THE TAVERN HAS NO LIGHT.

Most houses wouldn't be lit; it's too early for candles and too warm to need fires for heat. But there should be smoke from more chimneys – people still need to cook – and surely it's not late enough for every farmhand to be in from the fields?

LOOK, Wrath indicated with their head. THERE ARE SOME CHILDREN PLAYING OUTSIDE. THE WOMAN WATCHING THEM SEEMS OLD FOR A HUMAN.

Their grandmother? This feels off.

AGREED. LET'S KEEP FLYING. True to their word, Wrath continued on toward the nearest larger township.

By the third town, they were sensing a pattern. There was no evidence of any raiding. There were also far fewer people around than one would expect. Far fewer lights in homes. No horses or wagons, either. Between the towns, fields looked to have been left untended for days. It was unsettling.

HAVE YOU EVER SEEN A TOWN WHOSE MEN AND WOMEN HAVE MARCHED TO WAR?

No. If war came, I should think I'd be marching with them. What are you saying?

I THINK LUBREY MAY HAVE BEEN PLANNING WORSE THAN EXTORTION.

Gwen just stared, taking this in. Ava had been worried about rebellion, but Forquitte was now married to Jane Holyoake – surely that removed any grounds that might have got him allies in this. Did he really think he could go it alone?

WHY SHOULD HE NOT? HE HAS THE ELEMENT OF SURPRISE. HOW MANY SOLDIERS STAND READY IN YOUR CAPITAL? HOW PREPARED IS YOUR KING? YOU SAID THIS LUBREY HAS BEEN TAKING GOLD TO RAISE MEN. I THINK HE HAS RAISED THEM.

Extra gold could be used for so many things. If he wasn't needing it to fend off the ogres he could be well armed and well armoured; or he could merely have more troops. He shouldn't have enough to bring down the castle, but the Capital itself is lightly defended and there aren't enough supplies to withstand a lengthy siege. This could be very bad, Wrath.

Gwen was troubled. She wished she knew more about raising soldiers, and how long it takes to move them. She wished she knew more about where the King's allies were, and which units they could send. There was so much about war that no one felt she needed to learn in her first three months when the Realm was at peace.

LUCKY FOR YOU, YOU HAVE ME. Wrath didn't seem to need a voice to sound smug. DANGERS TO THE REALM WILL FALL BEFORE ME, YOU SAY? THE OGRES CAPITULATED TO THE MERE THREAT OF ME, AND NOW MY SPEED WILL TAKE OUR KNOWLEDGE TO THE KING.

And to my Ava.

Wrath's amusement flowed through the bond they shared.

The flight back to the Capital was swift and silent. Gwen could feel herself growing more nervous with every passing moment. Flying was fast but tucked out of the wind behind Wrath's shoulder blade it didn't feel it.

Wrath took a brief dip closer to the ground. From there the land rushing past was clearly many times faster than if she were on horseback. She tried to untense her muscles; she knew Wrath was reacting to her anxious thoughts, even though neither of them verbalised anything to the other.

Dawn was breaking when they spotted the armies. They were approaching from the north, from Lubrey, so it was the Earl's men they saw first. Trailing in a loose line were horses and carts full of food, arrows, extra pieces of leather armour, barrels filled with beer, wine, or water. There were carts filled with lumber, and carts with other building supplies. There were young lads riding mules herding cows ahead of them. There were older folk leading horses – perhaps in case a carthorse died? Or perhaps for light cavalry units? No knight would ride one of these.

They rapidly caught up to the marching soldiers. The knights made a surprisingly small part of the force – perhaps twenty fully armoured men rode in the vanguard. There were indeed light cavalry next; more of them, perhaps a couple of hundred or so, but still small compared to the rest. She'd always thought there were more cavalry in an army.

THERE ARE IF YOU PLAN TO MEET ON THE FIELD. THEY ARE LESS USEFUL IN A SIEGE.

Gwen nodded absently, still trying to tally up the force in front of her. A few hundred well-armed and armoured men (and women? From here she couldn't tell) in infantry units with swords. Many, many more in loose formation with pikes. And then, of course, were the units of archers.

She understood the archers. She had trained to be a part of a unit like this. Of course, it was far easier to take an untrained person and give them a pike than get them up to standard with a bow; she understood that, too.

She swiftly tried to count numbers. They weren't marching in formation, which made getting a good number hard. Several hundred of each, at least – a thousand, maybe? Two?

ALL TOLD THERE ARE FOUR THOUSAND FIGHTING MEN IN THIS FORCE, NEARLY HALF OF WHOM ARE BARELY TRAINED BOYS WITH STICKS.

You can count that fast?

YOU CANNOT?

Arming and armouring these men and women would have cost a lot of coin, but that would not account for all the gold Lubrey took from the King, let alone whatever he had in his own coffers. I suspect there are other forces.

WE HAVE COME FROM THE DIRECTION HE WOULD MARCH. BUT A CIRCUIT AROUND THE CITY BEFORE WE MAKE OUR REPORT WOULD BE WISE.

They flew on, more slowly now that they were taking stock of what was happening on the ground, but still far faster than even the swiftest horse. As they circled the city, Gwen noticed several smaller armies – groups of two to five hundred men in medium-quality armour (better than the pikemen, but not as good as the knights and their armsmen) under various banners. She recognised the emblems of three mercenary companies, and assumed the others were likewise hired blades.

I THINK WE HAVE AN ANSWER TO THE MYSTERY OF WHERE LUBREY SPENT HIS GOLD. The memory of words contained the memory of a dry tone. LET'S SEE HOW MANY THERE ARE.

When they got to the southeast quarter of the city, where the river flowed out, they found an even larger army than the one to the north. This one was under many banners, but the main one Gwen saw over and over was the three towers of Eastwall.

Duke Holyoake? But I met him. He seemed like a good man. A little self-absorbed, true, but loyal to his King. And Ava's been befriending Lady Jane. How could he turn like this?

Is THIS JANE THE DUKE'S DAUGHTER? Gwen quickly sent her assent. PERHAPS THE LYING CUR HAS CONVINCED HER FATHER THAT SHE IS BEING HELD AGAINST HER WILL.

It's possible, but I don't like it. If the other army is four thousand, how big is this one? Five? Six? And they have siege weapons already built.

FIVE AND A HALF. THAT MAKES AROUND TWELVE THOUSAND FIGHTING TROOPS THAT WE'VE SEEN UNDER ALL BANNERS. I THINK YOUR KING NEEDS TO HEAR ABOUT THIS. SHALL WE FLY OVER THE WALLS TO SEE HIM?

Yes. Let's.

They crossed the low stone outer city wall to fly over the Capital. The morning sun was still low on the horizon and the shadows still long, but it was clear the approaching armies had been seen. Citizens of the city were beginning to make their way to the castle, arms wrapped around their most prized belongings. They moved purposefully but with obvious alarm, like ants from a kicked nest.

The city wall would be no use at all against an army. At least, not with as few defenders as they had. There were some extra weapons in the armoury to give to willing citizens should it come to that – her rapid education had contained that much, at least – but there weren't as many as hands to hold them. There was also the issue of training. A spear in poorly trained hands was a weak weapon, but a spear in completely untrained hands could do more harm than good.

The citadel in the middle of the city, the castle with the palace at the centre, was far stronger. Its high stone walls would not house the whole city in comfort, but they could huddle there for a few days.

A few days was probably all the food they had, if their supplies from outside were cut off. The stores beneath the castle were sufficient to feed six hundred soldiers for months, but the civilians numbers in the tens of thousands. If not more.

As they flew over the battlements, she heard shouts from the guards. Details were hard to see in the early morning light, especially with the sun behind them, but it would be difficult to miss the fact that a dragon was flying over the walls. Gwen tried shouting and waving to let them know it was her, but she had no way to make herself heard.

LEAVE IT. THERE IS AN OPEN COURTYARD WHICH APPEARS TO STILL BE EMPTY. IT IS LARGE ENOUGH TO LAND IN. STAY MOUNTED UNTIL THEY COME FIND US AND ALL WILL BE WELL.

How sure are you?

SURE ENOUGH. IF I AM WRONG, WE CAN FLY AWAY. I KNOW YOU WON'T LIKE IT IF I HAVE TO FLAME MEN IN THE PROCESS. Wrath had the poor taste to sound amused by that.

They had landed for approximately two minutes when the Kingsguards appeared. The courtyard was open to the sky, as Wrath had said, and Gwen was clearly visible riding the dragon.

She was also still wearing her beautifully ornate suit of armour, commissioned by Princess Ava. Not all the guards recognised her, but even the ones who didn't knew she was important, and word spread through the ranks.

They lined the walls, standing at a respectful attention, as runners were sent to inform command of the presence of a dragon. No one who had to work the early shift was senior enough to deal with this.

It took perhaps fifteen minutes for a senior officer to turn up. He looked to be in his middle years, and no longer used to being awake this early in the morning. His uniform looked well maintained, though hastily donned.

"Your Highness," he began, saluting fist to heart. "Is there some reason you cannot alight from this dragon?" He didn't comment on it, but it was obvious he had noticed how calm the dragon appeared. His men, by contrast, were stiffly at attention, holding pikes pointed toward the perceived threat.

"I have news of the ogres and the approaching armies. Please send word to the King and Princess Ava." She felt no need to tell this officer of the Earl's treachery. It was for the King to decide how that would be handled.

YOU CODDLE THE MAN. HIS DEEDS SPEAK FOR THEMSELVES, AND ALL WILL KNOW OF HIS TREASON BEFORE THE DAY IS OVER WHETHER YOU TELL THEM OR NOT.

You are probably correct, but that is not my decision to make. Besides, spreading gossip in front of common guards would make all think less of me even more than of him. She dismounted, standing tall in front of the officer. She had learned that if you look like you know what you're doing people have a tendency to go along with what you want.

Human customs are strange. It is your choice, Protector.

"I see. Is there anyone else you would like me to send word to?" The man bore the look of one who just wanted some simple instructions to follow.

"Not as of yet. I think the King should hear our news before we alert anyone else." He wouldn't want her trying to run his kingdom for him while he slept, of that she was certain.

"Very good, Sir Gwendoline." He sent two of his men to run and tell Princess Ava and the King.

Ava came running in, out of breath, her eyes bright. She was still wearing her nightwear covered by a robe which she had hitched up so as not to interfere with her legs as she ran.

Had Ava always been this beautiful? Gwen was certain her princess was more lovely, more compelling, with every passing day. The time spent apart was no different. She was stunning.

"You, and… you." Ava singled out two of the Kingsguards as she slowed her pace. "Help my consort out of her armour." The men rushed to obey and had Gwen's breast- and backplate off before Ava finished crossing the courtyard. The rest of the armour followed quickly, and Gwen stood toe to toe with her love.

Their bodies pressed together as they drank each other in. They gazed into each other's eyes, hands cupping cheeks as they stood in silent rapture at their reunion.

Ava broke the silence first. "You love me," she said, wonder hanging thickly in her voice. "Despite everything you said, you truly love me."

264

"I do," Gwen replied simply. She let the sentence hang by itself for a second before adding to it. "I love you truly, madly and completely."

Ava's laughter held her amazement. Her eyes held tears despite her joy. "I never thought I would see you again. My love for you wasn't supposed to be enough; not on its own. But you're here. So it's not just words – you love me."

It was hard to remember that it was only yesterday that this same revelation had come crashing down on her. Watching Ava go through this, feeling her go through this, brought it all back to her. She tried to maintain composure, but a single tear fell down her cheek, matching the ones adorning her princess.

"You told me you didn't believe in love. I'm glad you changed your mind." Gwen smiled, overcome with emotion as her thumbs gently brushed her beloved princess' cheeks.

She leaned in and softly pressed her lips to Ava's. There was no tension, no fear, only love. She sensed the love flowing back along their connection and felt fulfilled.

One of the young lads the officer had sent returned, puffing.

"His Majesty would like to see Sir Gwendoline in his outer chambers, Captain. He would like to see Princess Ava, too. He said to leave guards with the dragon but with orders not to try to hurt it."

"Were those his exact words?" The officer – the Captain, apparently – was soft spoken but intent. Evidently he was feeling more awake than before. By Ava's startled reaction, she had forgotten they still had an audience.

"No, Captain. He said any man who tried to hurt the dragon would probably die without Sir Gwendoline there to stop it, and that he wouldn't trust some of the younger boys to realise that without a direct order."

YOUR KING THINKS YOU CONTROL ME? The memory of words was more feeling than sound. It *felt* indignant.

Only in the words of a young lad who isn't quoting him. Please don't leap to feeling insulted?

THESE MEN ARE LUCKY I LIKE YOU.

"I think Wrath will stay until we return, but please tell your men not to interfere if they choose not to wait." There. She hoped that would satisfy draconic pride well enough. The men knew she didn't control Wrath, and soon the King would as well.

"Shall we go face Father together, then?"

"Yes, let's." Gwen took a deep breath, dreading the upcoming meeting. "It would not do to keep the King waiting."

Chapter Fifteen – The Plan

It wasn't a long walk to the King's chambers, but their escort gave them enough space that Gwen could fill Ava in on the broad details of what had happened and what she had seen. Ava needed no convincing on the treachery of the Earl of Lubrey, but she listened attentively to each piece of proof Gwen offered.

"Your Majesty?" Gwen bowed as they entered King Harald's antechamber, her tone somewhat less than formal. It was hard to be totally formal with a man in a dressing gown. Even when that man was your King. Especially when that man was your father-in-law.

"Gwen! I see my daughter has already found you to welcome you home. I hear you tamed the dragon?" He sounded like he wanted her to elaborate, but she wasn't entirely sure how.

"Not so much. Their name is Wrath, and they think the line in our prophecy about dangers to the Realm falling before my wrath is about them. Dragons have their own prophecies, it turns out. They call me 'Protector'." She didn't add what Wrath had felt she was protecting the Realm from.

"How do you know all of this? Can it talk?"

She winced. She hated hearing him referring to them as 'it'. "In a way. It's more like they leave memories of words that I never heard spoken aloud." She needed to talk of the ogres and how many soldiers were approaching the castle, but it seemed her King wanted to talk about the dragon.

"They? There's more than one?" The King sat forward, clearly anxious despite the late hour.

"No – they're the only one. He or she seemed wrong, and I don't like using 'it' for a sentient being. Doesn't bother them, of course. Pronouns are human things." She paused briefly and continued. "What *does* bother them, though, is you thinking I control them. I don't. They're an ally; apparently dragons have always thought themselves the protectors of the monarchs."

"I… see." His pause was longer. "You believe the dragon, then? You don't think it's a danger?"

"Not to you or to me. They might be dangerous to your guards if one is stupid enough to attack them. Dragons don't value human life as a general thing – Wrath will try not to kill anyone because it bothers me, not because they have any moral objection to killing." She opened her mouth again to talk about the pressing issue of the approaching armies but was too slow.

"It doesn't place value on human life? How can you be so sure it's safe, then?" King Harald's gaze was intense.

"Because they're honourable. They don't value humans for the same reason we don't value cows, but neither you nor I would harm a cow belonging to someone we *do* value. Your Majesty, would you mind not calling Wrath 'it'? They say they lay eggs if you'd rather call them 'she'?"

268

The King stared at her. "I'm not even going to ask how that came up," he muttered. "Alright, so she doesn't find value in most human life, but she does value you. And because of this she will be gentle with other humans because they're... like your cows?" His tone was doubtful, but it was clear he was trying to understand.

At this point, Ava spoke up. "Father, Gwen went to treat with the ogres, to find out why they've been increasing their raids recently."

King Harald turned his attention to his daughter. "And I assume you have an opinion on what she was told?"

"Yes, Father. I do." Despite the early hour, and despite her lack of formal attire, Ava's presence commanded the room. "Would you instruct your guards to wait outside the door? The closed door, if you'd be so good."

King Harald lifted a finger at his guards, confirming his daughter's command, then raised an eyebrow at her impatiently.

"The ogre's commander initially gave simple reasons for his raids – mostly, that he and his followers enjoy doing it. But when pressed on why they went from very few raids to very many so recently, they were more forthcoming."

"They were raiding Lubrey, were they not?" He frowned. "And now we have armies approaching from that direction. My first scouts should return in a few hours with news."

"They weren't raiding Lubrey, Father." Ava was still quietly commanding, so Gwen left her own reports on the approaching armies ungiven. Ava knew as much as she did now, in any case. "In fact, Reginald gave them permission to take lands and raid just outside his own domain."

"They specifically said it was him, did they? Are you trying to tell me they recognise Reginald on sight? I find that a bit of a stretch." The King's tone was affectionate, but in the way one might be affectionate to a six-year-old. Gwen suddenly understood why her wife found her father so frustrating.

"Of course not, Father. I doubt they can tell one human from another much better than we can them – though I suspect you could tell their commander from their foot soldiers by dress, yes?"

"Of course. But an order coming from a lord rather than a soldier – or, rather, from a man dressed as a lord and not a soldier – is hardly the same as a command from Reginald in particular. So why do you think he is responsible?"

"Multiple reasons, Father." Ava's tone was getting cooler as she held on to her regal bearing. "For one, the ogre's commander was given advance warning of the movements of potential targets in the region by the same man who gave his word not to retaliate. That man was named "My Lord Lubrey" by his men – a detail I doubt an ogre would have the wit to invent."

"An ogre might not, but a human might. My child, is it not possible that another lord instructed his men to address him in this manner, to discredit an Earl whose star is rising so rapidly?"

Ava tensed so briefly at being called 'child' that Gwen thought no one else would have noticed. "It is possible, Father, but there are reasons I think it unlikely. For one, the physical description of the man matches Reginald Forquitte. For another, the raids we have independent witnesses of have happened between the ogres' mountain homes and Forquitte's lands – he is in the best position to keep his word of safe conduct for the raiding parties. Thirdly, there is the timing of the raids. They did not begin until after Reginald left to spend his betrothal at his estate, and there was a brief lull in their ferocity while he was here for our wedding. I suspect that lull came about due to a pause in the flow of information out of the lands of Lubrey. Finally – and I cannot believe I have to tell you this, Father – there is the little detail that four thousand of his men are as we speak marching to put us under siege." She took a deep breath. "With your permission, may I have a guard summon his wife, Jane Holyoake?"

The King nodded slowly, clearly troubled. "This all just seems so out of character for him. What would he have to gain?"

Gwen quietly left the room as he said this and told off a guard to go fetch the Countess. She returned, missing nothing.

"Out of character?" Ava's incredulous retort lacked her usual elegance but carried strength of feeling. "Father, I told you of his character when you began talking about him as a possible husband for me! This is not out of character one bit."

"Assuming you were correct, and not merely looking for a reason not to wed the man I chose for you, how would you connect his…" the King cast around for a suitable phrase. "Lack of delicacy with women, shall we say, to this act of treason? They are of completely different substance."

"But both reflect the same entitlement that is a key feature of his character. He feels entitled to everything – to women, to sport, to praise, to lands, to gold. He feels entitled to terrorise his neighbours in order to enrich himself. He is a bully, father, and if he cannot win by fair means he will win by foul. This is completely within his character."

The King was silent for so long Gwen feared he was going to reject his daughter's words. She kept her peace, following Ava's lead.

Finally, King Harald spoke. "I do not like it, but I see your point. It would seem I owe you an apology, my dear. I should have listened to you more closely when you were telling me of his disposition months ago."

"You should have." Ava's stern tone softened. "But if you had, I would never have run away, and if I had never run away I would never have met my Gwen. Perhaps the Gods stoppered your ears for a reason."

"Perhaps they did. And perhaps you can now tell me the rest of what you know of the approaching armies?" He directed the question at his daughter. Gwen wasn't surprised; Ava had already shown she knew their numbers and disposition.

"Four thousand Lubrey soldiers approach from the North. They are approximately half bow and half pike; though they have a few hundred swordsmen and perhaps half as many horse." Ava rattled this off with confidence. "Five and a half thousand Eastwall soldiers approach from the southeast. They have a similar makeup but bring three trebuchets and a ballista."

Her father interrupted her to clarify. "Which explains you sending for Jane. I see."

Ava nodded and continued. "There are also several companies of mercenaries approaching from various directions. Gwen was unable to recognise all banners, but they include The Varoux Guard, The Agyrian Grand Company, and The Five Hundred. All told, these add another two and a half thousand to the field, bringing the total marching against us to twelve thousand."

"Hmm." King Harald stroked his beard thoughtfully. "We could withstand a siege, here. Or we could if we could be sure Reginald would allow civilians to pass unharmed. As it is, we must allow the citizens to join us in the keep, and there is no way to get enough food in to feed them all."

"How long can we feed the city with supply lines cut?" Gwen suspected Ava was asking for her benefit.

"Four, maybe five days." He looked at his daughter sharply. "But you knew that already. So you know we either need to turn them away or else break the siege quickly."

"Well, Gwen tells me Wrath believes they're prophesised to protect us. And legend has it that dragons can defeat entire armies – it pains me to condemn so many innocents, but in war people die and it's better to be a few thousand soldiers than an entire city." Ava didn't look comfortable with this.

"The ballista is the only difficulty," the King mused. "The legends of dragons facing armies didn't include siege weapons."

Gwen spoke up. "It was only the Eastwall army that had siege weapons. Perhaps we should see what Jane has to say?" She paused, before adding, "I'd like to try to disperse the mercenaries without bloodshed, too, if I can. I doubt they knew they'd be facing a dragon when they accepted Forquitte's coin."

"Yes. I am very curious what Jane has to say." King Harald sounded less than pleased. "Her father was always a friend to us. It pains me to think they could be traitors, but today has been filled with such pain."

Ava held up a finger. "I think I can hear her approaching. Will you let me take the lead?" Her father nodded his assent.

A moment later Jane appeared in the doorway. She curtseyed formally. "Your Majesty. Your Highness."

"Come in and close the door behind you." Despite agreeing to allow his daughter to lead, Harald still gave the instruction.

Jane curtseyed again, less deeply but still with respect. "How may I be of service, your Majesty?"

Ava stepped in. "Jane. I think we can drop the formality, but we do need some answers from you." Her tone was warm but serious.

"Of course, Ava. I've been informed armies are approaching the city – do you need to know how long it will take for me to summon Eastwall to the Capital's defence?" Jane sounded crisp, competent, and helpful. And yet there was also an undertone of worry.

"It is in fact the matter of Eastwall's levies that brings us here this morning." Ava was delicate. "You asked if we needed *you* to summon Eastwall to our defence. Did you mean to ask if we need your father?"

Jane's brows furrowed. "I meant what I said. You know well that I've been running the Duchy in my father's name since I was old enough to be declared competent."

Gwen realised she did indeed know this but had not given it much thought. Everyone knew the old Duke was still in the deepest mourning, twenty years after his wife had died. It was an open secret that he had left most of the raising of his child to nannies and governesses, and allowed his seneschal to oversee much of his other duties until Jane was old enough to do all of them for him.

Rumour had it that he had declared his daughter competent at fourteen. Not unheard of, but most fourteen-year-old Dukes or Duchesses would still have a regent. It was a lot of responsibility to place on a child. She couldn't imagine asking Nicholas to rule a Duchy at his age.

Ava's brows furrowed. "Are you telling us that any order to raise soldiers would come from you and not your father? Would your Earls, Viscounts, Barons and Knights expect their marching orders to have your name on them? Or his?"

"Mine, your Highness." Jane adopted a more formal tone as her posture shifted. She was clearly uncomfortable and had no idea where this audience was leading. "My father's signature and seal would be authoritative enough, of course, but our vassals know well that he would not take an interest. His seal would be closely inspected for forgery, and most likely a runner would be sent to confirm in person any orders he gave."

Ava nodded slowly. "Does anyone else have access to your seal?"

"No."

King Harald interrupted. "How certain are you of that?"

Ava gave her father a sharp look and shook her head once. Gwen felt the currents of politics washing over her head, and resolved to learn more so she could be a better consort for Ava.

"I am... quite certain, your Majesty." Jane faced him calmly, but her tone had a hard bite to it. "There is only one copy of my seal, and it is locked in my personal box, underneath the bed in the rooms you assigned me. I check it each morning and each night. Beyond that, I sign my name and impress my signet to all orders of any importance." She held her hand up, back facing them. "As you can see, I still have it. No one can have issued orders on my behalf."

"I am so sorry, but I have to ask you this." Ava's tone was gentle. "Did you order Eastwall to ready siege weapons and march upon the Capital?"

Jane flinched, but less than Gwen had expected. She was an intelligent young woman; perhaps she had recognised where this line of questioning was going. "I did not."

"And yet they are here, five and a half thousand, siege weapons and all." Ava's face held compassion, but it was the face of a princess, not the face of Jane's friend. "Tell me. Did your husband ever speak to you of treason? Of rebellion against the Crown?"

Anger flashed across Jane's face. "No he did not. And you know how I feel for him – we have spent the past week together, Ava, and you have learned well that I would not have kept my counsel if he had."

"I know, Jane." Ava's mask slipped a little, and her concern for her friend showed through. "I know he was not your choice. I know you married for political advantage, and under pressure from your father. But I also know you're carrying his child, and I cannot imagine you would want your child to be born a traitor's bastard."

"Do you think I'd believe my child less a traitor's bastard if that traitor won?" Jane was incredulous. "You clearly believe Reginald is behind my armies being where they ought not to be. I do not know how he could have arranged for that, but I can tell you that him winning is neither my only nor my best path out of his treachery." She took a deep breath and continued in a more even tone. "Percival has offered me the Brother's Vow."

Gwen was confused. It was uncommon in the country, but not unheard of, for an unmarried man to wed his brother's widow; but it was only ever done if there had been no fruit of the union. If Jane was pregnant it shouldn't even be thought of – why was she bringing it up?

"He wishes to legitimise your heir?" Ava asked.

Jane shrugged. "He has always been sweet. And he is far closer to my own age, of course. Given a free choice I would have wed him instead, but a younger brother is a poor match for the only child of a Duke."

"You had no choice at all?" Gwen shouldn't have spoken, but she felt for the fiercely spirited young woman before her.

There was a touch of derision in Jane's laughter. "Of course not. How could I have? Your own beloved Ava could have chosen anyone she wished, yet but for your fortuitous rescue and the magical bond of 'true love', *she* would have ended up married to the brute. What chance did I have?"

Gwen continued. "Why would your heir need legitimising?" She almost apologised for her ignorance but remembered in time that as Ava's consort she shouldn't do that.

Jane hesitated, clearly weighing up how much to say. "Percival has been very good to me these past few months. He was a dutiful son while his parents lived, but he has not transferred that loyalty to his brother. He has believed for longer than I have known him that Reginald would one day be stripped of all titles and hanged, beheaded, or exiled for treason. He does not believe his brother to be capable of being satisfied with what he has. And a man who can never be satisfied will keep reaching for the sun until he is burned to ashes."

Gwen caught Ava's eye. The little nod told her she hadn't overstepped. It was good to be able to read each other so well.

"Stripping him of all titles would have to include nullifying your marriage," Ava mused. Of course it was true. If their marriage stayed valid, then he would have a title by means of being her husband. "And of course no one would expect you to stay in such a disadvantageous union even were it not mandatory. Still, your child can remain heir to Holyoake, can they not? Conceived in wedlock, even if not born into it?"

Jane regarded her for a second before speaking. "And of course it would be more beneficial to the crown should the two titles have two separate heirs, am I correct?"

"There is that. Though it is not our chief concern right now."

"No, it's not, is it?" Jane was keeping her composure a lot better than Gwen could have managed in the same circumstances. "Our chief concern are those armies approaching. What do you propose we do about them?"

"Since you didn't summon Eastwall, I should think you can order them to stand down easily enough." Ava had clearly come to this conclusion some time previously. "That would take almost half the soldiers out of the equation, along with all the siege engines. If they come to the city's defence it would be a distressingly even battle, but a lot better than where we currently stand."

"I can, and of course I will, but I would very much like to summon my vassal lords here – with your permission, of course." Jane's mouth was set in a flat line. "I would like each and every one of them to explain why they were marching on the Capital without receiving any orders from my hand."

Ava nodded. "Good. With the ballista stood down, Gwen can fly out and attempt to persuade the mercenary bands that they value their own lives over whatever gold they have been paid."

Jane's eyebrows raised at that. "Fly? Do you mean to tell me the wild story of your consort arriving home on the back of a dragon are true? I thought my serving maid was inventing stories again."

"All true, Lady Jane." Gwen's smile felt a little forced. "I expect Wrath will be willing to put the fear of... well, the fear of *us* into those mercenaries. I just hope I can persuade them not to be overzealous with the flame."

"Well," said Ava, clapping her hands. "It appears we have the beginnings of a plan. I'm not sending you out without food in your stomach, my love, so we'll have breakfast while Jane writes out her orders to her vassals."

"Just let me fetch my lockbox from my rooms." Jane was already walking toward the door. "If I could join you in breaking your fast, we can discuss what exact wording I should use."

Gwen had picked up just enough political instinct to realise this wasn't merely a request for food and advice. She hadn't picked up enough to know exactly what it was instead.

"Of course," said Ava. "Let's all eat together."

After breakfast the three women picked up their planning where they had left off. The letters were written, Harald and Ava had agreed that they could not be misconstrued, and they had been dispatched by fast messenger. The King had decided he could trust his daughter from here and left them to it.

"We still need to work out what to do about the Lubrey army." Ava was never one for small talk. If there was something that needed to be said it was big talk all the way. "The castle can withstand their siege, but our food supplies can't. What do you think we should do?" The question was directed at both of them.

"Forquitte will be with his army, won't he?" Gwen waited for Ava's nod before continuing. "Do you think I should try to find him from Wrath's back? Taking him out should make his army scatter."

"There's no guarantee of that." Jane was quiet but intense. "And he and his brother look very similar when wearing armour. I would be... very sad if Sir Percival died to dragonfire."

Ava looked thoughtful. "If we can get you to your husband, do you think he'll trust you at all?"

"I think that depends on how I get there." Jane rubbed her cheek in thought. "I doubt he'd trust me if I just turned up waving a flag of parley."

"I was thinking more of a daring escape." Ava's eyes were alight. "Do you have some armsmen you trust? Some people who could believably be bodyguards smuggling you out of your dreadful captivity to reunite you with your beloved?"

Jane mimed a retch at that. "Please don't. But yes, there are five men and one woman in my personal retinue who would be both believable as bodyguards and trustworthy not to betray our plans."

"Excellent. We saw the banners of Eastwall and locked you in a dungeon without waiting to hear an explanation. Your armsmen, of course, were incensed by this and made a daring rescue." Ava paused, thinking. "There's a postern gate just behind the kitchens. It would usually have two guards on it; your armsmen caught them by surprise and disarmed them without any deaths."

"And left them tied up in the pantry? I like it." Jane's grin was evil. "Reginald would not expect anyone to know I was gone for hours."

"There's still the matter of how to bring him back." Ava frowned in silence for a moment before brightening somewhat. "Would you have access to his food without him being too suspicious?"

Jane scowled. "Access? The man likes to punish me by forcing me to do his drudgery. He keeps telling me that one day I shall enjoy cooking his food and mending his clothes. We employ people for that – I have a duchy to run!"

Ava gave a sly smile. "Perfect." She laughed at Jane's glare. "I mean it, it's perfect. Can you act at all?"

"Not so you'd notice. Why?"

"Well, if he is so certain you will learn to love serving him, then being rescued from horrendous imprisonment at the hands of people you thought were your friends would be a perfect time to start, yes?" Ava had that look in her eye she got just before someone else got fleeced.

"I suppose it might give me access to his food, yes." Jane's frown cleared. "I assume you intend for me to put something in it?"

"Strong sleeping herbs." Ava nodded decisively. "If you think he would suspect you enough to use tasters, or make you eat it, lower the dose and inform your armsmen to bring you both back to the palace asleep. But if you think he's certain enough of his hold on you to eat first, give him enough to knock a bull out."

All three of them shared a smile. They had a plan.

Chapter Sixteen – Justice

Gwen finished putting her armour back on with the aid of a helpful guardsman. She was nervous, but her job would be the simple one. She just hoped Wrath was skilful enough to accomplish it without too many deaths.

IF YOU WANT THE HUMANS TO SURVIVE, JUST ASK. Wrath gave a yawn and brought their head closer to Gwen's. YOU NEED NOT QUESTION MY SKILLS.

Sorry. Gwen scratched them on the chin, earning her an indignant snort. *We need to scare off the mercenaries. I'd rather not kill them if we can avoid it, but ending the war is too important not to take the risk.*

CHILD'S PLAY. HUMANS RUN IN TERROR AT NO PROVOCATION AT ALL.

These ones have been paid to lay siege to the castle. Running may well mean never getting paid again. They will be more difficult to terrify than most humans, and more likely to try to fight back.

AH. A CHALLENGE.

Gwen would have felt better if Wrath weren't so satisfied about that.

They rose out of the unroofed courtyard, Wrath's wings beating far too slowly to feel real. Gwen realised they had never answered her question about how they did that.

DID I NEED TO? IT'S MAGIC.

Of course, Gwen replied with a touch of irritation. *But does it follow any rules?*

PROBABLY.

Gwen sighed. That seemed to be all she was going to get. Wrath had no curiosity for how their magic worked and seemed to find it amusing that Gwen did.

They flew in silence to where the largest of the mercenary companies, The Varoux Guard, was marching into position near the city walls. They were very orderly – they were known for it – and the sound of their footfalls was unnaturally loud as they all struck the ground in unison.

There was a shout from below as Gwen and Wrath were seen. A couple of hands raised, fingers pointing their way, but they quickly lowered again as orders were shouted. Crossbows were readied with impressive speed; men knelt on the ground to steady their aim as they raised them in rows.

STOP STARING AND DUCK.

Gwen obeyed hastily. She heard a single command, and the air was filled with a sheet of crossbow bolts. She felt one clatter against the knee guard of her armour and a chill went through her at the glancing blow. If she'd been peering around Wrath's neck one could have taken her through the eye.

Other projectiles bounced off Wrath. The sound of them clattering off their scales was like she imagined rain would sound if each drop was as large as a horseshoe.

Gwen stuck her head cautiously around the dragon's neck after the arrows had stopped. The kneeling men were standing bent over, winding their windlasses, and the next row had stepped forward to kneel in front. Another order was barked.

Do you have a death wish? Duck! And *stay* ducked.

Gwen ducked back behind Wrath's shoulder again, feeling like a coward as she huddled behind them.

It isn't bravery to risk your neck for nothing, it is foolishness. Now, hold on tight — I'll run a line of flame in front of them and see if they break.

If they don't?

I'll run a line of flame behind them on the way back. And if they still don't break I'll be forced to stop missing them.

I hope they're smart enough to run.

I'm not counting on it. *You're* not smart enough to stay ducked.

Gwen knew Wrath well enough by now to sense the affection behind their exasperation. She huddled down lower and held on tight.

She was glad she had. Wrath snapped their wings tight to their body and dove toward the ground. Gwen felt her stomach try to leave through her mouth, and her grip on Wrath's shoulders felt tenuous at best. The bolts plinking off their scales were also coming over their head.

Gwen felt one strike her helmet, knocking her head to the side and sending a ringing through her ears. She ducked her head lower to Wrath's back, pressing herself in close as her vision swam.

The roar of Wrath's flame was disconcerting. Their wings snapped open in a low, fast glide as flame poured out of their mouth, lighting the grass on fire in a line in front of the crossbows. Gwen thought she heard officers yelling at their men, "Hold, you mangy sons of a spavined mule! I said hold!" but it came from far away, as if through water.

Gwen shook her head, trying to clear it. The motion sent agony through her skull, and her stomach convulsed in protest. Her breakfast departed her, and she felt darkness creeping in the sides of her vision. She struggled to hold on to Wrath.

She struggled to hold on to consciousness.

THEY'RE BREAKING. Wrath's thoughts could barely make it through the mess of her own. WE WILL LAND IN THAT THICKET. SOMETHING IS AMISS, PROTECTOR.

Gwen tried to return her agreement, but thought was hard.

It would be so much easier to just let go…

Gwen tried to control her dismount as the dragon landed. She ended up half sliding, half rolling off their back and onto the ground. The world swam.

YOUR HELMET IS MISSHAPEN. TAKE IT OFF.

It took several seconds for the suggestion to make it through, but Gwen finally started fumbling at her face. She managed to get the bent metal off her head, and immediately the feeling of being underwater eased. Her vision cleared and the pounding through her skull became a localised area of pain where the bolt had struck.

She heaved again, but there was nothing more to come up. She removed a gauntlet to scrub her mouth with the back of her hand.

I WAS JOKING ABOUT THE DEATH WISH. I'D RATHER YOU STAYED ALIVE. Wrath's concern was touching, and Gwen felt her heart warm. LET ME KNOW WHEN YOU ARE READY TO FLY AGAIN. WE HAVE OTHER FISH TO FRY.

Running off all the mercenary groups took much of the day. Gwen didn't spend as much time with her head out now that she didn't have a helmet, though in truth no other company had organised lines of crossbows to threaten her. They made it back to the open courtyard in the late afternoon.

She barely had time to remove her breast- and backplate before Ava came racing in.

"Darling! You're home!" Ava ran across to embrace her. "Did you succeed? Where's your helmet?"

Gwen smiled ruefully. "You're going to have to have another one made for me, my love – it saved me from a crossbow and then I left it in a thicket."

"That's a fine way to thank it for saving you," Ava's fond laugh made Gwen's insides melt. "But you were successful? You're home in one piece; I was starting to get worried."

"The mercenaries are all leaving the field, so, yes. How did the rest of the plan go?"

"Without a hitch. Jane's vassals began arriving while she was out; she and her bodyguards returned with Reginald's recumbent frame around an hour ago." Anger crossed Ava's eyes briefly. "I was there for the start of her hearing with her vassals. She's still cursing them out – I suspect she will set some public expiation to ensure this never happens again."

"Do you know what happened, then?" Gwen was wondering how Jane's men ended up enmeshed in Forquitte's treason. They didn't seem to have a lot to gain by betraying both the King and their Duke.

Ava sighed. "Yes, and I even understand it somewhat, but Jane can't accept excuses. They entered a treasonous war in her name – there can't be a good enough reason for that."

Gwen waited, still holding her beautiful wife. Ava would tell her in her own time.

After a pause to snuggle in closer, the Princess continued. "Reginald had sent missives to all Duke Holyoake's vassals that they were to ready their armsmen and march on the Capital. Most obeyed without question – apparently they are under the misapprehension that a man may speak for his wife by default."

"I thought it was well-established law that Jane's control of Eastwall would no more go to Forquitte than his control of Lubrey would go to her?"

"Of course, and some of her vassals remembered that and asked for a good reason why they should summon their armsmen at his word. But altogether too many are men who assume they would speak for their wives and allowed his expectation of the same to go unchallenged." Ava's mouth twisted in distaste.

"And how did he answer those who did not automatically assume he spoke for his wife?"

Ava snorted. "By lying, of course. He claimed my father and I locked her up without trial and without cause. He claimed we did this out of animosity for him – and he used the fact that I broke our non-existent betrothal as evidence that I am both an oath-breaker and irrationally enraged at him."

"But you never gave your word – how did he persuade these men that you were an oath breaker?" Gwen would have assumed a man credulous enough to believe that would have also just followed the initial order unquestioned.

"A gentleman's agreement is viewed as much weightier by gentlemen." Ava pursed her lips. "In any case, several insisted they would not have begun the siege without evidence that their Duke's daughter was indeed being mistreated, and claimed that her calling them off before the siege began is evidence of this. They say they waited – in truth they were not given time to – and that no harm has befallen."

"Surely Forquitte knew he'd lose the bulk of his men when Jane stood them down?" Gwen asked. "Why would he take so great a risk when he could have left them in Eastwall and still had enough soldiers to lay siege?"

"He was confident his prophecy would be self-fulfilling. When we saw Eastwall armies marching on us we would assume them traitors, and we would mistreat them unfairly – just as he claimed we already had."

"But he didn't count on you being friends with Jane, did he?" Gwen smiled at that. Forquitte seemed to have no concept that women could care for one another's company. "It's strange, but I can completely believe that he wouldn't even consider that you might actually talk to her before locking her in your dungeon."

"I suppose it's just as well for us that he didn't." Ava's answering smile had the gleam of triumph that made Gwen's heart race. "As it is, he didn't question her rescue story. He also didn't question her change of heart about cooking for him – after all, he had just saved her from monsters who would lock her in a dungeon without hearing her side first, why wouldn't she want to reward him with service? The fact that she had previously called it demeaning just made it all the sweeter for him."

"Deidre was right after all, wasn't she? He did want to make himself King." Gwen shook her head and laughed. "Do you think he'll wake soon? I'd love to be there when he realises he's been beaten."

"Shouldn't be long, now. Let's get Jane and go wake our sleeping Earl."

They stood shoulder to shoulder. Three women standing over the supine form of the beleaguered Earl. He stirred, his manacle clinking on his ankle.

He raised his head and opened his eyes. From his position he would see Princess Ava, flanked by her wife and his. His eyes moved from one to the next, absorbing their regal postures, their united front.

He sat up, shifting his leg more intentionally, and ran into the tension of the chain. His features hardened for the merest moment before his face fell. It took a few seconds to regain his previous impassivity.

"I see," was all he said.

"Yes," said Jane. "You do."

Ava lifted her chin high. "You have been weighed in the balance, Reginald Forquitte, and found wanting."

Gwen said nothing. There was nothing more to say.

Gwen and Ava walked hand in hand down the passage leading to the open courtyard where they'd left Wrath. They'd left Forquitte alone in his cell, awaiting trial.

"I know he's going to be stripped of all titles," Gwen began, "but what will justice look like in his case?"

Ava sighed. "It will be ultimately up to Father, of course, but I suspect he will be banished rather than executed." She shrugged. "His brother will become Earl of Lubrey, and it sounds like Jane is planning to remarry. She doesn't have to, of course – she has an heir, now, if all goes well with her pregnancy."

"It sounded like she wanted to."

Ava nodded. "I hope he makes her happy. Reginald will be a pauper if he lives, and he will not be allowed to set foot in the Realm again. Beyond that, I have no idea."

Pride and love surged in Gwen's chest. She wrapped her princess in her arms and held her close. "You're going to make a good Queen one day."

Ava snuggled closer into her embrace. "To think, it was my father trying to circumvent the prophecy that started it going in the first place."

"I somehow doubt that that fact escaped him." She held her Princess close a moment longer before stepping back. "Come on – I've got a dragon to introduce you to."

"I'm pretty sure they're still there, but remember, Wrath is their own person and is no one's pet." She pushed the door open and led Ava into the courtyard.

"Just as well I'm with my gallant Protector, then, isn't it?" The smile in the princess' voice was reflected in her eyes.

"I think they view themselves as your protector – I'm more a general Protector for the Realm." She shrugged, a touch self-consciously. "Apparently dragons guard monarchs and heirs – and that's why they come when royalty is otherwise unguarded."

A thought struck Gwen suddenly that perhaps she *was* supposed to be Ava's protector. She'd protected her from a terrible marriage, at the very least. Could that be the true meaning of the draconic prophecy?

YOU WORRY TOO MUCH ABOUT UNDERSTANDING. PROPHECY IS NEVER CLEAR; JUST ACCEPT IT AND MOVE ON.

Of course, now they were close enough that Wrath was able to hear her thoughts again.

IF YOU COULD TELL THESE GNATS TO PUT THEIR STICKS DOWN, IT WOULD MAKE LIFE CONSIDERABLY MORE PLEASANT FOR ALL OF US.

Gwen had forgotten the soldiers were still there. She looked around to see if she could spot the ranking member. She didn't know the insignia, and was worried she'd get it wrong, so she addressed them all. "Thank you, that will be all. Please return to your duties – it must surely be time for a change in shift?"

The men glanced at each other before each apparently decided the consort could damn well dismiss them if she wanted to. Besides, it *had* been a long day, and it was well past time for the shift to change. They each saluted, not in unison but close enough, and they smartly left the courtyard.

"Did Wrath just call those men gnats?" Ava's voice was very low, though the men were well out of earshot.

"You heard them?" Gwen was amazed. She'd thought she was the only one.

"Not... exactly. There were no words. But I got a fleeting image of a gnat holding a pointy stick. I had to assume that's what a soldier with a halberd looks like to a dragon."

"Wow. Alright. Yes, they asked me to tell the gnats to drop their sticks. It isn't hearing for me, either, but there are words."

SHE'S THE PRINCESS OF PROPHECY. HER FATE IS TIED TO MINE. OF COURSE SHE CAN UNDERSTAND ME — AT LEAST SOMEWHAT.

Gwen looked at Ava expectantly. She spoke hesitantly. "I... that was more difficult. I think they were talking about me. The image was of a princess and a dragon – not me and Wrath, but it could have been meant to represent us? Stylised. A golden glow surrounded both of us. Prophecy? I think we were talking. This is hard." She grimaced, looking slightly frustrated.

"No, no, you got all the important points. Wrath said your fate is tied to theirs because of prophecy, and it is natural that you are able to at least partly understand."

"What are the dragon prophecies? How are we tied?"

HARM WILL BEFALL BOTH YOU AND THE REALM IF YOU LEAVE IT BEFORE BEARING AN HEIR OF YOUR OWN. I AM PROPHESISED TO SAVE YOU FROM THAT HARM. THE PROTECTOR IS PROPHESISED TO SAVE THE REALM FROM IT.

Ava's jaw dropped. "I'm... bound to the land until I bear an heir?" She looked stricken and turned to Gwen. "But we hadn't even decided if that was ever going to happen. And I'm not even sure I ever want to... accept a man's help getting pregnant. But I want to see more of the world one day. Did I understand correctly? Am I destined to stay here forever?"

YOUR WOMB SHALL QUICKEN SHOULD YOU WILL IT. YOUR CHILD SHALL BE THE PROTECTOR'S. DRACONIC MAGIC IS SUBTLE; THERE IS NO NEED FOR THE MESS THAT MALE HUMANS PRODUCE.

This time both women gaped. There were so many questions.

Luckily, they had all day.

It was later. They had spent a considerable time with the dragon, and then gone to the armoury to store Gwen's plate until next time. On the way they'd sent a couple of Kingsguards to go see if they could find the abandoned horses. Now, they were on their way to the royal baths.

Gwen and Ava were holding hands as they walked. The interlock of their fingers felt really nice, and Gwen felt strangely nervous. The revelation that all of this was real had finally sunk in. It was wonderful, but also terrifying. She finally felt like she had something worth holding onto; something that would be dreadful to lose.

"When did you know?" She asked, suddenly.

Ava startled but seemed to understand what she was asking. "That I loved you?" Gwen nodded. "I didn't know for sure until you left. I was coming around to the idea that maybe love was real, maybe I could learn to love you, given time. And then…" She trailed off, staring off into the distance.

"And then you missed me when I was gone?" Gwen guessed.

Ava snorted. "No. If it was just missing you I'd have put that down to lust. I knew I wanted you from when I first laid eyes on you."

"Really?" Gwen was surprised. "You sounded so disappointed when you saw me and realised I was a woman."

"To be fair, I was planning on marrying my rescuer whoever they were. Seeing you were a woman made me concerned it might be more difficult to persuade you to go along with it. If I seemed disappointed it was only that my plans had become more challenging – or so I thought." She grinned wickedly. "Imagine my delight when you suggested pretending love. You even suggested asking a friend, which made it clear you didn't have the distaste for two women marrying that a lot of country folk seem to."

"Actually, I didn't realise all your friends were women. When your first response to that was Deidre I nearly had a heart attack." Gwen's smile was rueful. She had been so naïve.

"Oh wow. I'm actually glad I didn't know that." Ava laughed, though it sounded a little strained. "I don't think I would have proposed to you if I'd known you were only thinking males when you suggested friends."

"One thing, though." Gwen was genuinely curious. "If you were just after a marriage that was easy to get into, why not accept James' proposal? I mean, yes, the man's a git, but he clearly

294

wanted to marry you, was willing to make up any story to make it stick, and at that point you didn't even know if I was willing. Why stay with me?"

"Honestly? I was already hoping I'd manage to seduce you while we were faking a romance. True, I didn't know if it would work, but as you so rightly pointed out that young man was... not a great choice. I wasn't going to throw away the hope of having you for the certainty of having him." She smiled. "I think I mentioned at the time that I was glad you were the one to save me and not him. I meant it. I mean it even more now."

"Alright, so we've established that you recognised lust for me right away," Gwen smiled, enjoying knowing that. "Which, to be honest, is impressive. I definitely wanted you very early on, but I kept lying to myself about it for... well, I don't know how long for. Maybe I didn't even admit to myself how much I wanted you until we were betrothed. Some thoughts just felt dangerous." Her smile turned a little self-conscious. "How did you know you loved me?"

Ava turned serious. "When the prophecy said you'd die if you weren't protected by mutual love, I was terrified. The thought of losing you ripped my heart out, and I could barely breathe. I couldn't understand why you were going anyway – I just wanted to run away with you and protect you."

"Oh, Ava," Gwen stopped walking and pulled her in, cupping her face tenderly in the hand that wasn't entwined with hers. She pressed the softest of kisses to her lips.

"Anyway." Ava brushed a tear away, putting a smile on her face. "After you'd left I went and had a lengthy discussion with my mother. I told her everything – how we'd agreed to a sham marriage because it suited both of us, and how that meant that you weren't the prophesised hero after all and were riding to your death. How we'd made friends over the months. I even told her, a little, of our arrangement. No details – no need to look at me like that – but that we were being… physically intimate."

"And what did she say?"

"That we might have started out faking it, but that if I was in so many knots over losing you then I clearly loved you. She said I was too cynical; she believed me that we started out as fake, that I wanted not to marry Reginald and you wanted to help your family. But she said it was plain as the nose on my face that we love each other, and that I needed to trust that the prophecy would protect you."

"And did you?"

"No!" Ava laughed ruefully. "I accepted that I was completely in love with you. But I didn't think her logic was sound about you. She said you looked to be in love – I knew you to be a decent actor when you put your mind to it, so I discounted that. She also said that if you didn't love me you wouldn't have been willing to ride to your death for me."

"That seems like good logic to me, honestly." Gwen smiled. "I wouldn't give my life for just anyone, you know."

"Well, it did at least make me hope you'd survive. After all, if my fears were well founded and you didn't love me, maybe you'd just run as soon as you were far enough out of the city that running away wouldn't spark a rebellion? I figured it was better to know you were safe but that I'd never see you again than believe you were riding to your death out of a sense of honour or obligation."

Gwen felt her lips twitch in faint amusement. "Would it disappoint you greatly to know that running away occurred to me? The honour of my word was part of what kept me from doing it, but mostly I was worried that if I got caught in my cowardice then you'd be the one to pay the price."

"I'm not disappointed at all. I'm glad you actively chose to go on – that you knew you could run. I'd hate to think you didn't realise you had a choice."

"I will always choose you, my love." Gwen pulled their joined hands to her lips, and kissed Ava's knuckles gently, one by one.

It had taken longer to reach the baths than Gwen remembered, but perhaps that was because they were taking their time and talking. Or perhaps it was because she was both excited and anxious to bathe with her beloved again. To bathe with her for the first time in the knowledge of how they felt about each other. It was surreal, and wonderful, and terrifying all at once.

Fresh towels, sweetly scented soaps and clean, soft clothes awaited them when they arrived. Gwen hadn't noticed Ava request this – had someone else anticipated their need? Whoever it was, she was grateful. Her undergarments were decent if not pretty, but they smelled as much as the rest of her. There were surely many things in life worse than putting on foul clothing after washing the stench from your body, but right now it was difficult to think of more than one or two of them.

"I'd ask you to help with my clothes, but I'm only wearing a robe over my nightgown. May I instead offer to help you with yours, my gallant knight?" Ava's smile was teasing, but full of love.

"I'd like that," Gwen admitted, turning to face her, and holding her arms out wide. Ava stepped in and started unbuckling her gambeson for her. When she was done, she pushed it off her shoulders and stared. Underneath, Gwen's bare chest gleamed in the candlelight.

"No undershirt?" Ava breathed, her eyes taking in all of Gwen's soft curves.

"That was my undershirt." Gwen's smile was gentle, but she could feel her heart begin to race. She reached out and undid the tie holding Ava's robe closed around her.

Ava stood very still as Gwen disrobed her. Silence stretched as clothing fell, and the princess was breathing heavily. She licked her lower lip, eyes roaming Gwen's body as they stood naked before one another.

Ava's hand reached out, her fingertips lightly stoking the outer edge of Gwen's breast, trailing across and underneath. "I thought we were here to make me presentable for your bed, my princess?" Gwen tried to put a hint of tease into her tone, but she knew she sounded breathless and aroused. "At this rate we're not going to make it back to the bedroom."

"*Our* bed. And there's no rule saying we can't have both, my love."

"Shall we at least make it into the bath?" She offered her hand, and Ava took it. They descended the marble steps into the steaming water.

When they were submerged, they dropped hands and turned to face one another. Gwen could see her own shy nerves echoed on Ava's face, as well as the blush she knew matched that suffusing her own cheeks. They stood like that, a tableau of new lovers, for all they'd been enjoying each other intimately for months.

"Would you like me to wash your back?" Ava's smile was achingly sweet. Gwen nodded, not trusting herself to speak, and turned to find the soap and cloth. She handed them to Ava, who began gently rubbing soapy circles all over her back and shoulders, her free hand trailing fingertips across the slippery skin. Gwen shuddered and submitted to the tender ministrations.

A gentle nudge of fingers bade Gwen raise her arms, and Ava soaped her up and down her sides. Gwen's skin pebbled in the wake of those gentle hands, wanting them to finish washing away the accumulated dirt of many days on the road, but also feverishly imagining them getting sidetracked to more pleasurable pursuits.

By the hitch in her breath, Ava was having similar thoughts. Her fingertips wandered slowly, even as her main hand made efficient work of removing the grime that had gathered on Gwen's body. At last she appeared satisfied with her efforts and let go of the soapy cloth. It drifted unheeded down to the bottom of the pool.

At the unspoken signal they surged toward each other, waves forming in the bath as they pressed into one another, water splashing out over the side. Neither cared to check if any of it reached their clothes and towels. Hands found hips and waists and necks as their bodies merged. Their kiss was urgent, full of need, desperate to show love as well as the desire that had been out in the open for months. They deepened the kiss, and Gwen wasn't sure who was setting the pace, but she knew that she wanted it.

She wanted it all.

Their legs tangled as they kissed, each with a thigh pressed into the other. This was familiar; they'd brought each other pleasure like this before, and Gwen was beginning to rock without conscious thought. Ava pulled back slightly. "Wait," she said, and her breathless voice intensified the throbbing Gwen already felt between her legs.

"What do you need?" Her own voice was breathless, too. She didn't care.

"I..." Ava blushed and cleared her throat. "I've wanted... for a while. But it seemed too intimate." Her blush was as deep as Gwen had ever seen it. "But you love me. And I love you. So... this?" And she raised herself up on tiptoes, her hand between them spreading them both as she moved to press them together.

Gwen understood an instant before they made contact. Intimate was right. The feel of Ava's swollen clit pressing up against her own made her vision swim. Her hips began undulating of their own volition and the smooth slick feeling of centre pressing into centre was almost enough to unravel her on the spot.

It wasn't the most intense thing they'd ever done. Not even close. But knowing what this meant to Ava, knowing how much she wanted this, wanted it because she loved her... it was enough to take Gwen's breath away. Her world shrank to just the feeling of them pressing themselves into each other, rocking in time, their breathing rising into pants together, their chests pressing as they heaved. She welcomed the heat coursing through her, her toes digging into the marble base of the bath involuntarily, her climax growing within her.

When it arrived, it flooded them both at once. Their panting became wild cries as they came, hard, connected in every sense of the word. Tremors and shocks passed through both of them, easing slowly as they came back to reality.

"I love you, Ava," Gwen's voice was full of wonder, her fingers gently pushing a stray lock of hair back behind Ava's ear.

"I love you, too, Gwen." Ava's voice held all the love in the world as she snuggled in close to her wife.

Epilogue – Happily Ever After

"Ma! Ma! Matilda's being mean!" The footsteps of the young Prince Henry pattered down the hall, followed by the trail of his favourite blanket.

"Am not!" Princess Matilda was two years older than her brother, and she stood making use of every inch of her extra height. Her small fists were on her hips, and she scowled at him in a huff.

"Are so! You won't let me play knights and dragons with you!" His lower lip quivered. He thought himself a big boy, and big boys weren't supposed to cry.

"Well, four is too little to be a knight. We said you could watch, though, didn't we Edlyn?"

Edlyn Holyoake was a year older than Matilda, though not quite so tall. "Maybe he can be your squire?" She always was the peacemaker.

"Don't want to be a squire. If I can't be the knight, can I be the dragon?" His eyes held a hopeful light. He loved dragons. He kept trying to talk to Wrath, but they never spoke back to him.

"Don't be silly, Henry. If we tried to ride you you'd get hurt." Matilda had the haughty demeanour of a child who thought she was much older and wiser than she was.

"See, Ma? She's being mean!" His wail was plaintive.

Gwen sighed. Motherhood was wonderful, though there were times she wished she and Ava had waited a couple more years. Or at least had a larger gap between children. She loved them both more fiercely than she could imagine, but she could live without the constant bickering.

"Henry, why don't you go find Will and ask him for some archery lessons?" The farrier was surprisingly good with a bow, and even more surprisingly patient with the young Prince. Much more so than his sister was.

"Real bow and arrows?" He perked up at the idea. Real weapons were always more exciting than pretend ones.

"Yes, my love. You need to learn how to use them sooner or later; it might as well be now." She smiled and ruffled his hair. His dark curls were so much like hers had been at that age, much to his grandfather's delight.

He scampered off, pleased with this turn of events.

"What? Mother, why is Henry allowed to use a real weapon? You never let me practice with a real sword!" Matilda's indignation was righteous, as befitting a six-year-old princess.

"His bow will be too light to cause real harm, and Will will be watching him. If you want to learn the bow I can ask Elfrida to take you for lessons; I'll do it myself when you come of age." She didn't address the issue of real swords. They'd had that conversation before, and she saw no benefit in going over it again.

Matilda's eyes lit up. "Really, mother? Do you think she would?" Her enthusiasm was very sweet – she admired Elfrida and would follow her like a puppy if the young squire didn't make herself scarce quite regularly.

"I think she might if I asked her nicely. Edlyn, too – if you want to, that is?" Gwen was sure Elfrida would be happier taking both of them than Matilda on her own. The young Princess' hero worship could get tiring, but she tended to keep it more under control when her best friend was with her. Will, on the other hand, had been very clear that he was willing to take one child but had no confidence in his abilities to keep two or three out of trouble. She wondered how he would cope when he had children of his own.

302

"I think I'd like that." Edlyn was less keen, but she was young enough that the assent was probably genuine. She liked spending time with Matilda, though she didn't have the martial focus her friend did. When it was her turn to choose their activity she chose painting or embroidery. Gwen was just glad her daughter was learning a little of both worlds.

"Alright, I'll talk to her later today. If you two are finished playing Knights and Dragons, Master Avery would like to see you for your lessons."

And Gwen would get to spend a little time with her wife.

She found her wife in the smallest of the audience rooms, with her ladies in waiting, Eveline, Deidre, and Jane. The husbands were there, too. Gwen still didn't know Lord Mountfeather well enough to be comfortable calling him by his first name; Deidre had introduced him by title, and while the man was unfailingly polite at all times, he did tend to fade into the background with the furniture. The Earl of Lubrey was another matter. Percival was affable and smiling, and six years after his marriage to Lady Jane still seemed unable to believe his luck.

"Darling! So good of you to join us. I take it the children are at their lessons?" Ava swept across the room to greet her with a kiss to each cheek. The showy displays of desire had cooled years ago, to be replaced by genuine affection. Not that things had cooled down a great deal behind closed doors.

Gwen's smile was warm and loving. "Of course, my love. Letters for our daughter and archery for our son." She broadened her smile, ignoring the others in the room for the moment.

"Already? I know you said Will was willing to take one on, but I thought Matilda would beat him off the mark." The affection in her eyes still made Gwen's heart sing. She hoped it always would.

"Matilda asked to learn too, of course, but she'd rather Elfrida taught her. Besides, she does need to learn her letters – she's going to be Queen one day."

Ava laughed. "Don't say that too loudly around my father. Henry is the apple of his eye – and enough lords choose a younger son to inherit that he thinks we will, too."

"Well, you don't have any siblings, so it's not as though he can disinherit you in a fit of pique." Gwen let enough mirth into her voice to make it clear to the others she was joking. Ava wouldn't need the tone. It was one of many things she loved about her wife.

"True enough. Come, sit with us, and eat. The others were asking after you." She led the way to the chairs, where the servants brought them refreshments.

"I trust Edlyn wasn't too much of a handful this morning, your Highness?" Percival's voice was surprisingly deep when she had first heard it, but he'd been around long enough that it was no longer strange to Gwen.

"Your daughter is a delight, my Lord. But can we drop the formalities? You know my name's Gwen." She had to remind him every time. She probably always would.

"Of course, Gwen. Was Finn with you today? Or was he off bothering the cooks again?"

"Your son wasn't with us, so I'll assume he's been watching the cooks at their work." She smiled. The boy was five years old, and when he wasn't trying to copy his sister in everything she did he was down in the kitchens using his baby blue eyes to con titbits out of the cooks.

"He and Matilda get on very well, don't they?" His smile was disarming.

"Usually, yes, though I didn't see them together today." She was being cautious. Percival wasn't subtle about hoping his son would marry well – and there was no better marriage for him than the young princess. But Ava was adamant that their children would marry for love – or for whatever reasons they chose – and she wasn't going to promise either of them to anyone at their age. And she also liked Percival too much to tell him to knock it off, so here they were.

Besides, maybe Matilda would choose him after all. Stranger things had happened.

"My uncle, Baron Xorth, sends me to speak with you on matters of sovereignty and trade, your Highness." Xago was significantly younger and smarter than his uncle, though perhaps not as fierce a warrior. He had learned to mimic more typically human manners of speech, and he could not always be trusted to be perfectly straightforward.

In other words, he was just like any other lord.

Gwen stood behind Ava as they received him. Technically King Harald should be doing this, but he was withdrawing from these duties more and more to allow his daughter to take the reins of the Realm. Also, he liked spending his afternoons with his grandchildren.

"We are listening, Xago. What would Lord Xorth have of us?" Gwen loved hearing her wife use the royal 'we'. Maybe she should be past enjoying the overdone arrogance of royal politics, but Ava's regal hauteur still made her knees go weak.

"Baron Xorth wishes to enact a tax on trade caravans passing through our lands. He feels that the current peace is beneficial to all, but perhaps less so to our family than to those who cross freely under our watchful and benevolent protection. It has come to his attention that these trade caravans do not always even call him Baron – he has been referred to as ogre with no honorific, and he wishes to restore the respect he is due. If your Highness permits it, he intends to enforce this respect personally."

Xago probably thought he was being subtle. For an ogre, perhaps he was.

"I see. And how, exactly, does Lord Xorth envision this respect? How does he intend to enforce it? And what is the precise nature of the tax he is proposing? They are connected, of course, but how?" Ava knew the answers. Gwen could see the shape of them, and Ava was always so much more attuned to the political winds. She would know exactly what he was aiming for. She was going to make Xago spell it out anyway. Best not to leave any loopholes large enough to ride an ogre raiding party through.

"In person. He intends – with your permission, of course, your Highness – to send forth tax collectors to meet any traders enjoying his protection. He intends to send them in pairs, with ceremonial escorts drawn from the Baron's own elite guard. Their ceremonial uniforms and armaments will be to ensure the merchants understand the respect due to a Peer of the Realm. The tax will, as your Highness has so astutely ascertained, be an amount determined based on the trader's own standing. An amount that will demonstrate respect, but not one that the merchant will be unable to pay."

"I see." Ava snapped her fan open and then shut again. This wasn't her own habit, but it was common enough in the aristocracy that using the mannerism added to an air of noble detachment. "Are you talking a percentage of the funds the merchant is carrying, then?"

Xago bowed his head politely. As tall as he was, he had to exaggerate the motion. "That is correct, your Highness. A percentage of the gold and goods the merchant is carrying – Baron Xorth will not be tricked by merchants carrying no gold in their caravans." That wasn't the first time he's called his uncle Baron rather than Lord. It was an odd affectation, but ogres were odd in many other ways. Perhaps he wanted to remind everyone that the lordship was a Barony, a hereditary peerage and not a mere honorary title.

"And what percentage exactly are you proposing?" Ava was cool and regal in her questioning. Gwen would have laughed at him by now – but her wife had more patience.

"An amount to be ascertained on a case-by-case basis, your Highness." His bow was full and deep this time.

The fan snapped open and shut in quick succession. "No. That is not taxation. If you have a proposal for a tax, specify the amount and let the merchants know before they make their travel plans. The plan as you currently propose it will look identical to the resumption of ogre raids as far as the merchants can tell. And the proposal as it stands leaves too much leeway for Lord Xorth's elite soldiers to decide the best way to curry favour with the Baron is to set the tax at one hundred percent." It wasn't the soldiers. This was a political lie. It was Xorth himself who would order the taxation to become robbery.

Ava continued. "If you wish to propose a reasonable tax, give full details to the master of the Royal Guard. He will assign heralds to declare it to the merchants, and he will assign Kingsguards to protect your tax collectors about their duties. They will be kitted out in full regalia, of course, so the honour of your uncle the Baron will be satisfied. He will not have to live without his elite personal guards merely to protect bureaucrats. But no taxes will be levied by surprise – all merchants will understand the amount they need to pay before they leave, and they will have the chance to carry the gold or choose another route as suits them best."

Xago bowed again, this time to hide a grimace. "As your Highness commands, of course. The merchants must be prepared. But you need not trouble yourself to protect our tax collectors – Baron Xorth is eager to demonstrate the might of his household guard at each stop."

"No, Xago." Her tone was gentle yet firm. "Your uncle would be most displeased to lose his Barony because a merchant reported him as taking more than was his due. Enough lords are uneasy with Lord Xorth being a Peer that they might vote to strip him of titles on the flimsiest of evidence." She waited for him to raise his eyes to hers before continuing. "The presence of the Kingsguards, in full regalia no less, will demonstrate your uncle's might in a different way. It will show that he has the full backing of the Crown, and any insult to him will be met by King Harald's men."

Xago pondered this, calmly meeting her gaze. Finally he bowed again. "The minstrels will sing songs of your wisdom, your Highness. It shall be as you command."

"Sir Gwen! How are the Dragon Queens this evening?" Elfrida's grin was infectious as she scratched Wrath affectionately behind their ear.

Gwen winced, glad Queen Constance wasn't there to hear. Not that she appeared to mind, of course. Technically the princess' consort was also a princess, but the minstrels who sang of Gwen, Knight Protector of the Princess and member of the Order of the Dragon had decided that calling them Queens sounded better. It was far too late to change how the public referred to them now, of course.

"Elfrida! We're wonderful. How's your training coming along?" Gwen forced down the wince and replaced it with a big, broad smile. Elfrida had recently graduated from page to squire and was the first Gwen had officially taken charge of as one of her chivalric duties.

"You'd know if you did more of it yourself." Her tone was teasing rather than actually upset. Elfrida got to learn from many knights rather than just one, and multiple masters meant she got away with spending much more time with Wrath than she might otherwise.

OF COURSE. MY COMPANY IS MUCH BETTER THAN ANY HUMAN'S, AND MY PROTÉGÉ IS ASTUTE ENOUGH TO SEE IT.

"Hah! You just had a thought complaining about how long I spend with Wrath, didn't you? I'm getting better at hearing them; you'd better watch out." Her grin was broad, and she seemed proud of herself.

"Not complaining. Just remembering how much time you like to spend together." Gwen allowed her fondness to seep into her words. At some point over the years Elfrida had become personal page to her and Ava, and they'd grown rather fond of each other. It seemed natural that she'd take her on as squire when the time came.

"Good. Because you don't go flying often enough since Henry was born."

SINCE THE FIRST WHELP, TRULY.

Gwen laughed. Wrath and Elfrida were a perfect match. "Have they let you fly them yet?"

NO. BUT SOON.

"No... what?" Elfrida's eyes lit up. "Soon? Really? Wow!"

"Dragons don't measure time as we do, Elfrida. 'Soon' could mean anything." Gwen was cautious, not wanting her squire's over eagerness to dampen their bond.

SOON IS SOON. I SUSPECT SHE WILL BE READY THIS SEASON. WE SHALL SEE.

Elfrida deflated slightly, but still seemed excited. Apparently she had hoped 'soon' meant this week; she may even have thought today. But this year was still exciting.

"I'll be good, you'll see! I don't weigh as much as Sir Gwen, either, you'll hardly notice I'm there!"

Gwen laughed, a rich, deep laugh. It was true – Elfrida was over a head shorter than her and very slightly built – but she'd seen Wrath pick up a cow in each talon while on hunting raids, and she suspected the difference between her weight and her squire's would be hardly noticeable.

SHE WON'T HAVE THE WEIGHT OF YOUR INFLATED EGO, PROTECTOR.

Gwen's laugh became a guffaw. "*My* inflated ego? Wrath, that's like the sun complaining a campfire is burning too brightly."

"Will I be Protector someday?" The question was sudden, but Gwen had the feeling Elfrida had been wondering for a while.

"I don't know. It's what Wrath calls me; something in their prophecies. I don't think it's the sort of title that gets handed down – Wrath?" She tossed the question at the dragon.

IT'S A TITLE FROM PROPHECY, YES, BUT MY PROTÉGÉ CAN DO THE SAME JOB ONCE SHE'S TRAINED. IF SHE WANTS TO BE CALLED PROTECTOR, SHE CAN BE.

Well, that was uncharacteristically tactful. Gwen felt a little overwhelmed.

She saw Elfrida gazing adoringly at her dragon companion, and suddenly felt like a third wheel to their precious moment. She thought about excusing herself, and then realised she had no need to.

The Realm would have a protector after her. The line of succession was secure. With a full and happy heart, Gwen set off to find her beloved. Her Princess Ava.

Her Dragon Queen.

End Note – Would You Write Me A Review?

If you've made it this far, I truly hope you enjoyed the ride. Whether you did or not, I would greatly appreciate you leaving an honest review wherever you bought this. People are always more willing to try a book if they can read someone else's opinion on it – I prefer seeing some reviews myself before I take a chance on a new author. So please, even if it's only a sentence or two, I would dearly love you taking the time to leave your thoughts.

I don't currently have any plans to write more books – but a positive reception to the tale of Gwen and Ava could change my mind. If you want to get in touch, my twitter is @KathleenDePlume and my email is kathleendeplume@gmail.com

Acknowledgements

I scoffed at people who said writing was never a lone pursuit – how much more solitary can you get? And then I wrote a book.

I'll try to keep this short.

Firstly, I would love to thank my wonderful wife, without whom this book would never have happened. She told me every day how proud she was of me, and she was the one who pushed me to polish my work and seek external help and guidance. Without her I would still be sitting with a half-finished first draft and some vague notes.

Secondly, I would like to thank all the wonderful volunteers who beta read my self-edited draft. The pure positivity combined with a genuine desire to help me improve spurred me on, encouraging me to make improvements, polish my lore, and squash those pesky typos.

(Any remaining typos and anachronisms are all my own fault!)

A special thanks to Dee, my plot doctor, who helped make the prophecy feel real, and the Princess feel badass. Without her help, the ending would be rushed and unsatisfying – thank you for your patience, Dee, as well as for your wisdom.

Finally, I would like to thank everyone who helped with the aesthetic elements of the book – the fantastic cover art being the biggest one of these. Without that help this book would be a shadow of what it is today.

What I tell you three times is true: Thank you. Thank you. Thank you.

Printed in Great Britain
by Amazon

80247797R00181